But I'm (Not) A Villain

Eric Demarest

To Debbie

    Thank you for making my life fun, and for pushing me to be a hero on the days I don't feel like one.

    I love you.

1

Matt

"I'm not a hero."

I've been saying that a lot lately. Any time I start to think I'm important, or that I can save the world.

Right now, I'm saying it to Rob as we walk through downtown Chaplain. Not that it's much of a downtown. The sun glints off the dirt-smudged laundromat window up ahead. We stride over the uneven sidewalk past the door of the Golden Dragon, and I catch a whiff of burnt egg rolls. A couple cars flow by, and a dozen or so people are strolling around; for Chaplain, that's a busy day.

"Well, *one* of us is a hero," Rob says to me, flashing a smirk through his mahogany cheeks. "We got the bastards, didn't we? So if it's not you, I guess it's me. Or maybe Phillip here."

I almost startle when I turn to see Phillip walking beside me. He blends in so well, even I forget he's there half the time. His gray hoodie is pulled up, like always, over his pale skin and spiked black hair. He just seems to fade into the crowd the moment you see him.

"What do you think, Phillip?" I ask him. "You think we're heroes?"

Phillip shrugs, although he does let a hint of a smile slip for just a second.

"See, Matt?" Rob points to the news article on his phone. "Crossman goes on trial next month. It doesn't matter that he owns the factory and half the town. He decided killing people was a good business model, and because of *us*, he's not gonna get away with it."

"I know what we did, and I'm proud of it," I insist.

"So... *why* aren't we superheroes?"

I sigh. "Because no one knows it was us who did it. And nobody *can* know."

"You always do know how to take the fun out of everything," Rob quips. "I still say they should throw us a parade."

A lady walking a tiny fluff of a dog strolls by us, almost running right into Phillip because, of course, she doesn't see him. Phillip casually steps around her without missing a beat, then leans in to glance at the article on Rob's phone. "It is pretty cool seeing that. Of course, if Tess were here, she'd hack in and get the real inside scoop on what's going on."

Rob laughs. "No kidding. She'd tell us what the judge had for lunch yesterday. I don't know how she turned autism into a superpower."

"It's not because she's autistic," I say, "she's just crazy good with her phone. Although I still don't know how she..." I trail off and shake my head. "Hell, I don't know how any of us can do what we do."

That goes for me, too. I've never understood my Ability. I'm just glad I found a few people who accept me for it without looking at me like the freak I am.

We keep walking over the cracks in the sidewalk, past a lady texting on her phone and a guy carrying some takeout home for dinner. I don't really know any of these people, but I've seen them around. In a town as small as Chaplain, everyone has seen everyone around.

Across the street, an older lady steps out of the liquor store holding a pack of hard lemonade in one hand and chugging on an already open bottle in her other hand. She half-trips over her own foot, so I'm guessing that isn't the first one of those she's had today. Hey, I don't judge. I've seen my dad put down a lot more than that in his lower moments. The lady stumbles to the curb, where there's a delivery truck parked and a dolly loaded with cases of beer waiting to be hauled into the store. She stops for a second, looks at the beer, and then glances back and forth to see if anyone's watching. I'm pretty sure she's thinking about stealing some of that beer, and yeah, I would judge her for that. Finally she decides against it and she steps into the street—but she doesn't bother to look around the truck.

A car speeds toward her. The driver's got his head down, probably texting. The lady sees the car and totters, frozen in place. I'm not fast enough to get to her before it's all over, but there's something else I can do.

I reach out my hand. My palm tingles, and with my Ability I grab onto the bottle in the lady's hand. It doesn't matter that it's fifty feet away, I can feel the hard surface of the glass as solid as if I'd physically grabbed it, and I pull. The lady's hand is clenched tight around the bottle; it jerks but she holds on. The car hurtles closer. I pull harder, and the tingle in my hand rages. The bottle bursts out of the lady's grip and flies toward the car like a fastball, and shatters against the windshield. The driver's head pops up from his phone, he finally sees the lady and his eyes bulge out. He slams on the brakes and the tires squeal, and the lady screams. The car's only a few feet from her now. It skids to a screeching, jolting stop, the bumper rocking down and back up again close enough to itch the lady's kneecaps. I let out a long breath.

The lady totters unevenly. She drops the case of lemonade to the pavement and starts to tip backward. It looks like she's going to go down hard and probably break a hip, when suddenly something catches her.

I squint to see what kept her from falling. At first, I only see a shadow... but then I catch a glimpse of Phillip's hoodie. I'd been so focused on what I was doing that I hadn't even noticed him rushing into the street toward her. Looks like no one else noticed him either. He gently props the woman back up. She stares bug-eyed at the car that almost ran her over, then spins around to see who caught her. But Phillip's already becoming a ghost again, slipping away into the crowd that's formed on the sidewalk. He glances at me and gives me a thumbs-up before disappearing.

Rob whistles beside me. "And you save the day again."

I give him a look, but have to force myself to hide a smile. "I'm *not* a hero."

"Well, between your magic trick and Phillip's disappearing act, you got the job done. Of course, if Tess were here, she would've just hacked into that car's override controls and stopped it herself."

I chuckle. "Yeah, that would've been a lot easier."

I glance at the crowd gawking at the action. The lady in the street looks like she's going to hurl, and the guy driving the car has rushed up to her and is babbling "I'm sorry" as fast as he can get it out. The rest of the folks on the curb are talking with an agitated edge, eyeing the spiderweb pattern in the car's windshield from the broken bottle.

"Well," Rob says, "I guess it's time for me to use *my* superpower."

"What's that?"

"Cleaning up after you," he says with a wink.

Rob spreads his smile wide enough to pop the dimples in his cheeks and strides casually into the street, up to the lady still standing there. "Wow, that was a close one. Good thing you thought to throw that bottle at the car."

"But I *didn't* throw it!" the woman exclaims. "How did it—"

"Of course you did," Rob says nonchalantly. "Just basic instinct, I guess. I don't know if I would've been as quick as you. Good thing you threw it and got his attention."

The lady looks at him skeptically, but then Rob flashes that grin again. And a few seconds later, the lady's nodding, saying how her reflexes took over, and the people on the curb are saying she's got a good arm on her and she should try a career in baseball. Rob's good. It's funny; he's told me how he feels self-conscious, being the only one in our group without a special ability. But he does have a superpower—his charm. He can talk his way out of just about anything.

I stride off down the block with one last glance at the lady in the street, grateful that I could help... and grateful that no one knows about it.

But as I walk away, something tugs inside me. Part of me wishes people *did* know. I guess a parade wouldn't be so bad, or even a little thanks, but it'd be nice to just be *understood*. To not have to hide who I am. But this isn't a comic book. If people saw that in the real world, out in the open, they wouldn't cheer. They'd freak the hell out, and I'd get run out of town... or dissected in a lab somewhere.

So, I keep it hidden, like my mom taught me. Like she had to do herself. I'm just glad I have a few people I can share it with, who didn't run away when they saw. I guess I should be grateful for that.

I pass the coffee shop—our pathetic little version of one. It's basically a shed with a big square hole cut out of the front where you can walk up to make your order. I decide, what the hell, I saved a lady from getting run over so I deserve a muffin. I step up to the counter, where Tracy Burke sits slumped behind it, trying to feign interest. I take in the smell of coffee, and milk that's about to go bad.

"Hey, Tracy," I say. "One blueberry muff—"

That's as far as I get, when someone thuds into me from the side. Someone small, but it's still enough to throw me off balance. I land on my ass on the pavement.

I look up to see who knocked me over. Her ice-blue eyes lock onto mine, and I find myself staring. She looks my age, but I've never seen her before—and like I said, I've seen *everyone* around here before. The girl bends down over me, her wavy hair draping over her shoulders, a mix of blonde and brown and red that I can't quite put my finger on. A faint layer of freckles specks her face.

"Sorry," she says in a voice that makes me wonder if she actually means it. "Here, let me."

She reaches out her hand. I hesitate for a moment, then take it, surprised at how cool her skin feels. Her eyes squint shut for a second as I pull myself up, then she smiles. The smile looks pretty on her through those freckles, but it feels forced, somehow.

"Thanks," I mumble. "Did you, uh, want to order?"

"Small coffee to go," the girl says to Tracy without taking her eyes off me. I can't tell if it's creepy or if I like it.

No... I like it.

Tracy putters behind the counter and comes up with the coffee and a prepackaged muffin that's probably expired. I hand a couple bills to Tracy to pay for my muffin, and the girl does the same for her coffee. She keeps looking at me.

Okay, it is getting a little creepy now.

"I, uh, haven't seen you around here," I say, for lack of anything better.

"We're just passing through," the girl says.

" 'We'?"

She flinches for a second, like she wishes she hadn't said that. "My friends and I," she says casually without elaborating. "Nice little town you have here."

"It's home." I shrug. "Everybody knows everybody."

"Hmmm." She nods, studying my face. "But do they *really* know you?"

I freeze and stare at her. "What?"

"Sometimes it feels like everyone knows you, but no one knows the *real* you. That can be hard, can't it?"

Something about the way she says that cuts right through me. "Wow, I, uh..."

"Never mind." A calm smile spreads through her freckles. "I'm Ash, by the way."

"Oh... Matt," I say. "Matt Pine."

Ash nods. "Well, Matt Pine, I guess I'll see you around."

She turns and walks toward the corner where there's a beat-up car parked. I watch her walk away, her hair swishing back and forth. I still can't quite decide what color it is.

"How will I see you around?" I call out to her. "I thought you said you're just passing through."

Ash turns and gives me a long, sly look. "You never know, do you?"

She finally breaks her gaze with me and gets in the car. I glance down at the counter, only to realize she stole my muffin.

Huh. Maybe something new can happen in Chaplain after all.

2

Ash

Her hand touches his, skin to skin, and the Pain rushes in. Not her pain, but his. A faint throbbing in his hip from where she'd knocked him down—he must be a wimp for it to hurt like that, she'd barely touched him—but that's not where the real pain is.

Isolated... misunderstood... hiding himself. There's more behind that, much more, loss and doubt and self-loathing. He's managed to put some of that behind him, but it still lingers, still rushes through their touch into her.

She's used to the flood of Pain by now, but this one is... different...

Ash blinks as she helps the boy up and forces any expression off her face as they talk. This one could be useful. She should plant a seed.

"... no one knows the *real* you," she says. "That can be hard, can't it?"

His face twitches, the look she always gets when she cuts someone right to the core. Good, she'd gotten it right. She makes sure to keep a straight face as they introduce themselves.

Matt Pine. She stores the name away.

She walks back to the car after picking up her coffee and his muffin. She feels him still watching her as she walks away. Good.

Ash pulls the car door open with a creak and slides into the driver's seat, frowning at the frayed seat cover. It infuriates her that after all she's done, with all she can do, this piece of shit is the best she can afford. She rips the plastic wrapper off the muffin and takes a bite, grimacing with a mouthful of stale processed *blah*.

"You make a new friend out there?" comes a deep voice beside her.

She turns to Heath in the passenger seat. His forehead creases down like it always does, the dark olive skin stretching back over his shaved head. He shifts his bulky shoulders in his seat. He's the same age as Ash, but as big as he is, he could pass for a twenty-year-old easy.

"Maybe," Ash answers vaguely.

Heath holds his stare on her. "So what did you and your 'friend' talk about?"

Ash points to the gray plastic disc of Heath's cochlear implant, clinging conspicuously to the side of his bald scalp, and the wire trailing to the other gray piece behind his ear. "Don't pretend you need to ask me. I know you heard everything we said out there. Hell, I'll bet you could count his pulse from here."

"It doesn't always let me hear everything, you know," Heath retorts. "Some frequencies—"

"It's not *supposed* to let you hear everything," Ash says, cutting him off. "Lucky for us, yours doesn't work like it's supposed to. Or should I say, *you* don't work like you're supposed to. But none of us do, do we?" She tosses the muffin to him. "You eat this. It's awful."

Heath's forehead creases a little more. "He gonna be your next fling?"

"Of course not," Ash says, then smirks. "Well, maybe later. But either way, we need to stick around here a while."

"We're staying?" Leah asks from the back seat in her thin voice. "We never stay anywhere for very long."

Ash turns to look at Leah. Her dark hair hangs around her face, her skin so pale it's almost colorless. Leah's a year younger than them, and she looks it. Her thin shoulders hunch forward, and she won't make eye contact.

"You're right, Leah," Ash says. "We don't usually stick around. I'd planned on putting this speck of a town behind us as soon as we'd filled up the gas tank. But plans change."

"All because you met a boy?" Heath grunts.

Ash reaches out, her hand lightly grazing the dark skin of Heath's forearm. She closes her eyes and lets the Pain rush in.

"Jealous?" She opens her eyes with a sly smile. "You're jealous, Heath?"

He frowns and turns away.

"The point is," Ash says, "that boy is different."

"Oh, yeah?" Heath won't look at her, his voice unimpressed. "Different how?"

"Different like *us*."

3

Matt

The Chaplain High lunchroom buzzes with the usual conversation and the clatter of cheap trays on cheap tables. I make my way across the faded floor tiles which have been here since at least four presidents ago and drop into my seat. It's not that it's "mine" exactly, but it's the same one I sit in every day. Rob's already in "his" seat beside me, chewing on his just-came-out-of-the-freezer hamburger. He smiles through a face full of ketchup and mayo. Phillip's there too, though it takes me a second to notice him like usual.

"Hey, guys," I say. "Hey, Tess."

"*Hey,*" Tess says from across the table, her fingers flurrying over her phone. It's her phone saying the words for her, to be clear, saying what she types into it; that's how she talks. It's no big deal, we've gotten used to that. She holds her phone up close to her face, the glow reflecting off her eyes. She doesn't look at me—she doesn't like eye contact—but we've gotten used to that too. Tess pulls her hand away from her phone just long enough to give me a quick wave before going back to tapping. I'll bet she's got two dozen tabs going on that thing right now, looking at who-knows-what, probably about to override a nuclear missile launch.

I used to say that as a joke, but after seeing half the stuff she can do... well, you never know.

"*I heard there was some excitement downtown yesterday,*" Tess says with some more taps.

I cough. "Yeah, a lady almost got run over. Fortunately she, uh, threw a bottle to get the guy's attention—" I glance back at her grey-blue eyes, knowing she sees everything even though she doesn't actually look up at me. "You already know it was me, don't you?"

"*You're a terrible liar,*" Tess says with a subtle smirk.

"Well, Phillip helped too, and then Rob smoothed everything over like he always does. I wish you'd been there, though."

"*I could've overridden the car's controls.*"

"Called it," Rob says.

I shake my head, and look up when I catch a glimpse of red hair. Emily. She strides toward us, smooth and confident—not like she used to walk, all timid on those gangly legs of hers. They're not gangly anymore, of course, and her teeth are nice and straight since she got her braces off. She's not wearing the plain, baggy clothes she used to wear, either; now, it's a striking green sweater that hugs her tighter than... well, I force my eyes back up to her face before I can finish that thought, or before someone accuses me of being a perv. She smiles, broad and full with those newly straight teeth, and I can't help but smile too.

Then my smile drops when I see who steps out from behind her. Scott moves up and nudges against her with the shoulder of his letter jacket as they walk. Emily gives him a smile that makes me twinge, and they walk together to our table. Scott pulls out a chair for her, smooth as always, and she slides into it. Rob gives me a not-so-subtle wink. I do my best to shrug it off as Scott drops himself and his dumb, swoopy hair into the seat beside her.

"Hey, guys," Emily says, her smile still full.

"Hey, Emily," Rob says. "Always good to see you back here."

"Are you kidding? I've known you guys since kindergarten. You can't get rid of me that easy, just because I made some other friends too." Emily flashes her eyes at Scott, and I twinge a little more.

"We had to say hi," Scott says. "Getting to know you guys is a great perk of dating this one over here." He gives Emily's arm a squeeze before fist-bumping Rob and Phillip. He holds his fist out for me; I reluctantly give him a limp tap back. *Sorry, Scott, you don't fool me as easy as these other chumps.*

He pulls out his phone. See, there you go, he's already bored with us. Then he turns to Tess. "You make your move yet, Tess?"

"What do you mean, her move?" I ask him.

"We've been playing an online game of chess." Scott taps his screen, then throws his arms up. "Whoa, you took my queen! How do you always do that?"

"*You'll get me next time,*" Tess says.

Scott laughs. "I doubt it. What's this, ten losses in a row? And that one time, I'm pretty sure you let me win."

Tess's poker face is impressive, but, yeah, of course she let him win.

Then Scott starts talking to Phillip about some movie they both watched on TV last night, and he pats Emily's arm but he's not even feeling her up or anything. Damn, it's hard to hate this guy; but I'm still going to give it my best shot.

"Oh, crap," Emily says. "I forgot, it's Tiffany's birthday today. I really should go say hi to her."

"That's right, we totally should." Scott gives her arm another pat.

"Sorry to bail on you guys. We'll come by again tomorrow, okay?"

"No worries," Rob says. Phillip and Tess give her a wave.

Emily stands up, and Scott pulls her chair out for her. He carries her tray for her, too, like she doesn't have arms of her own. They stroll away together toward Tiffany's table—the cool table. Tiffany's one of Emily's new friends. One of the cheerleaders who didn't know Emily existed a few months ago, but now... damn it, I think they're actually friends. I stare after Emily as she walks away, trying to pretend that it doesn't bother me how Scott is looking at her; and trying to pretend I'm not staring at her ass.

"Dude," Rob says. "I thought you were over her."

I pull my eyes back to our table. "I thought I was too, but it's not that easy. Emily and I grew up together, and it took me so long for those feelings to bubble up to the surface. And then when I finally told her how I felt..."

Rob's dark brown eyes look intently at me, his usual joking pulled away. "Sorry to say it, man, but Scott's a great guy for her to be with."

I let out a sigh. "I know he is, and I know I shouldn't give him the cold shoulder like that. I'll get over it. Eventually."

"If it helps," Tess says, "I can really whip him in our next chess game."

I laugh. "Thanks, Tess."

Rob turns to look toward the lobby. "Hey, who's that?"

I glance over to the lunchroom entryway, under the banner telling us how bullying is bad and the one next to that saying to join the debate club. I see the lone figure striding in underneath those, her steps direct and confident. Her wavy hair flows as she walks, looking more brown in this light but still hard to pin down exactly what color it is.

That girl from yesterday.

Ash.

I can't help but stare at her as she strides in, and neither can anyone else. Chairs squeak against the floor as everyone turns to look at her, and a chorus of not-so-subtle gossip rushes through the room. Ash keeps striding in like she owns the place. She marches a straight line, straight toward... me.

She reaches our table, drops herself into an empty seat, and stares at me with her icy-blue eyes. "Hey," she says.

"Well, hey there," Rob says back sarcastically. "Good to see you again. Oh, wait—who are you?"

Ash never takes her eyes off of me. "I met Matt at the coffee shop yesterday."

Rob's cheeks spread in a massive grin. "Oh, *really?*"

I cough awkwardly. "We, uh, didn't *meet*, exactly."

"What else would you call it?" Ash asks.

"I mean, we just..."

Rob's smile keeps spreading until his dimples pop. "It's funny how Matt never mentioned you. You want to introduce us to your new friend, Matt?"

I force a deep breath. "Guys, this is, um, Ash."

"Pleased to meet you," Ash says, though she doesn't stop staring at me.

Rob reaches a hand out, still grinning. "I'm Rob. *Very* pleased to meet you."

When Ash shakes Rob's hand, her eyes narrow for just a second.

Phillip leans forward slightly, and Ash startles. "Where'd you come from?" She quickly wipes the surprise off her face; I get the feeling she doesn't like being surprised very much. "And who're you?"

"Phillip," he says blandly, studying her with his pale green eyes.

Ash looks him over for another moment, then stretches her arms out. Her hand brushes against Phillip's forearm, a little too obvious to be an accident. He flinches, ever so subtle. Then Ash glances at Tess. "Does your other friend talk?"

I hesitate. "Tess takes a while to warm up to new people."

Tess keeps her eyes on her phone, her face free of expression.

I glance around to see everyone in the room watching us. Or watching Ash, at least. They're pretending not to, but doing a lousy job of it. Even Emily, with her sideways glances in Ash's direction. For a second, I almost wonder... is she jealous? But there are bigger questions on my mind.

"What are you doing here?" I ask.

"That's a rather forward question, isn't it?" Ash says. "Can't a girl stop by to see a friend?"

"Well, of course she can," Rob says with a smirk. "Now when you say 'friend,' you mean—"

I kick him under the table. "I thought, uh..."

"I told you I'd see you around," Ash says.

"You said you were just passing through."

She shrugs, swishing the waves of her hair. "Plans change. I might be sticking around this school after all."

"You're *enrolling* here?" I say, doing a terrible job hiding the shock in my voice.

"Maybe." Ash smiles, clearly enjoying herself. "I was just talking to your principal about that."

Phillip leans forward, his hoodie casting a shadow over his pale face. "Don't parents usually handle that?"

"Parents." Ash stares at him with narrow eyes. "What are they good for?"

"I can think of a few things," Phillip says.

"Good for you." Ash's voice goes cold. "I take care of myself."

Something dawns on me. "You're traveling through here on your own, aren't you? No parents?"

"*Emancipated minor,*" Tess says, her fingers flurrying over her phone.

Ash glances at her suspiciously. "Very good. At least your friend's phone talks, even if she doesn't."

Ash reaches toward Tess. I dart my hand out and grab her wrist to stop her.

"Tess doesn't like to be touched," I say, forcing a firmness to my voice.

Ash's mouth tightens and she glares at me. For a second, I wonder if she's going to reach back and slap me in the face. Then she smiles in an eerily knowing sort of way.

"Well," she says, her voice smooth as glass. "I guess I'll see you all around."

Ash slides up out of her chair and strides out of the room, savoring everyone's eyes on her.

And damn it, I can't help but watch her walk out either.

4

Ash

The car rolls to a stop on the cracked pavement of the parking lot, weeds sprouting up through the faded paint of the lines. Ash squints through the windshield at the row of motel room doors. The chipped stucco walls are patched in at least two shades of tan; the roof looks like it should have been replaced ten years ago.

"Is this the best we can do?" Ash asks to no one in particular.

"It's not the worst place we've stayed," Leah says quietly from the back seat.

Ash exhales. "All right, fine. I'm pretty sure this is the only motel in this pathetic town anyway. Heath, what can you tell me?"

He doesn't respond, staring out the window, the dark ridges of the back of his bald head toward her.

"I asked you a question, Heath."

Still nothing. Leah hesitantly reaches forward from the back seat and taps his shoulder. Heath turns back to look at her. Leah's hands flurry, her thin fingers speaking soundlessly in sign language. Heath glances at Ash, who glares daggers at him. He stares back, undaunted. Ash whips her hands in a sign of her own, the gestures sharp, *"Turn the damn thing on."*

Heath nonchalantly reaches up and flips the switch on his cochlear implant. "You rang, Your Highness?"

"You have a job to do," Ash snaps. "We've talked about this."

"We *have* talked about this. It gets tiring to leave it on all the time, remember?"

"You never know when something will happen that you have to be ready for. When it's off, you can't—"

"Heath," Leah says. When Heath looks back at her, she signs to him, *"Please, for me. We need you."*

Ash takes a breath and forces her voice to calm. "Leah's right. We're in this together."

Heath's shoulders relax. He reaches back and squeezes Leah's hand. "All right. Ash, what do you need?"

Ash nods toward the building. "Is there anything useful you can tell me about what's going on in there?"

Heath's eyes narrow, concentrating. "TV's on in room 102, I can't make out most of it but there are a lot of explosions. The guy in 103 is arguing with his girlfriend about buying too many shoes." He smirks. "Room 106 is either gutting a pig, or they're having sex."

Leah shrinks a bit further back into her seat.

"I meant anything about the *office*," Ash huffs.

Heath shrugs. "Sounds like whoever's breathing in there has asthma, and they're drumming some majorly bony fingers on a cheap countertop. Oh, and there's a clock ticking."

"So nothing useful, then. Fine, I'll do it myself."

"You really want to camp out here for more than a night or two?" Heath asks. "Do we even have enough for that?"

"I said I'll take care of it," Ash snaps. "I always do."

"Fine."

Ash throws the door open and steps out, squashing a weed that had forced its way up through the pavement and twisting her foot on it for good measure. She strides up to the office door, the *Vacancy* sign in the window looking like it's been sitting there collecting dust for quite some time.

The door chimes as she pushes it open. The air smells stale, and the dark, drab wallpaper isn't doing anything to help the atmosphere. Ash scans the small room and finds the source of the ticking—Heath was right about that, at least—a hideous cuckoo clock that looks like it was ninety-nine cents at a flea market.

An older lady sits behind the counter, drumming her fingers on the fake wood countertop. She forces a smile through the wrinkles on her cheeks and straightens her glasses. "Welcome to the Chaplain Motel," she says in a soft, raspy voice. "Checking in?"

Ash forces a smile. "Yes, please."

"And how long will you be staying?"

"I'm not sure yet."

"Well, I suppose we can keep it open-ended. But I will need a security deposit up front on a major credit card."

As the woman reaches for the computer keyboard, Ash slides her hand forward. Their fingers graze each other. Ash takes in the Pain.

Arthritis in her hip... no good. Wait—there it is—loss.

"A deposit?" Ash says, fumbling for her wallet. "Uh, sure, let me see what I have... oh, this trip has just been so hard now that I've lost him."

The lady stops typing, and her face softens, smoothing out the wrinkles. "Oh my, you're so young to have lost someone. Are you traveling alone?"

Ash nods, willing her eyes to tear up. "We used to take trips together all the time... my dad and me, I mean. It was just the two of us since my mom died years ago. But it was okay, because Dad worked so hard to make things fun for us. He'd pick out a place we'd never been and we'd just go. I didn't think about the planning or the... the money. Dad handled all that. But now he's gone too," Ash says, making sure her voice falters at just the right moment. "I'm on my way to Boston now to stay with my uncle, but my transmission went out, and I have to get it fixed before I can go on. That's why I have to stay here, but I didn't plan on this. Dad would always know what to do when something like this happened, but without him, I just..." She sniffs and waits for the reaction she knows will come.

"There, there," the woman says, patting her arm with a bony hand. "It's all right. You know, I went through the same sort of thing when my husband passed a few years ago."

Ash makes sure to keep the knowing smile off her face as she looks up at her, wiping at the pretend tears in her eyes. "You did?"

"Oh my, yes. Harold used to handle all the books and the reservations, all of that. When he passed, I didn't think I could keep up with this place. But I sat down and figured it out, and here I am."

"So it gets easier? I hope it does. Let me, um, just get that deposit for you... I just hope I have enough left on my credit card..."

The woman looks at her, a warmth shining through the cataracts in her eyes. "You know what? Why don't we forget about the deposit."

"Really?" Ash says with a surprise that sounds almost sincere.

"It's the least I can do with what you're going through. In fact..." She chews her lip for a moment, then opens the cash register with a *ching* that echoes off the dusty walls. "Why don't I give you a little something to help you out? Our little secret."

"Oh, I couldn't let you do that," Ash protests halfheartedly.

"I insist. Put it toward that new transmission." The woman hands a few bills to Ash with a wink that creases the wrinkles around her eye.

Ash beams. "That's so kind of you. That helps so much."

The woman pats her hand again and slides a room key across the counter.

Ash takes the key and the money and turns to leave, her smile dropping away as soon as she walks out the door.

5

Matt

I walk past the clang of lockers and a jumble of rowdy conversations, everyone glad that the final bell rang and it's time to get out of here. Believe me, I don't feel like hanging around the school any longer than I have to either. I'm halfway down the hall when I bump right into someone and send the pile of books they were carrying tumbling to the floor.

I instinctively bend down to pick up the books, and then come face to face with Emily.

"Oh... uh, hi," I say, my voice suddenly squeaking. *Real smooth, Matt.*

"Hi," Emily says awkwardly. "You don't have to—"

"It's cool, I want to." I wrangle the fallen books together. We both stand up, shuffling our feet on the scuffed floor tiles. A handful of other students brush past us on their way out the door.

"So," Emily says, not quite looking at me, "who's your new, uh, friend?"

"That girl at lunch?" I say defensively. "I just met her— I mean, bumped into her at the coffee shop. And then she showed up here. She's not really my friend. Not like you." I suddenly feel my face get warm. "I, uh, just mean, you and I have known each other a long time."

"We do go way back, don't we?" Emily brushes her hair back over her shoulder; she never used to do that back when she had the braces and the gangly legs. "You remember in first grade, how you used to give me your milk at lunch every day?"

I chuckle at the memory. "Oh, yeah. And Rob used to trade his chips to Phillip for extra dessert every Friday."

"Right, I forgot about that!"

"It was no big deal," I say with a shrug. "You liked milk, and I didn't."

"It was sweet of you. Oh, you remember when your mom found out? She made you drink two milks a day for a week to make up for it, so you'd 'grow up big and strong!' " Emily laughs, then it fades. "Oh... sorry to bring up your mom like that."

"It's okay." I drop my eyes for just a second. "You were there for me when it happened. You guys all were."

"We've been through a lot together, haven't we? Even now that we've grown up, and we've made some new friends too."

I think about Scott holding her hand and then chew my lip. "Yeah."

Emily darts a glance at me, but won't look at me straight on. "So, your new friend, Ash—she sure seems interested in you, for just having met you and all."

"Why shouldn't she be?" The question comes out more defensively than I'd planned.

"No reason." Emily shuffles her feet a bit more. "Just made me curious, I guess."

We stand there, not quite looking at each other, neither of us sure what to say. I wonder if she's actually jealous of Ash, wonder if she ever thinks of me as more than the awkward kid who gave her his milk when we were six. I told her how I feel a while back, of course, but that was a train wreck. And now she's with Scott.

"I guess I'd better head home, then," Emily says.

"Oh. Yeah, sure."

"Can I, uh, have my books back?"

I look down, suddenly realizing I'm still holding them. "Oh, right! Sorry."

I hand the stack back to her, almost dropping them again like the clumsy moron I am. Emily stuffs them in her backpack and throws it over her shoulder. I glance down at that sweater of hers one more time as she turns to leave.

"I'll, uh, see you tomorrow," Emily says.

I watch her walk away, mentally kicking myself. Rob's right, like he usually is. I need to let her go. Emily and I are friends, that's all. I take a long breath before I start toward the door.

I immediately bump into someone else. I don't even see anyone; then Phillip seems to materialize under his hoodie, his green eyes staring at me from his pale face.

"You've gotta stop sneaking up on me like that," I blurt out.

"What's with that Ash girl?" Phillip never says much, so when he does talk, he cuts right to it.

"I don't know." I start walking again.

"Why is she transferring here? Where'd she even come from?"

"Like I said, man, I don't know."

"She's really emancipated? On her own?"

"I guess. Good for her, right?"

"I wonder," Phillip says.

"So we have a new girl at school, so what? It's only news because nothing ever happens around here."

"Sure." Phillip takes a long pause. "She seems awfully interested in you."

"Why does everyone keep saying that?" I say, my voice rising a little. "Can't I be interesting?"

"I just—" Phillip gives me a pointed look. "Be careful, okay?"

"It's cool, man. But thanks, I guess."

We step out the door into the sunshine. Rob's already outside, and he waves me over.

"Come on, Matt," Rob says. "The taxi service is heading out."

A tiny sting of something flicks against my cheek, and I instinctively brush it off. "Taxi service, huh? I hope you don't have the meter running."

"Who says I ever turned it off from yesterday?"

Something hits my cheek again. Was that a pebble? I glance to the side to see who's messing with me. A bunch of the football players are hanging around, but they're not laughing or pointing at me or anything. A couple volleyball players walk by, and there are some band nerds chatting, but no one looking guilty. I start to look away when I catch a glimpse of wavy hair through the crowd, that brown-blonde color I can't quite put my finger on. I only see her from the back, and she's walking away.

"I'll, uh, catch up with you guys later," I say, staring after her.

"What, you're doing the loner thing today?" Rob asks.

"I just... need to check something out. I'll see you tomorrow."

"Your loss, man. I just got the hatchback detailed."

I'm already pushing my way through the crowd, following that hair I can't name the color of as it slips around the corner of the building. I make my way around to follow her, trying to hurry without looking like I'm hurrying. When I make it around the corner, I don't see her anymore.

"Ash?" I call out.

I feel another ping, this time on my ear. I rub it and then catch a glimpse of her disappearing through the bushes across the street. I pick up my pace, then jolt as a car horn blares and tires screech beside me. I sheepishly mouth an apology to the driver of the car who's giving me the finger, and hurry out of the street and through the bushes.

I get to the playground of the old elementary school. I glance at the rusting monkey bars and the swing set with one of the chains broken and the swing dangling. The pea gravel crunches under my feet. Something small flicks against my right cheek, then my left one. As I sweep my hand in front of my face, my hand brushes against a bunch more little specks. Suddenly I realize they're some of those pebbles from the ground, but they're... floating.

I track my gaze across the playground and notice dozens of the pebbles hanging weightless in the air like a cloud, hovering there.

"What the—"

Ash steps out from behind the tunnel slide on the playset, smiling through the sparse freckles on her cheeks. "I thought this might get your attention."

"Are you doing this?" I ask, staring at the floating rocks.

"Don't be coy with me. I know you've seen things like this before. Or should I say, you've *done* things like this before."

I suck in a quick breath and stare at her. "What?"

"You didn't think you were the only one who's different, did you?"

My heart stops when she says that. I stare at her, my mouth moving but nothing coming out.

Ash steps toward me, brushing aside some of the hovering pebbles like insects. "But, no, I'm not the one doing this. Come out here, Leah."

Another girl steps out. Thin, almost frail-looking. Pale, paler than Phillip even, with hair black as ink hanging down over her shoulders. She walks slowly, each step hesitant. Her eyes are down on the ground, but she makes a quick glance at Ash.

Ash gives her an approving nod. "You can drop them now."

Leah's thin fingers twitch, and suddenly the pebbles in the air tremble and fall, skittering into the rest of the gravel underfoot. I watch in awe, and my voice drops to a whisper. "Man, I wish I could do that."

Another figure emerges from behind the playset, and I involuntarily take a step back because this guy is huge. His shoulder muscles stretch at his shirt, and his shaved head is accentuated by his dark olive skin. His mouth is a tight line, a freckle or a birthmark standing out just above his lip. As he stands there glaring at me, I wonder if I'm about to get beat up.

"You wish you could do that, huh?" he says in a deep but quiet voice.

I startle. "Wait, you heard that?"

"What exactly do you wish you could do?" he continues without answering my question.

"Seriously, I whispered that, and you were forty feet away."

He gives me a hard stare. "Like Ash said. You're not the only one who's different."

Ash motions toward the big guy. "This is Heath. He has good ears, but the manners... not so much."

Heath seems like he has a resting irritated face as he keeps staring at me, and I wonder again if I'm going to get beat up. Then I notice something on the side of his bald scalp, a circle of gray plastic sitting above his ear.

"Wait, you have a hearing aid," I say, the words coming out before I can even self-filter. "How did you—"

"Cochlear implant," Heath says.

"What?"

"It's not a hearing aid. Uninformed idiots call it that, but it's not. Cochlear implant."

"Oh... right..."

"And your next question," Heath says, "will be something stupid like, 'Those help deaf people hear, right?' "

I swallow, glad he spoke before I did because, yeah, that's about what I was going to say. "Well, I mean, I just thought those implants would let you hear some things, but not, you know... everything..."

"Right," Heath says. "I shouldn't be able to hear all this stuff, should I? Because surprisingly enough, you're right about that. For *normal* people, cochlear implants might let them hear some sounds, but not nearly as much as most people think. Definitely not enough to let me hear what you whispered a minute ago." He gives me a hard look, the dark skin of his forehead creasing. "But people like us aren't normal, are we?"

I stare back at him. "Well, uh..."

"You never answered my question," Heath says. "What is it you wish you could do?"

I involuntarily glance toward Leah. "I just... you were doing that with all of those rocks at the same time? Holding them steady like that?"

Leah shrugs faintly without looking up.

"You know," Ash says in a sly voice, "you don't seem nearly as surprised by the floating rocks as most people would be."

"What?" I sputter. "Of course I'm surprised. Don't I sound surprised?"

"I knew you were different like us," Ash says. "I just wasn't sure *how*, exactly."

"What do you mean, different like you?"

Ash shakes her head. "You're slower than I thought you'd be. Do you need another demonstration? Leah." The last word comes out sharply, like a command. Leah hunches a little further down, and her fingers twitch. The dangling swing on the playset suddenly pushes out a few inches on its own, setting it rocking back and forth on its single chain.

"Don't pretend this is something new to you." Ash steps toward me. When I flinch back, she says, "Don't worry. Everyone else out there, they don't understand. We can't show them who we are, just like you can't show them who you are. But we're not like them, and neither are you. That's why I knew I could show you."

I stare agape at her. "But how did you—"

"...know?" she finishes for me. Ash smiles as she closes the distance between us, and reaches her hand up toward my cheek. I'm in too much shock to pull away as her fingers brush my skin.

Her eyes flicker shut for a second. When they open again, the blue seems more intense than before. "So much pain."

"Pain?"

"You have a gaping loss in you," Ash says. "You were young then, weren't you?"

I swallow hard, pushing down thoughts of that night staring at the burning house.

"That's my gift," she says, her face softening. "Or my burden. I feel others' pain."

"But how did you know I'm... different?" I ask, partially to get the image of the burning house out of my head.

Ash shrugs. "Pain takes a lot of forms. You feel like you can't be yourself, hiding because you're misunderstood."

I stiffen. "I don't—"

She holds her hand up. "Of course you're misunderstood. We all are, because we can't tell all those normal people what we can do. If we did... it would end badly."

I swallow, remembering what my mom told me about hiding my Ability. How people don't understand things that are different.

"It's okay, Matt," Ash says. "I know. *We* know. You don't have to hide anymore."

I stare at her, counting the freckles on her face, not able to meet her eyes. I try to decide if her tone was sincere. I look over at Heath; his face is still blank and stern. Leah glances at me, just for a moment, but I see a glimmer in her eyes before she looks back down.

Do they know? I mean, really *know?* I want to believe it more than anything, but I can't quite make myself.

"I think I'd better go," I say, trying to hide the regret in my voice.

Heath takes a step toward me, but Ash subtly raises a hand and he stops. "It's okay," Ash says. "It takes time to open up. We'll be waiting when you change your mind."

I take a hesitant step backward, my foot crunching against the gravel, then another step, and another, before I finally peel my eyes away from her and turn to walk away as fast as I can without running.

It's all I can do to not look back.

6

Matt

The school hall is quiet as I plod my way back inside. The place is almost empty now, because I'm the only moron going back in after the bell has rung.

The image of those floating rocks swirls in my head. I never thought I'd see something like that—not if it wasn't me doing it. I never thought I'd find someone else like me.

When Rob, Phillip, and Tess found out, and accepted me for it, I thought that was the closest I'd get. Phillip has his disappearing act, and Tess does her hacker thing. And it felt like they were superheroes with me, but it's not the same. What they can do doesn't defy the laws of science and nature. Even among the rejects, I'm still the only freak.

I reach the door to the science room and look inside. Mr. Plask sits hunched over his desk, pecking at his computer. I knew he'd be here;

sometimes I think he sleeps in this room. He scratches at the tufts of his hair, all scruffed up like it usually is. The glow of the screen glares off his glasses.

"Mr. Plask?" I say, knocking on the doorframe. "You busy?"

He looks up, looking only moderately startled this time, and smiles. "Matt! What brings you here?"

I step slowly into the room. He watches me silently. I grab a chair and drag it up to his desk, the legs squeaking against the floor. I sit myself awkwardly in it, fiddling with my hands.

"Have you ever wondered," I ask him, "if there could be others out there like me?"

Plask's expression is hard to read because his eyes are warped and oversized behind his glasses. "When you say 'like' you, you mean—"

I reach out my hand, and with a tingle of my fingers, his pen flies up off the desk and into my hand. His mouth curls up. "Just wanted to be clear," Plask says.

I set the pen down and rub my hands together. "I appreciate that you've kept my secret and that you—and my other friends—don't look at me differently, knowing what you know. When I caught that bottle of acid and you saw what I could do, I thought my life was over. You showed me it's not; in fact, maybe it's just getting started. But I still figured I was the only one like this, that I'd still be alone. But now..." I can't make myself finish.

"Well, of course I think there could be others."

"Really?" I ask, surprised by the quickness of his response.

"I always believed, hoped, in the possibility of something incredible. And then I found you." Plask smiles. "Besides, we already know there was someone else. You inherited your Ability from your mother, didn't you?"

I swallow as my mind goes back to that storage unit where I found her old things and finally pieced it together. She had the Ability too, but I'll never be able to share that with her, to talk to her about what it means and what I want to do with it. She died years before I ever knew.

"Yeah, my mom had it," I say, composing myself. "But that's just because we share the same DNA. I'm talking about someone else, someone... not from here."

Plask raises his eyebrows. "What's bringing all this up, Matt?"

I open my mouth to tell him, but I can't. This is too much, and it's not my secret to share. "I don't know," I say, trying to sound convincing. "I guess I've just been wondering what it would be like to have someone like me, *really* like me, to share it with."

Plask nods slowly. "I suppose I can understand that. I'm... sorry if I haven't been supportive enough."

"What? No. I mean, you've been great. You made me believe in myself when I didn't think I could."

He smiles. "I'm glad to hear that. But finding someone else with an Ability like yours..." He scratches at the tufts of his hair. "I do believe they're out there, Matt, but how to find them? I don't know."

The unspoken words are on the tip of my tongue—*what if I already have?* I can't ask Plask that, so I don't. But the more important question, the one even I can't answer, is...

Can I trust them?

I wander around town for a bit after that. Given the size of Chaplain, it doesn't take too long for me to walk home, even when I take the scenic route. I trudge past our tiny excuse for a post office, past the liquor store with its gaudy display of neon beer signs flashing in the window. Past all the houses I've walked past a thousand times, and the old oak tree that gets a little more crooked every year. I make it to my house, up the uneven front steps, and push my way through the front door. I hear a clinking of bottles as I step inside.

"Dad?" I call out.

"Oh, hi, Matt. In here."

I drop my backpack with a thud on the living room carpet—one of us should really vacuum in here—and make my way to the kitchen where I find him pulling out a bottle from the fridge. Dad holds it out in front of him as he unscrews the cap, making sure I get a good look at it; he doesn't say it out loud, but we both know he wants me to see that it's a soda and not a beer. I give him a subtle nod.

"You, uh, want one of these?" he asks.

"Sure. Thanks."

He hands me his bottle and opens the fridge to pull out another for himself, leaning a hand on the scuffed countertop. He scratches at his cheek, which is sagging a little with his age, but I have to admit, it has more color than it did a year ago. "How was your day?" he asks. "You, uh, had a test today, right? English?"

"Math, actually, but yeah. It went okay. I'm still a little fuzzy on quadratic equations, but—" I shake my head and take a swig of the soda. "Never mind. You don't want to hear about that."

"No, I do. Really." His voice sounds almost sincere. "Quadratic equations? You know, I think I remember some of that from my high school days. If you want, we could look at that together later?"

I smile. "Sure, Dad," I say, though I know we probably won't. Baby steps. We're just now getting to where we pretend to take an interest in each other; to *really* take an interest, to talk about big stuff, that takes time. "How was your day?"

He nods, sending his stray string of hair swishing. "Oh, fine, fine. I mean, everyone's worked up about the buyout of the factory, but I'm sure it'll work out. It was to be expected, you know, considering."

By "considering," he means because the former owner, Seth Crossman, is currently in jail, awaiting trial on fraud and murder charges. Dad doesn't know I'm the one who put him there, and he probably never will.

It's okay. Like I said, baby steps.

"Sorry it's up in the air," I say. "I hope it's not too stressful."

"No. No, I'm okay." Dad takes a long swig of his soda; I hope he's not craving something stronger.

"Cool," I say. "I'm gonna go do my homework."

Dad nods. "Okay. I was actually about to leave to meet with my sponsor from, uh, rehab."

I nod back at him. "I'm... proud of you, Dad."

He smiles. "Thanks."

We stand there awkwardly for a minute, trying to decide if we're supposed to hug. I decide we're not quite there yet and I turn to start toward the stairs.

"Matt?" he says.

I turn back. "Yeah?"

"Are you really okay?"

I swallow. No, I'm not okay, but this isn't about math tests or pimples. This is about my Ability. We don't talk about that. He knows—I think he does, at some level, under years of repression and denial. I know he saw me move that action figure when I was a kid. Didn't he? But he pretended not to see, or he convinced himself he hadn't, and we've never said a word about it since. Part of me wants to finally say it out loud; that I'm different, that I may have finally found other people who are different like me. But I push it back down again and shake my head.

"I'm good," I say.

He nods, pretending to believe me, and heads out to his meeting.

7

Matt

Rob's hatchback coughs and clunks as it struggles to carry us toward school. Rob watches casually out the window at the row of houses that are all trying to pretend that they don't need new roofs and a whole lot of paint.

"You finish that Spanish homework?" Rob asks.

"Sort of," I reply, watching a stray dog pee on a parked car. "Those verb tenses always trip me up."

"No joke. I have enough trouble just speaking English." Rob squints through the windshield. "Dude, what's that?"

I follow his eyes to a trail of smoke rising at the end of the next block. We drop into silence as a few more houses pass by, and the smoke gets thicker and darker... making it clear this isn't just a barbecue. I can see the flames now, churning out from the house on the corner, clawing with glowing fingers from every window, belching out the smoke. Half a dozen people stand on the opposite corner, watching, murmuring to each other. Rob skids the hatchback to a stop at the curb and we pile out.

"You already call 911?" Rob calls out as we hurry up to the group.

An older guy with a face full of gray stubble nods. "Ten minutes ago."

Everyone in the group grumbles at that—*How can the fire department take that long? What do our taxes pay for? Are they going to let the whole block go up?*—But we all know the deal around here. They have to come in from the next exit down the highway, because we don't have our own fire station.

I point a shaking finger at the burning house. "Is anyone in there?"

A lady in a jogging outfit shakes her head. "Nah, that house has been empty for six months. I've been wondering if it would ever sell."

"Not gonna happen now," the old guy says.

The crowd murmurs some more about that, but I don't hear them. I can't look away from the house as the fire rages, my mind spiraling back to the night when it was my house burning and the fire department took too long to get there that night too. Except that night, the house wasn't empty.

I can't fight off the image of the burning roof caving in, that image that has replayed in my mind more times than I could possibly count, the moment that removed all doubt that the person inside was gone. The rafters creaking and splintering, the shell of the house swallowing it up, the flurry of sparks churning into the sky. *She's gone.* The image repeats, the crunch of the charred wood louder this time as it collapses. *She's GONE.* The rush of flames into the sky is like an inferno. And it repeats again, over and over and over.

"Dude," Rob says, pulling me out of my trance. "Maybe we should get out of here."

He gives me a look that says he knows what's going on in my head, and he knows the best thing for me to do is get the hell away. I nod, feeling numb, and we climb back into the hatchback and leave the flames behind us as we finally hear a siren approaching from the distance.

We don't say anything for the next few blocks, our silence punctuated by the uneven rumble of the engine.

"It's not the firefighters' fault," Rob says. We both know he's not talking about that abandoned house back there. "You know how far they have to come to get here."

"That night was a long time ago," I tell him, my voice void of emotion. "I'm okay."

We don't say anything the rest of the way to the school. The engine coughs a few more times and the houses flow by outside. I look past the houses and the trees to the gray sky overhead.

We pull into the school parking lot and come to a stop with a squeak of the should-have-been-replaced-a-month-ago brakes. I push my door open with a creak and start to step out when Rob puts a hand on my arm.

"You sure you're okay?" he asks.

"Dude, I told you—"

"I don't just mean about that house back there. You were off before that, too."

He's right, of course. This thing has been gnawing at me from the inside, but it's not something I can talk about. Not to him. "I'm fine," I lie.

"Is it something with your dad?"

"Nah." I start walking toward the school building, Rob following behind me. "Things with him are better than they've been in a while, actually. Not that it's saying much."

"Wait, this isn't about Emily, is it?"

I bite my lip. "No. Seriously, Rob, I'm fine."

He wouldn't understand. He accepts my Ability, or says he does, but I don't know if he *understands* it; I don't know if anyone does, or can, unless they have an Ability too. Someone like…

Ash.

For just a second, I think I see her almost brown, almost blonde hair through the crowd of kids up ahead. Part of me wants to see her again, but most of me is glad I don't have to deal with her right now. I'm still not sure how I feel about her.

I jump when someone suddenly appears right next to me. "What's on your mind?" Phillip asks.

"Don't sneak up on me like that!" I blurt out. "And why would there be anything on my mind?"

"Don't know, but isn't there?"

Rob laughs. "That's exactly what I said."

"So you noticed it too?" Phillip asks.

"Guys," I say, "there's nothing to notice. I'm fine."

We push through the doors and I start down the hallway with everyone else, intent on getting to class so I don't have to think about any of this. I meet Tess going the other way, walking with slow steps. For a second I think maybe I can walk past without her noticing, since she's got her head down looking at her phone like always, but even without looking up, she says, *Something bothering you, Matt?*

"See?" Rob says, stepping up behind me. "We all see it, so you might as well tell us what it is."

"Look, guys, it's just—"

I glance down the hall and see a wavy trail of red-brown-blonde hair again. I must really be obsessing about Ash if I keep imagining her everywhere like this. And this time it's super vivid, because behind her I even see a big, bald, dark-skinned guy, and a thin, pale girl with black hair...

Crap.

Ash strides up to me, very real and very *here*.

"Ash?" I sputter. "I didn't think... I mean, I didn't think you'd be..."

Rob looks back and forth between her and me and then pops a sly grin. "Ah. So *that's* what's up."

Ash casually brushes back her hair. "Why so surprised? I told you I was transferring here."

"You, uh, said you were *thinking* about it..."

"Well, I thought about it, and I did."

Rob eyes Heath. "And you brought friends this time. Is this your *other* boyfriend?"

Heath's scowl doesn't break. "I'm not her boyfriend," he says in monotone. "Are you Matt's boyfriend?"

I glance back and forth between them, feeling the awkwardness almost sticking to me. "Uh, guys, this is Ash," I say, suddenly not sure what to do with my hands. "Wait, never mind, you met her already. Sorry. But these two with her are Heath and Leah."

Rob and Heath look each other over suspiciously. Leah is looking intently at a chipped spot on the floor tiles.

"And, uh," I say, "this is Rob, Phillip, and Tess."

Ash looks at Tess, wrinkling her nose. "Ah, yes, the girl who doesn't talk."

"*I can talk just fine,*" Tess says, her fingers hitting the phone screen a little more forcefully than usual.

"Speaking of girls that don't talk," Rob says, "it's Lisa, right?"

Leah flinches back a step, her eyes still on that chip in the floor. She shakes her head slowly.

Phillip nudges Rob. "Leah, not Lisa."

Leah smiles at him... almost.

"*Nice to meet you all,*" says Tess.

"So," I say, shuffling my feet, "you *all* transferred here?"

"Yeah," Heath grunts. "And we're ecstatic about it."

Rob straightens up. "What's that supposed to mean?"

"You seem like a smart guy. You figure it out."

"Now, Heath," Ash chides, "we talked about this."

"*You* talked," he says.

Her smile disintegrates—barely for a moment, but the heat from her eyes is unmistakable. Heath looks away, and then Ash's smile is back. Rob and Phillip share a look.

"So, uh, Ash," I say, "you really transferred yourself? You're really emancipated?"

"Sure," she says.

"And them?" Phillip asks, nodding toward Heath and Leah.

Ash smiles a little wider. "I helped them get emancipated too."

"What does that mean, you helped them?" Phillip looks at Leah, but she won't meet his eyes for more than a second.

"It means what it sounds like it means," Ash says. "They needed some help, and I gave it to them. Like right now, we need to get to English lit, I believe. Let's go, guys." She starts down the hall, then turns back. "You know, Matt, you could come with us."

"With you? But I have math this period."

She shakes her head. "You know what I mean, Matt. You have more in common with us than you do with them."

Ash walks away. Heath lumbers after her; Leah hovers awkwardly for a moment, then scurries on behind. I'm left staring.

Rob taps me on the arm. "What the hell was that?"

"Nothing," I say, a little too quickly.

"That was *not* nothing. And not just the way Ash was trying to get her hooks into you. Did you see how she shut Heath down like that?" Rob nudges Phillip. "You saw that too, right?"

Phillip's mouth creases, considering his response, but the bell rings before he says anything.

"Gotta get to class," I say quickly, glad for the excuse to get out of here.

Rob grabs my arm. "We're not done here, dude."

"I'll catch up with you later." I squirm out of his grip and hurry down the hall. I feel Rob's eyes on me but I don't look back.

I hurry into the classroom and slide into my seat just as Mr. Harkin launches into something about parabolas. As much as I don't want to listen to that right now, at least I don't share this class with Rob, Phillip, or Tess, so I don't have to deal with their questions for a while. I'm about to pull out a pencil to at least pretend to take notes when my phone buzzes. I pull it out to see a text from Rob—*I repeat, what the hell was that?*

Okay, maybe I'll have to deal with this sooner than I thought. I rough my hand through my hair trying to come up with a response; at least I don't have to worry about Harkin yelling at me for using my phone in class, since there's zero chance he'll even notice. He's already waist-deep into one of his tangents that's way above our heads.

"... see, the fascinating thing about this problem is how it applies to all sorts of things, like jets or even rocket propulsion. I bet you didn't know this, but..."

Everyone in the room is either staring ahead blankly or on their phones too. Clearly this isn't as fascinating as Harkin seems to think it is. I suck in a long breath and type a message back to Rob.

MATT—that's just how ash talks, dont worry about it

ROB—what's that about you having stuff in common w/ them? You just met them!!

MATT—I guess we both enjoy long walks on the beach

ROB—you know what i mean. Why is she so in2 u?

I'm about to respond with something snippy like *why shouldn't she be, I'm not such a bad catch, am I?*, when I get another text—from Phillip.

PHILLIP—i'm concerned about u, man. ash seems to know a lot about u already

God, this is going to be a long day. I add Phillip to the chat with Rob.

MATT—rob, phillip, i appreciate you looking out for me, but i'm fine

ROB—who said i was looking out for you?

I snort and send him back a middle-finger emoji. Then my screen flashes to yet another text, this one from Tess.

TESS—What did she mean, more in common?

I let out a long sigh and then add her to the group chat too.

MATT—look, guys, i dont know what ash was talking about. it's not a big deal

ROB—seems like a big deal

TESS—Is there something we should know about her?

I type three different responses but delete all of them before I hit send.

PHILLIP—just feels like she's trying to get you for herself

MATT—what? dont worry, you're my crew. Always will be

ROB—don't forget it

PHILLIP—you're our crew too man

I send a thumbs-up emoji and slip my phone away, wishing that were the end of it. Not just for their questions, but for the ones that keep swirling around inside my head. If only it were that simple.

8

Matt

After deflecting the slew of text messages asking why Ash is so into me and then trying to follow Harkin's way-over-my-head lecture, I'm more than ready to get out of class. Everyone else seems to be ready too, and as soon as the bell rings, we all pile out in a stampede.

I scan the crowd in the hallway, hoping I won't bump into Rob, Phillip, or Tess for them to give me any more crap. I don't see any of them, so I'm in the clear for a bit longer. But my eyes catch on a small figure at the end of the hall. Her black hair drapes over her ghostly pale skin, down over her thin shoulders.

Leah.

She walks alone, shuffling along with timid steps, hunched over, her eyes darting back and forth. The crowd flows around her on either side, everyone sidestepping to keep her at arm's length as they move past, giving her suspicious glances for just a second but making sure to avoid eye contact. Leah keeps her eyes down on the floor and keeps shuffling, as if she knows full well that she doesn't belong.

Chaplain doesn't do great with outsiders, not that we do so well with the regular folks either. It's mostly just awkward until Kyle Draughton shows up, our prick of a football team captain. He struts right up to her, says, "New in town, freak?" and slams into her with his shoulder without even slowing down. Leah totters from the blow and her stack of books drops to the floor in a tumble.

Kyle throws his head back in a laugh and keeps on walking without looking back. The other kids keep walking, too, some of them laughing along with Kyle, a few at least trying to hide it, but none of them bother to stop or help Leah, or even look at her.

"Hey!" I yell, my face hot. I rush down the hall, pushing past all the indifferent jerks. I want to grab Kyle by the neck and feed him his letter jacket, but he's already disappeared around the corner. I couldn't really take him anyway, but that's another story. I skid to a stop beside Leah. "Are you okay?"

She nods slowly, her black hair swishing.

"I'm surprised you're not with Ash and Heath," I say. For once, I'm disappointed that Heath isn't here; he could've knocked Kyle's head off, and I'd pay good money to see that.

Leah's mouth quivers for a second. "I got lost looking for the bathroom," she says, barely audible.

"It's just down the next hallway." I point, making sure she sees. "New places can be hard, I get it. The good news is, our pathetic little school isn't big enough to be too complicated. Give it a few days and you'll get to know the place fine."

She kneels down in a slow, shaky motion, like she could topple over any second, and fumbles to pick up her books. I drop down with her.

"Hey, let me help you with those." I reach out to wrangle the books. "And don't worry about Kyle—that jerk who knocked into you. He's like that with anyone who's new. Or... different."

Her eyes flick up to mine, just for a second—little brown-green pools against her pale face. "Did he ever do anything to you?" she asks me timidly.

My mind reluctantly goes back to all the times Kyle tripped me in the hall or played keep-away with one of my books. "Yeah. But why would you think that?"

"Because you're different too. Aren't you?"

I look at her, unsure how to respond. The herd of kids keeps shuffling past around us.

"Ash says you're like me," Leah says. "I don't know if I can believe her. I don't think anyone else is like me. That's why people like him..." She rubs her shoulder where Kyle hit her.

I force a hard swallow. Am I ready to share my secret with her? But the pain on her face... "You're not the only one," I tell her.

Leah looks up, and our eyes meet. I can feel her searching, needing it to be true but too scared to believe it. And before I can talk myself out of it, I reach out my hand.

My fingers tingle. Her pencil, on the floor with her fallen books, rolls to my hand.

The other kids walking past barely pay attention to us at all, much less notice a pencil rolling a few inches, but Leah sees it just fine. Her eyes grow wide, and she looks at me dead on for the first time.

You're not the only one.

The corners of her mouth twist up, slowly, into a smile. Almost a smile, at least. She reaches out her hand and her fingers twitch, and the pencil rolls back toward her. I can't help but smile too.

Then Leah's timid mask washes over her face again, and she looks back down at the floor. Her hand darts out and grabs the pencil, and she scoops up the books with her arm and scurries up and turns without looking at me, hurrying off down the hall. I watch her go, feeling the residual tingle in my hand. Knowing that we shared something a lot bigger than flicking a pencil.

You're not the only one.

Ash

The car door creaks like a coffin in an old horror movie as Ash climbs her way in, settling into the duct tape over the seat. She watches all the other students pile into their pretty little cars that their daddies bought them, and Ash mutters an f-bomb under her breath.

"About time you got here," says Heath in the passenger seat. "I'm ready to get the hell away from this school."

"Why, Heath," Ash says in mock surprise, "did you not have a good first day? Did one of the big kids take your lunch money?"

Heath grunts. "We've never bothered with school in any of the other places we've been through. Why is this one so important? It's pathetic here."

Ash looks out at the students, all huddled in their superficial cliques. "I told you, we need to get to know our new friend. And to do that, we need to fit in."

"You think we fit in?" A harsh edge comes out in Heath's voice. "Here, or anywhere?"

"You know what I mean. And remember, *he* doesn't fit in either. That's the point. That's why we need him."

"So let's throw him in the trunk and be on our way."

"We need him on our side first. We need him to understand he's the same as us."

"*Is* he the same as us?" Heath says. "Will he fight for us, or will he run away and look out for himself?"

Ash reaches out toward Heath's wrist, but he pulls his hand away.

"Fine," she says with a huff. "Besides, I don't have to touch you to know it all goes back to your brother."

Heath turns toward the window.

"We're not like Brian," Ash says firmly. "We fight together. You fight with *us*. Remember?"

Heath looks at her for a long moment, then nods.

Leah reaches up from the back seat and gently touches Heath's arm. "We have to stick together. To protect each other, from..." She trails off, and her eyes flick downward.

"That's right, Leah," Ash tells her. "There are a lot of threats out there for people like us. That's why we need each other."

Leah starts trembling. Heath looks back and smiles at her. As much as Heath ever smiles. "If anyone wants to get to you," he tells her, "they've gotta go through me."

Ash nudges Heath and gives him a sharp look. "That's why you need to stick with us."

"I didn't say anything about leaving," he snaps.

"You were thinking it."

"I was *thinking,*" Heath says, "that I don't trust your new boyfriend."

"Matt won't hurt us," Leah says softly. "He's like me."

Heath chews his lip. His eyes soften as he looks at Leah. "All right. I'll give him a chance, for you. But I'm not sold on him yet."

"I'm telling you," Ash says, "we need him."

Heath turns to her, his eyes hardening again. "He'd better fight for us."

"He will."

9

Matt

I step into my bedroom and drop my backpack onto the carpet where it's fraying in the corner. The image of that pencil rolling back and forth keeps running in my mind, over and over, and the image of Leah's face smiling. Smiling because she'd finally found someone else like her.

I never thought I'd find anyone like me either. Didn't think anyone else like me was even out there... except for the person I'd lost before I knew what we shared.

The picture on my nightstand draws my eyes. My mom's dark hair draping over her narrow shoulders. Her smile frozen in time.

"Hey, Mom," I say. "Big day today."

I watch her eyes in the photo, waiting for her to respond. If only.

"I found a girl today, someone I never thought I'd find." I stifle an awkward laugh. "Not like that... I don't think so, anyway. But someone really special all the same. Someone like me." I fight down a swallow. "Someone like *us*."

I reach to the nightstand with the scratched finish and slide open the drawer with a squeak. I carefully reach my hand inside and lift out the superhero doll.

Her red and gold breastplate shines in the light, and her arms look as strong as ever. I imagine my mom holding this the day she discovered her Ability... is that how it happened? Or did she buy the doll after, when she decided she could be a superhero too? I wish I knew.

"It's hard carrying this thing that no one else understands," I say. "No one understood you either, did they? Not even Dad. God... what would that be like? To fall in love with someone and never be able to tell them, always hiding it..."

I suddenly think about Emily. Not that I'm in love with her... well, she's certainly not in love with me. But either way, in all the years I've known her, all the times I've wanted something more with her, I've never been able to tell her who I really am. Will I ever be able to tell her?

"I do have some friends. People who understand me... or at least try to. I'd thought when I was finally able to tell them, when someone else knew about me, that was the best I could hope for. And it's been great, but now I've met someone who's actually *like* me, three people in fact, and I don't even know what to think anymore."

The doll's fierce eyes stare back at me, and I almost hear my mom's voice coming out of her mouth.

"I'm not going to ditch my friends or anything," I respond, like Mom had actually scolded me. "It's just, I don't know how to handle this. Rob, Phillip, and Tess are like my family. I've shared everything with them ever since they found out about the real me. And they've accepted me... I think. But what would they think if they found out there are other freaks like me?"

I stare at the doll's mouth, waiting for an answer that I know will never come. Then I look back at my mom's picture, her face starting to blur through the tears in my vision.

"I wish I could've talked to you about this before I lost you. I wish I could introduce you to Leah, and Ash, and Heath. Well," I add with a chuckle, "maybe not Heath. But I know you'd accept them, and they'd accept you." I look up from the photo, over the cluttered mess of my bedroom, and let out a long breath. "But I'm being stupid, right? Rob, Phillip, and Tess will accept the others. I know they will, because they accepted me."

I set the doll next to my mom's picture, my gaze darting back and forth between them. "Thanks, Mom."

The lunchroom buzzes with the usual gossip, the smell of burned meat particularly strong today, as I walk to our table and slide into my seat. Phillip smiles at me from under his hoodie. Tess takes her hand off her phone long enough to give me a wave.

Rob frowns, the lines creasing in his narrow forehead.

"What's the matter with you?" I ask him.

"You're not going to sit with your *other* friends?" Rob says with an edge.

"What's that about?" I snap.

"You know. The people you have more in common with."

I get ready for another comeback, but Phillip gives me a look with his soft green eyes that shuts me up. I exhale. "Come on, Rob, don't be like that. You know you guys can't get rid of me that easy, right?"

Rob sighs. "Fine. I just don't get why—" He stops and glances toward the entryway. "Well, looky who it is."

Ash strides into the room, with Heath and Leah following behind her. The buzz of conversation gets louder and everyone glances in her direction. Ash makes her way straight to our table. "Room for three more?" she asks, although it doesn't sound much like a question.

Rob does his best to glare at her. "Actually—"

"Sure," I butt in. Rob gives me a look. And there isn't really room, because there's only one empty chair. Ash gives a gloating smile to Rob and sits herself in the chair, casually crossing her legs.

Leah stands behind her, shuffling awkwardly with her tray. Heath noisily clears his throat.

"Heath," Ash says. "Get some chairs."

I'd say he frowns, except he pretty much always looks like that. He slaps his tray on the table and skulks over to where Jessica and her gang are sitting, grabs two chairs without asking or saying a word to them, then stomps back and drops the chairs next to Ash with a thud. He plops into one and grabs his fork, shoveling a bite of meat loaf into his mouth. Leah hovers for a moment before timidly sliding into the other chair.

"Uh, hi," I say.

Phillip nods. "Nice to see you all again."

Heath gives him a curt nod between bites. Leah's eyes flick to Phillip for a second before they go back to the floor.

I glance around the lunchroom. Everyone's still watching us, but they're trying to be subtle about it—including Emily, who's sitting beside Scott at the cool table. I slide my chair a little closer to Ash, hoping for a reaction. Emily masks her feelings and looks away.

"So, what are we talking about?" Ash looks straight at me when she says it.

Rob coughs. "*We* were talking about Pete Johnson's disaster of a new hairstyle. Care to weigh in?"

"Actually," I say, "there is, uh, something I wanted to talk to you guys about."

Everyone at the table turns to look at me. The clatter of lunch trays carries on around us.

"Yeah?" Rob asks.

I fumble with my hands. "Ash was right when she said I have something in common with her. With all of them."

"What, you guys got matching tattoos?" Rob says.

Ash narrows her eyes at me.

"Not like that," I say. "There's just something about me... uh, about *us*—"

Ash grabs me by the shoulder and yanks me back in my chair. "What the hell are you doing?" she hisses at me. "Remember what I told you, about normal people not understanding?"

"I was just going to tell them—"

"Stop. Just stop. They don't need to know that."

Phillip and Rob share a look. Tess taps a little quicker on her phone.

"They do need to know," I say. "They're my friends."

"Friends." Ash's voice has a cold edge on that word. "But are they like us?"

"Why does that matter?"

"Are they *like* us?"

I squirm in my seat. "Not exactly."

"Then they don't, *exactly*, need to know."

"Seriously," Rob says, "what the hell are we talking about?"

"Look," I say, "maybe they're not... different, like us, but they can still do things most people can't, and they stood up with me when no one else would. More important, they accept me."

Ash sucks in a long gasp. "Oh my God. They *know* about you?"

"Well, yeah. They're my friends."

"Are they?" Ash darts accusatory glances between Rob and Phillip and Tess. "What do you keep Matt around for, huh? You like having your own circus freak? Make the monkey dance for you?"

Rob's face tightens and he leans toward her. "Do you really think—"

Heath reaches out with a thick arm and shoves Rob back. Rob pulls back a fist. Heath pulls one back too, his bicep clenched tight and ready to pop. I shove myself between the two of them before they can kill each other.

"Hey, calm down," I grunt as I push them apart.

"He started it," Rob mutters.

"You want me to finish it?" Heath barks back.

"Look," I say, "there's nothing to fight about here. These guys accept me."

"The hell they do," Ash says. "Unless they're like us, *really* like us, they don't have a clue. They might pretend to be your friends for a while, as long as it's convenient. But sooner or later, it'll all come out. 'Normal' people will never understand."

My mom's words haunt me when she says that. She'd told me the same thing. She'd told me to hide it. I glance around the room at everyone sneaking nosy looks in our direction and wonder if she was right.

"You can't go spouting your secret to just anyone, Matt," Ash says. "And Christ's sake, you told them about *us*, too?"

"Not yet," I say. "But you pretty much did."

Her mouth hangs open, then clenches tight. She glares at Rob and Phillip and Tess, who all sit in stunned silence. Ash pushes up from the table, her chair grating angrily against the floor. "Well, I'm sure as hell not going to stay here to do party tricks for you people. You shouldn't either, Matt. I told you—you have a lot more in common with us than you do with them."

She storms toward the door. Everyone in the room watches her.

"So, uh," Rob says, glancing at Leah and Heath, "when Matt says you guys are different like him, he means…"

Leah hesitates, glancing at Ash like a scared puppy. She gets up from her seat and takes a step to follow, but she turns back. She reaches out her hand for just a second.

Her fingers twitch, and Phillip's fork jumps three inches to the right. Then she hurries out after Ash while everyone else at the table stares at the fork like it sprouted legs.

"Heath!" Ash shouts from across the room, stomping her foot.

Heath looks at her, leans back in his chair, and crosses his arms over his thick torso. Ash gives one more huff and stomps out of the room, with Leah scurrying behind her.

"What the literal hell?" Rob says. "Am I the only one who saw that?"

"Leah's really like you, Matt?" Phillip asks.

"*Telekinetic*," Tess says.

"Yeah," I say, looking down. "She is."

"I guess I didn't think there'd be anyone else like that," Phillip says.

I swallow. "Me either."

Rob eyes Heath suspiciously. "Are you gonna move some forks around too?"

"I've got someplace in mind I could stick them if you want me to," Heath quips.

"Look, guys," I cut in before one of them throws another punch. "I didn't think there was anyone out there different like me. When I found you—" I look at Rob, Phillip, and Tess. "...when you saw what I can do and you didn't run away... and when I saw the things you can do too—"

"But we're not *like* you, are we?" Rob says, an edge to his voice.

"What's that supposed to mean?"

"Just like Ash said. We can do stuff, but not *special* stuff like you. We've been your second-rate sidekicks, but now you've found the real thing, right?"

"It's not like that, Rob."

"Isn't it?"

"I think," Phillip says, "what Rob means is... maybe you think Ash is right. That you think you have more in common with her than with us."

"Of course not," I protest.

Heath clears his throat.

"Okay, but... well, I am different from you guys. Different from everyone. It's not easy to carry that sometimes, and even though you accept me, you'll never really *understand* it. And now I've finally found someone else who..." I trail off, because I see the hurt in Phillip's eyes and Rob won't look at me. I can't read Tess's face, but I'm pretty sure she's ticked at me too.

"So, is this when the witch hunt starts?" Heath says, his voice deep.

"What?" I ask.

"*Witch hunt,*" Tess says. "*Refers to the Salem witch trials in 1692.*"

"I know what it means, Tess, I just don't know why—"

"Ash is right," Heath says. "You all say Matt's your friend, but he's not like you. Deep down, what he *is*, he's not like you. And sooner or later, that difference is going to rear its head in an ugly way. It always does."

"You speaking from experience?" Rob asks.

Heath's expression stays flat and hard.

"Whatever happened to you, we're not that shallow," Rob says.

"We just don't want to lose our friend," Phillip says.

"Noble of you to say," Heath says. "You may even mean it... for now. But it's always the same. Even if it's someone you know, someone you say you care about, it doesn't matter. Sooner or later, you'll dump Matt out with the trash, just like happened to us."

Phillip pulls his hoodie back, drawing the shadow off of his face. "We're different than most people, you know. We're all rejects here."

Heath shakes his head. "Not like this."

"It doesn't mean we're going to start a witch hunt."

"No?" Heath leans back and then points to the table in the far corner of the lunchroom. "That guy over there just called me chrome dome. Not the most original insult I've heard, but still. That girl next to him used a word for Ash that I won't repeat. And that scrawny dude back there in the hallway said Leah looks like she escaped from a mental ward."

Rob darts glances back and forth. "You're joking, right? No way you heard all that."

"That's how you're different, isn't it?" Phillip asks, the green of his eyes intense. "Your hearing?"

"*Not scientifically possible with a cochlear implant,*" Tess says.

"No joke, sister," Heath says. "I *should* be able to pick up a few abstract sounds if they're loud enough, maybe a couple words one of you dipshits is saying if I'm lucky. That's what *should* happen with this thing. But here we are." He leans back. "By the way, someone just flushed a toilet in the little boys' room down the hall."

"Jesus," Rob mutters. "So what's Ash's party trick, then?"

"The point is," Heath says, glaring at him, "everyone here is already against us, and that's just for being from out of town and looking a little different. If they knew what we really are? How do you think that would go?"

He looks straight at me when he says that. I drop my eyes because I know. I've had the same flashes of fear when I thought someone would find out. When someone *did* find out.

"Look, it might be a witch hunt with all of them," I say, gesturing to the rest of the room. "But the people at this table are different."

"No, they're not," Heath says. "Everyone's the same. Except us."

He pushes himself up and lumbers out, and everyone watches him. I can't hear as well as Heath can, but he's right about one thing. I'm guessing everyone in the room has plenty to say about him.

10

Matt

The main school doors slam into my shoulder as I barrel my way out of the building and into the sunlight. I don't bother listening to whatever Principal Stokes yells behind me. I'm not usually one to cut class like this, but right now, Stokes can kiss my ass. What is bothering me is that I barely said anything to Rob, Phillip, or Tess before I bolted from the lunch table. But they won't hold it against me. They're real friends, right?

Either way, I don't have time to think about that. I need to find Ash and Leah. Heath too, I guess. My eyes scan the parking lot as I run, looking for Ash's car, terrified I'm going to see it burning rubber out of the parking lot and never coming back. I run past all the rusted pickup trucks and the cheap little compact cars, praying I haven't lost the chance to ever be with people like me.

Then I see her. Ash stands stiffly next to her piece-of-crap car, hands on her hips, her forehead creased down. Heath leans against the car, his arms casually folded, and Leah stands hunched over a few steps away, but my eyes go back to Ash. The waves of her hair billowing over her shoulder. Her eyes cold as frost... then she sees me, and just for a second, they glimmer.

"Matt?"

"You didn't leave!" I sprint up to her and skid to a stop, huffing to catch my breath. "I was afraid you guys had left."

"We should have," Heath says.

Leah looks up at me for just a second and I almost catch a hint of a smile before she looks down again.

Ash's forehead creases a little tighter. "I thought you'd still be in there, with your..."

"My friends?" I finish for her. "Look, I'm not going to ditch them or anything, but—"

"You shouldn't have told them," Ash says, her voice clipped.

"Look, I'm sorry I told them about you guys... or I was about to. It's your secret, not mine."

"I told you that you can't go spouting off about that to everyone. Remember?"

"I know. I'm sorry."

Ash folds her arms across her chest. "You shouldn't have told them your secret, either."

"They accept me," I insist.

She gives me a pointed stare, the cold blue of her eyes intense. "If they accept you so much, then why'd you come running out here looking for us?"

I look down at a weed growing out of the pavement, not sure how to answer that.

"You don't need them, Matt," Ash says. "They're only going to hold you back." She glances back at her car. "We should leave, and you should come with us."

"Leave?" I take a step back, trying to digest that. "Leave and go where?"

"Doesn't matter," Heath says. "Anywhere."

"But I can't just leave. My friends, my dad..."

"Does your dad understand you?" Ash asks.

I look away.

"I'm telling you," Ash says, "you don't need any of them. You don't need to be stuck in this town, waiting to be hunted down like a freak."

"But to just *leave?*"

"I told you, he's not ready," Heath says. "We should leave without him. We've gotten by on our own for this long."

A faint sound escapes from Leah's throat. We all turn to her.

"If Matt is staying here, then I want to stay too," Leah says.

I smile at her. "Thanks, Leah. I never thought I'd find someone else like me."

"Touching," Heath says. "But we can't keep sticking around here, waiting for them to get the pitchforks and torches ready."

"Just stay a little while, can't you?" I beg. "Give them a chance? Give *me* a chance?"

Ash glances at Heath, who's still glaring, then gives me a skeptical look.

"Please," Leah asks her quietly.

Ash looks back and forth between us. She reaches out and brushes her finger across my forearm, and her eyes narrow. "What did you do to your shoulder?"

I rub it self-consciously. "I, uh, banged it on the door when I ran out here."

She gives me a look that tells me she felt a lot more than the ache in my shoulder, and the corners of her lips curl up slightly. "What the hell. Does this pathetic town of yours have a pawn shop?"

"Uh, yeah. What's that got to do with—"

"You want us to stick around, and I have to pawn something. Get in the car."

Ash's car isn't exactly a smooth ride, but it's still better than Rob's hatchback. I'm crunched into the back seat behind Heath, with Leah beside me but leaning over to the side as far as she can to keep her distance. She still won't look at me except for a few quick glances. The rusty suspension creaks underneath us.

"So," I say to break the awkwardness, "seems like you guys do a lot of traveling."

"You could say that," Heath says.

"Where'd you come from before this?"

He chuckles, scratching at the wide bridge of his nose. "It's not like we keep track. Just keep moving."

"You never stop and stay a while?"

"Not unless Ash meets a boy," he says, turning in his seat to give me a look.

I deflect the comment, just grateful they've stuck around. "Doesn't it get old, always being on the move?"

"It can get lonely," Leah says softly.

Ash clears her throat and Leah looks out the window.

"Well, uh," I sputter, trying to change the subject, "where do you stay, if you're always traveling?"

"Wherever we want," Ash says.

"You mean wherever we can afford," Heath chuckles. Ash shoots him a look.

We pull up to Chaplain Pawn and Ash slides to a stop, straddling two parking spaces.

"How do you afford anything?" I ask. "I mean, you've really been traveling around the country without your parents, just taking care of yourselves?"

"We're better off without them," Ash scoffs. "My parents never did a damn thing to help me. They just wanted to *fix* me so I wouldn't be a bother to them anymore. Well, now I'm not."

I glance at Leah. "What about your parents?"

She looks away; I'm pretty sure I catch a flash of fear in her eyes.

"Best not to ask Leah about her past," Ash says.

Heath shifts his bulky shoulders in his seat. "Not everyone has had a nice sheltered life in your perfect little town."

That comment lands like a rusty knife, right between the memories of my mom dying and my dad lying slobbering drunk on the floor. "If you think I've—" I stop myself and take a deep breath before I say something I'll regret. The whole point was to not drive them away. "Look, I just meant, how do you pay for stuff?"

"As a matter of fact, that's part of why we're here." Ash opens the glove box and pulls out a small case. Popping it open, a diamond necklace glimmers inside. "We need to sell this."

"Whoa!" I exclaim. "Are those diamonds real?"

"Real enough to pay the bills for a while."

"Where'd you get that?"

Heath chuckles. "Ironically, from her parents."

Ash shoots him another look that tells me the necklace wasn't a sweet sixteen present, and she climbs out of the car. I fight off a twinge of hesitation, and follow her.

Chaplain Pawn isn't much to look at, not that anything in Chaplain is much to look at. The store name is printed in peeling letters across the window, and it looks like that window could use a good cleaning. Ash marches through the door, sounding the chime. The rest of us slide in behind her.

My nose tickles at the musty smell inside. The old floorboards squeak under my feet. I look over the shelves of decade-old TVs and various other obsolete electronics, porcelain knick-knacks... pretty much just junk. A couple of guitars and a banjo hang on one wall. I chuckle as I remember coming in here when I was twelve for a junky old electric guitar that one summer I decided I was going to be a rock star. Needless to say, that didn't pan out, and I sold the guitar back for five bucks in the fall. I look to the front counter where the owner, Mrs. Blake, stands watching us with a look somewhere between suspicion and boredom. She hasn't seemed to age a day since I bought that guitar from her, but that's only because I think she was born old and will stay that same level of old until the end of time.

Ash marches straight up to the counter and pops the necklace case open. "How much will you give me for this?"

Mrs. Blake squints at it. "What, more costume jewelry?"

"Are you kidding? This is real."

"How would a kid like you get a real diamond necklace like that?"

"What's it to you? Just tell me how much you'll pay."

As they continue to argue about the necklace, I glance over at Leah, who's looking at some engraved silver spoons. The way she's looking at them, I think she must really like them. I'm thinking about offering to buy one for her when she makes a quick glance to the front counter—Mrs. Blake is bent over staring at the necklace now—and in one quick motion, Leah grabs a spoon in each hand and stuffs them in her pockets. I blink a couple times, trying to convince myself if I really saw that.

"I told you, the diamonds are real," Ash is saying. She reaches out her hand toward Mrs. Blake's arm, but Mrs. Blake pulls back just before she can make contact. Ash frowns.

"Okay, maybe it is real," Mrs. Blake admits. "But I can still only give you two hundred for it."

"Are you *kidding?* It's worth at least ten times that."

Mrs. Blake shrugs. "In the right market, maybe. Not around here."

Ash puts on her best sad face. "I really need the money right now. If you could just—" She reaches toward her again just as Mrs. Blake pulls her hand up to scratch her nose, and Ash swipes nothing but air. Ash drops the sad look and scowls. "Fine." She snaps the case shut and stomps over to where Heath is thumbing through a collection of old comic books.

"Still can't unload that thing, can you?" Heath quips.

"Just shut it. You get anything over here?"

He shakes his head. "These are all junk."

"What about you?" Ash asks Leah, who shuffles over. Leah slides one of the spoons up out of her pocket, just enough to see the silver shimmer, then stuffs it back down again.

"It'll do. Matt, you find anything you like?"

I glance behind me, almost wondering if she's talking to someone else. "Are you seriously asking me to—"

The door chimes, and a short, skinny lady walks in. Mrs. Blake perks up.

"Oh, hi, Jan!" Mrs. Blake says. "I still owe you for lunch yesterday, don't I?"

Jan smiles like she's trying to be polite, but yeah, she did just come in to get her money back. Mrs. Blake opens the register with a *ching* and hands her a couple bills.

Heath nudges Ash with his elbow. "6723," he whispers.

"Now we're talking," Ash says.

"What?" I ask him.

Heath shoots me an irritated look. "The code for the cash register, genius."

My jaw drops a little. "What?"

"She whispered it under her breath when she punched it in."

"But what are you planning to—"

Ash gives me a *zip-it* gesture and glances to the front of the store, where Jan has pulled the plug on small talk and is walking out the door. Ash glances toward a corkboard on the far wall where a bunch of old postcards are held with pushpins. She flicks a finger toward the board and snaps, "Leah."

Leah looks down and hunches her shoulders a bit more; then she twitches her fingers, repeatedly, like a spasm. The pins on the board pop themselves out in a flurry, and the postcards go fluttering to the floor.

The motion catches Mrs. Blake's eye and she struggles up off of her stool. "What in the Sam Hill..."

As she moves toward the scattered postcards, Ash slides to the front counter. I glance back and forth, trying to figure out what I'm supposed to do. In the time it takes me to decide, Ash punches the code into the register. Leah flicks her fingers and a porcelain figurine drops from a shelf and crashes to the floor. It's perfectly timed to cover the sound of the register opening, like a well-choreographed dance. Ash pulls the money out in fistfuls. Leah and Heath move quickly toward the door, but not before Leah snatches a few more of those spoons and Heath reaches over the display counter to grab a gold watch. I stare in a daze as they walk out the door, realizing that when Mrs. Blake finishes picking up the postcards and the broken figurine, if I'm still standing here, it's not going to look good for me.

I bolt out the door, wondering what kind of hero I've become.

11

Matt

Ash's car whines as it carries us away from the pawn shop. I squirm around, not able to get comfortable, but it's not because of the duct tape on the seat.

"What the hell was that back there?" I demand.

Ash turns to look at me, raising an eyebrow. "What?"

"What do you mean, 'what?' The stuff you stole!"

"I told you, if you wanted something for yourself, you should've swiped it while you had the chance."

"That's not what I—" I squeeze my fists together. "For Christ's sake, you just made me an accessory to a robbery!"

Heath chuckles in a low rumble. "I told you he was a goody-two-shoes."

Leah turns one of those silver spoons gently in her hands. "I don't like doing it."

"We've been over this, Leah," Ash says. "We do what we have to. You need to accept that."

I stare at Ash dumbly. "So that's how you pay for everything? Ripping off people like Mrs. Blake?"

"Who's Mrs. Blake?"

I slam my fist into the door, putting a fresh dent in the plastic upholstery. "The lady you just robbed!"

Ash shrugs. "You saw how she tried to lowball me on that necklace."

"That's your excuse?"

She exhales, blowing a stray wisp of hair away from her face. "Look, we *needed* it, all right? How else are we supposed to eat?"

"That's how you want to live?"

"It's how we *have* to live," she says flatly.

Heath clears his throat. "You may not understand this, living in your gilded little cage in Home Town, USA, where everything is handed to you. Some of us don't have it so easy."

I feel my nostrils flare, my mind flashing with the burning roof caving in on my mom. "You think I haven't had a hard life?"

"Don't tell me about hard."

"The point is," Ash cuts in, "we do what we have to, so we can survive. It doesn't do any good to grow a conscience. Besides, we'll never see that lady again."

"Well, *I* will!" I yell.

"Seriously?"

"This is a small town! Everyone runs into everyone around here."

"That's why we should leave town," Heath says.

My mouth hangs open. "That's why you move around so much, isn't it? You coast into town, pull a few smash-and-grabs, and then skip out before you attract attention. Rinse and repeat. Is that it?"

Ash glares at me, her look like frostbite. "It's what we *have* to do."

"Maybe Matt's right," Leah says timidly. "Maybe we don't have to—"

"Remember what they did to you, Leah," Ash says fiercely.

Leah's face contorts in fear. She looks down, and her mouth pinches tight.

"You're so worried about those people out there?" Ash says. "They're sure as hell not worried about us. They've beaten us down our whole lives, all because we're different. Don't tell me you haven't felt it too, Matt," she adds. "Being shunned and cast out, having to hide yourself and praying to God no one finds out."

I swallow. "It doesn't give you the right to—"

"We have the right to *survive*," Ash snaps. "God, that's all we've been doing. Barely getting enough to keep the gas tank full in this piece-of-shit car. We deserve more, Matt. We should take it."

"Take... what?"

Ash pounds the steering wheel. "Damn it, Matt! The world hates us. They're *scared* of us. And you know what? Maybe they should be. Because we're better than them."

"Do you really believe that?"

"Don't you?" Her voice hardens. "Don't you want to finally fight back and take what's yours?"

The energy in my hand ignites like fire, and the emergency brake handle jerks upward on its own. The car screeches to a jolting stop in the middle of the street. The truck behind us blares its horn before swerving around us, and the burly driver scowls through his beard at us and gives Ash the finger.

Ash spins toward me and glares. "What the hell?"

"I need some time to think about this." I throw the door open and step out.

"You're not like them," Ash calls after me. "Sooner or later, you'll figure that out."

I force myself to not look back as I walk away, but what scares the hell out of me is I can't help but wonder if she's right.

Ash

She watches Matt walk away and grips the steering wheel tight until her fingers hurt. "He'll be back."

"Do we even *want* him back?" Heath says.

"We can't be choosy, Heath," Ash says. "There aren't many of us out there."

"We've gotten by with the three of us so far."

"That's just it. We've *gotten by*. We need to work up to something better."

"And you think he's the answer? That gangly, awkward son of a—"

"He's like me," Leah says quietly from the back seat.

Heath turns around to look at her. "I get that, Leah. But he's too big a risk."

"He needs time," Ash says.

"We don't *have* time," Heath snaps back. "What, we keep hanging around here until he changes his mind, waiting for them to hunt us?

You heard him. Everyone knows everyone around here. And now his friends know about us. You know what will come of that as well as I do."

"We'll deal with it."

"And we just knocked off the pawn shop. If we hang around too long, someone will connect the dots to us."

"We'll be fine."

"Are you listening to me? We need to—"

Ash glares at him. Without a word, he stops and turns to look out the window.

"Don't worry, Leah," Ash says. "I know how important Matt is to you. We'll get him back."

Heath clenches his jaw, then turns to look at Leah. "We'll get him back. For you."

"But you said he was a risk," Leah says.

"You're my sister," Heath says. "I've got your back. Always."

Leah smiles.

Ash clears her throat. "*I'm* your sister too, right?"

Heath shoots her a look. "You're my sister."

"Don't you damn well forget it."

A horn blares as a car skids to a stop behind them, where they're still stopped in the middle of the street. Ash slams the emergency brake handle down with a huff, and then the engine whines to pull them on their way.

12

Matt

My head hurts the whole walk home. It's not like it's a long walk, and it's a nice day—the leaves rustle in the breeze, that crisp sound when they're just starting to change color, and the sun shimmers in between the trees, and Mrs. Harris waves at me as she's checking her mail—but I don't care about any of that. I keep wondering if Ash, Leah, and Heath bolted out of town as soon as I jumped out of their car. And I keep wondering if that's what I want.

I get to my front door and step inside, and my thoughts are interrupted by the smell of burned chicken, along with an accompanying sizzle. "Dad?" I call out.

"In here."

I step into the kitchen and find him hunched over a pan on the stove, intently watching a couple of chicken breasts as if he's expecting them to sprout feathers. He glances up at me for just a second before going back to the pan. "Hey, Matt. I'm, uh, making dinner."

"Okay, but usually for you, that's more of a microwave thing."

He laughs. "I know, but I've been living like a bachelor for too long. I've got to think about you, too, and..."

... and Mom's been gone for a while now. I know that's how the thought ends, but neither of us says it out loud.

"Well, thanks, I guess." I wave my hand to waft away the smoke. "I, uh, think that side is getting kinda black."

He grimaces and wrangles the tongs to flip the chicken breasts over. A year ago, I wouldn't have imagined he'd ever be sober long enough to do this. That said...

"No offense, but do you actually know what you're doing?"

"Of course not!" He laughs. "The recipe said to 'brown' the chicken. I didn't even know what that meant! Why didn't they just say to cook it?"

"Well, it smells good anyway," I fib. I'm about to walk away and head upstairs because, well, that's how our relationship usually works. But now he's gone through rehab and he's cooking dinner, and... maybe we can actually talk? Because I really need to talk to someone.

"So, uh, how was your day?" I ask him.

He glances up at me, seeming a little surprised that I haven't left already. "Oh, fine. Fine." He scratches his cheek with the tongs. "Uh... how was yours?"

"Fine."

We stand there for a moment as the pan sizzles.

"How's everything at the factory?" I ask. "You know, with the buyout?"

"Oh," he says, a little surprised at the question. "Things are okay, I guess. We met the new owner. Well, it's not official yet, but you know. He seems like an okay guy. And there isn't any talk about layoffs or transfers or anything, so fingers crossed."

"Great," I say.

He pokes at the chicken with his tongs, glancing at me out of the corner of his eye. "How's... school?"

"Same as always." The chicken sizzles some more. Then I let out a long, heavy breath. "Well, okay, not really."

Dad's eyebrows pop up.

"There are some new kids in town."

"New students in Chaplain?" Dad chuckles. "I'll bet they're feeling like outsiders."

"That's just it. The new kids are... different."

"Different how? Like, from California?" He chuckles again.

"Different like... me."

"Hmmm?" His face doesn't register any reaction. He pokes at the chicken again. "Do you think this is done? It looks done to me."

He pulls the pan off the stove and steps around me, squinting at the recipe laid out on the counter. He grabs some stalks of celery. I shuffle there awkwardly.

"The thing is," I say, "they're like me, but they have a different, um, outlook about it than I do."

"Well, everyone's different." Dad grabs a knife and chops at the celery, coming close to whacking off two of his fingers.

"But how can they help me understand this if they see it completely differently?"

"See what differently?"

"The *thing,* Dad, the thing I—" I huff out a frustrated exhale. "They steal things with it."

"Steal things?" He blurts out, finally reacting. "That doesn't sound like a group you should get involved with, Matt."

I chew my lip. "What if I already *am* involved with them?"

"What?" He whips his head up to stare at me. "What did you do?"

"Nothing," I say defensively. "I... this is about who I am. *What* I am."

Dad squints at me, creasing lines around his eyes. "You're not making any sense, Matt."

"Look, these new kids, they understand me in a way I didn't think anyone ever could. And I screwed it up, and now I've probably lost that."

"What do you mean you lost it?" He grabs a bell paper and turns it around in his hand. "How am I supposed to cut this?"

"I yelled at them for what they did, and they're probably on their way out of town right now." I rub my hands together. "But what if I was wrong about all that? What if they're just doing what they have to?"

"What are you talking about?" He turns the pepper over again in his hand. "Seriously, how do you cut this? Do I go sideways, or across the top like—"

"*Dad!*" I yell. He drops the pepper. "I'm *different.* And these kids are different like me."

He looks at me for a long minute. "Are you trying to tell me you're gay? Because you know that would be okay, right?"

The frustration sighs out of me in a long breath. "I wish it were that simple, Dad." For a second, I think about just walking away. I force myself to stay put. "Look, we need to talk about this for once. We need to get past this."

"Get past... what?"

I look him straight in the eye. "You remember that thing I did with my action figure, when I was six or seven? How I made it move?"

His eyes dart back and forth, looking for something besides me to focus on. "I, uh..."

"I know you saw that. Maybe you've repressed it or made yourself forget, but deep down, you know. I need you to remember, Dad. I need you to say it out loud for once."

He still won't look at me. "Matt—"

"Mom could do it too. Remember? I got it from her."

Pain wells in his eyes. "No, Matt."

"I'm sorry," I say, then my face hardens. "Damn it, no, I'm not sorry. This is who I am. I need you to understand it. Or at least try to. Please."

He stares at me, and I can't tell if he's searching for the memory or trying to push it away. I think about walking away, just laugh it off, say this was all a joke and forget the whole thing. There's still time for that. But that would leave me in the same place, and I'm so tired of that place.

I reach out my hand, and with one last hesitation, I let my fingers tingle. The saltshaker, all the way on the other side of the counter, slides toward me. Dad's eyes follow as it grates along the countertop, slow and even, right to my hand. I pick it up, then set it down in front of him with a clack that echoes through the room.

Neither of us says anything for more heartbeats than I can count.

"Can you talk to me about this, Dad?" I ask him, forcing the tremor out of my voice.

He won't look at me. He shakes his head.

"Please, Dad," I beg. "You don't understand what it's like to carry something like this. What it's like to—"

"Stop," he cuts in. "I can't... I don't know how to..." He shakes his head again, a jerky spasm. "I have to finish dinner." He grabs the knife and whacks at the pepper in an awkward flurry.

"I've needed to tell you this for a long time, Dad. Mom had it too, but she's gone—"

He spins toward me, jabbing the knife in my direction. "Leave your mother out of this!"

My fists clench involuntarily. "Do you think there was something *wrong* with her?"

"I loved your mother, Matt."

"That doesn't answer my question," I spit back at him.

"I... I can't do this." He goes back to chopping the pepper wildly into haphazard chunks.

"Mom was *special*," I say forcefully. "I'm..." As hard as I try, I can't make myself finish that thought.

"Can you, uh, get the box of rice out of the pantry?" Dad says, his voice quivering, his eyes looking everywhere but at me. "I, uh, got brown rice. Some people don't like brown rice as much, but it's supposed to be healthier..."

I turn and walk away because I can't go on pretending anymore, and I'll be damned if I let him see me cry.

13

Ash

Ash rolls over on the cheap mattress, every spring and lump digging into her back. The motel room is dark and quiet around her, full of stale, musty smells, but her mind is far away from there—the place it always goes, that same memory frozen in time, always repeating, always forcing itself back into her head like a splinter.

She was nine or ten, her legs dangling off the plastic stadium seat. The sky was gray overhead. The crowd murmured around her. She smelled nachos and heard the crunch of the man chomping on them a few seats over. "Get your hot dogs!" a guy yelled as he labored to climb the stairs. The umpire bellowed something from behind home plate, though she couldn't hear what he said and wouldn't have known what it meant anyway. The loudspeakers echoed with warbly organ music.

Ash squirmed back and forth, the seat's hinges squeaking underneath her, and her stiff blue jeans pinched between her skin and the hard plastic.

"Sit still, Ashley," her dad chided beside her. "The people here are trying to watch the game."

Ash nodded politely and smoothed out her jeans so they wouldn't pinch her leg anymore. She hadn't wanted to wear the jeans at all; she wanted the dress with the pink stripes, but her dad had scolded her and said that's not what people wear to a baseball game.

The crack of a bat echoed through the stadium, and Ash looked up to see the ball soaring up and away.

"Wow! That's a great hit!" Ash cheered.

Her dad shook his head, his eyes still on the field. "It's a foul ball. Remember what I told you about those big yellow posts out there?"

"I, uh..."

"The ball has to be inside those posts. Otherwise, it's a foul."

Ash fiddled with her hair. "And... what does foul mean?"

Her dad turned and looked down at her. "I explained the rules to you, remember?"

She kept twisting her hair until it started to tangle. "I'm trying, but there's a lot."

He sighed. "We'll need to go over the rules again later, then. You'll need to know those when you try out for Little League next spring."

"*I'm* trying out?" Ash felt her eyes pop wide open. "But I thought baseball is for boys?"

"I found a co-ed league," he said matter-of-factly. "It'll be fun."

Ash's shoulders slumped forward. "I thought I might try swimming instead."

"It'll be fun," he repeated.

That's what he'd told her about coming to the game today, too. She'd wanted to go to the pet store, to see the puppies. But this wasn't so bad, she told herself; they were still spending time together.

Ash perked up when she saw another food vendor climbing the stands, this one carrying big billowy puffs of pink and blue. "Cotton candy!" She clapped her hands. "Can I get one, Dad?"

"Don't you want a hot dog instead?" he asked. "Hot dogs are baseball food."

She shook her head, whipping her tangled hair back and forth. "Cotton candy, cotton candy!"

The lines on his forehead creased, and then he sighed. "Oh, all right."

He waved the guy over and handed him some money. The man pulled a tuft of the pink candy out for Ash. She smiled and grabbed for it, and as she grasped the paper cone at the bottom, her hand brushed against his. She flinched.

The man didn't seem to notice, and trudged on his way up the steps. Ash stared after him and rubbed her hand, almost dropping the cotton candy.

"Be careful with that!" her dad scolded.

"My... feet hurt."

"What?"

"My feet hurt," Ash said. "Like I've been standing and walking all day."

"What are you talking about, Ashley? You've just been sitting here."

She kept watching the man with the cotton candy plodding up the steps in his heavy boots. She wondered how many times he'd climbed those steps today.

Her dad suddenly cheered and the crowd roared along with him as another crack of a bat rang out. Ash ignored it and stomped her feet against the concrete floor.

"What are you doing?" her dad asked gruffly.

"Now my feet feel fine," Ash said. "But they were so sore a second ago, right when I touched that man's hand."

"What are you talking about?" He looked back out at the field and then frowned. "Damn! A double play, and I missed it!"

"I'm telling you, Dad, when I touched him, my feet hurt! Why would that happen?"

"How should I know? Look, I'm not buying you new shoes again. We just got you those."

Ash rubbed her hand absently, not even bothering to eat her cotton candy. "Weird stuff like that has been happening lately. Like, when I tagged Billy at recess the other day, all of a sudden my tooth hurt like crazy. And when I touched Sarah..." She shook off a shudder. "... I got all sad about Grandma dying. But Grandma's not even sick or anything, so why would I be sad about her dying?"

Her dad cupped his hands around his mouth and yelled down to the field, "Why'd you swing at that? That was way outside!"

"Dad!" Ash yelled. "You're not listening—"

Ash grabbed his hand, and the feeling tore into her. A tug in her chest, a gnawing of something unfair, something not the way it was supposed to be. But there was more this time. An image of her room back home, but instead of the bottles of nail polish and the stuffed animals and the posters of horses on the walls, the room was full of baseball gear and remote-control trucks. And she saw *herself*, but with shorter hair and a squarer jaw. Her skin felt cold against her dad's hand, and the Pain flowed through their touch straight into her heart and made it ache. Ash yanked her hand away, and her cotton candy tumbled to the floor.

"You wish I was a boy," she said, shuddering.

Her dad's eyes shot wide open and all the color left his face. "What? Of course not—"

"You don't just wish it, you... you think I stole your chance to do the things you're *supposed* to do with a kid." Ash's chest burned with pain, but now it was her own pain, not his. "Are you really that disappointed in me?"

He stared back at her, his eyes still wide, until he forced them to narrow. "You don't know what the hell you're talking about! You can't possibly know that I... I mean, I *don't*..."

Back in the musty motel room, Ash finally fights the memory away, tossing violently on the lumpy mattress. She throws off the itchy blanket and rubs her arms. A yellow flicker of light cuts its way in through the window from the malfunctioning lamppost in the parking lot. Her breaths are quick and heavy in the quiet room.

"You reliving that day again?" Heath says, his voice deep against the quiet. He sits up on the fold-out cot on the other side of the room. The flicker from the window glares off the back of his head.

Ash nods, then tries to get her hands to make the sign for *"I'm fine,"* but she can't remember that one and her hands are shaking too much.

"Don't worry with the sign language. It's too dark for that anyway." Heath pulls the sound processing unit for his cochlear implant off the nightstand and slides it behind his ear, fixing the plastic disc against his scalp. "And besides, I already know you're not fine."

Ash thinks about snapping back that of course she is, but she knows neither of them will believe that. She listens to Leah's soft, even breathing in the other bed and tries to steady her own.

"I've been through shit like that too, you know," Heath says. "We all have. I understand."

"Thanks," Ash says, careful to keep her voice even. "You know the really pathetic thing? With as bad as things got after that, that baseball game was actually one of my better moments with him."

"You at least had a few good memories before it all went to hell, didn't you?"

Ash grinds her teeth. "Don't try to paint things better than they are."

"I'm just saying—"

"He showed me who he really is. Everyone out there has. It's us against them."

Heath sits there silently, the light from the window flickering against his face. "You sure you're okay?"

Ash flaps the blanket and rolls over. "Go back to sleep."

14

Matt

Some geese honk overhead in the early morning sky as I step up to the school building. I shake my head, trying to get out the image that's been stuck there the whole walk here—the saltshaker sliding across the countertop, and then the look of fear and shame in my dad's eyes. It repeats in my head, over and over. I chew my lip because I know that image isn't going anywhere anytime soon. I push the door open.

It's quiet inside the school. The noisy crowd won't get here for a few more minutes. I pass the custodian in the hallway, wheeling his squeaky mop cart which wafts a smell of disinfectant. I give him a polite nod. He pushes on past like he doesn't see me.

I get to the science room and look in through the doorway. Mr. Plask hunches over one of the lab tables in the back of the room, his back to me. He scratches at his hair, the haphazard clumps sticking up everywhere. Some glass beakers clack as he sets them out on one of the tables. His movements are awkward and jerky. He scratches his hair again. I watch him for another second and think about turning and walking away, but then I see the image of my dad's face full of shame again, and I force myself to take a step into the classroom.

My hand tingles and one of the beakers flies off the table toward me. Plask spins around, startled, his eyes bulging wide through his glasses. The beaker slaps into my hand, then my shoulders slump heavily forward.

"So it *does* freak you out," I mutter, squeezing my fingers painfully tight around the glass.

"What?" Plask sputters. "No, you just surprised me, is all."

The grating of the saltshaker across the countertop runs through my head again. The image of my dad's face sneers at me.

"Don't deny it," I say. "It freaks you out. *I* freak you out."

"You don't, Matt, it's just—" Plask darts a nervous glance toward the door. "Should you be doing that in here, where someone might see?"

I grit my teeth a little tighter. "Because it would freak them out too, right?"

"I just thought... you didn't want people to know."

"Of course they shouldn't know!" I slam the beaker on one of the desks so hard it cracks, splitting a jagged line through the glass. "Because I shouldn't be able to do this. *No one* should be able to do this."

Plask shuffles his hands awkwardly, looking like a nervous praying mantis. "Science is full of things that *shouldn't* happen, Matt. That's what makes the world interesting."

"So that's it?" I say. "I'm 'interesting'? Is that why you keep me around?"

"I... I never said that." He's doing his best to meet my stare, but his eyes keep darting away. "Did something happen, Matt?"

Another image of my dad's face jams itself into my head. "I just needed to know what you really think of me."

Plask is rubbing his hands furiously now. "If this is because I haven't talked to you as much lately, it's only because I realized it's not... not fair of me."

"What's that supposed to mean?" I demand.

"I don't have anyone else." Plask finally looks up at me. "I saw you and your gift, and I thought... maybe I could..." His eyes go down again. "It wasn't fair. You have people."

That damn saltshaker grates through my brain again. My dad's face stares at me frozen in shock.

"Yeah," I mutter. "I should have people, shouldn't I?"

Plask stands there, shifting uneasily. He takes a hesitant step toward me and holds out a jittery arm, almost like he's going to hug me; then he drops his arm.

"I'm sorry," he says quietly.

I look at him for a long time, trying to convince myself that I believe him. "I'm sorry too."

Plask smiles a little. "You sure you're okay?"

My dad's face sneers at me in my head. "Sure."

I shake my head one more time to jar the image loose. If only.

"Sorry," I say. "I shouldn't have bothered you with this."

"I'm always here, Matt, but... you should really talk to one of your friends, your dad..."

"Right," I say, masking the pain in my voice. "Thanks."

I step out into the hallway, where everyone is starting to stream in, and merge numbly into the crowd. As I look at all the faces, I realize I'm looking for one face in particular, one face I know won't be there. Ash.

That's why I've been pathetically begging my dad and Plask to accept me. Because I *had* someone who accepted me, who understood me in a way no one else can... and what did I do? I got on my moral high ground and ran her off. Why did I have to—

"What gives, man?" Rob steps up next to me. "I went to pick you up this morning and you ghosted me."

"Sorry," I say, my voice flat. "I had something I had to do."

"Something with your *other* friends?"

That comment twists the knife a little further into me. I grit my teeth but can't bring myself to say anything.

Phillip appears beside us and gives me a questioning look. "Something wrong, Matt?"

I shake my head. "You don't want to hear about it."

"Yeah, we do," Phillip says.

Rob raises an eyebrow.

"We're always here for you," Phillip says. "Besides, we haven't gotten to hang out much lately. Maybe after school, we could—"

My feet skid to a stop because through the crowd, on the other side of the hall, I see Ash's brown-blonde-red hair. It hangs in waves over one shoulder as she leans against the lockers. Heath leans next to her, towering over her and everyone else, and Leah hunches beside him. Ash's eyes lock onto me across the hallway.

Without a thought, I bolt forward straight toward them, leaving Rob and Phillip behind me and passing a herd of other kids. I ask, breathless, "You're still here?"

Ash lets a hint of a smirk through her poker face. "Yeah, Captain Obvious."

"I thought you'd leave town after what I said to you yesterday."

"We should have," Heath grunts.

Leah glances up at me, her pale face peeking out from behind her hair. "I'm glad we didn't."

I smile at her. "Me too."

"Are you sure?" Ash says, her smirk fading away. "You sure had a lot to say yesterday."

I shuffle my feet. "So did you. Look, I still don't feel right about what you guys do, but maybe we can—"

Before I can finish, Ash grabs me by the collar, pulls me in close, and plants her lips on mine. I'm so shocked I don't even realize what's happening, and then I'm shocked because, damn, it feels *good*. I kiss her back, hard, savoring the soft warmth of her lips. Finally, she shoves me in the chest to push me away and break the kiss.

"Easy, tiger," Ash says, her smirk breaking wide open.

"What was that?" I sputter.

"Don't tell me you didn't like it."

"I did, I just..."

Heath shakes his head. "Ridiculous."

Leah looks away, hiding behind her hair again.

I suddenly remember we're in the middle of a crowd. I turn around, somehow hoping no one saw that. Fat chance.

Everyone stands frozen, staring at us. Whispers rush through the hallway with wildfire intensity. Rob locks a furious stare at Ash, then at me, then back again. I catch sight of Phillip, his face washed out and passive, before he disappears into the crowd. For just a second, I have the urge to run back to them and apologize for blowing them off—again—but then Ash puts a hand on my arm, and I can't help but smile like a dumb son of a bitch. Rob glowers and turns away.

Then I see Emily among the other shocked faces in the hallway, standing beside Scott, her jaw on the floor. Her crimson lipstick punctuates her shock. When Ash winks at her and smirks, Emily turns to give Scott a quick kiss on the cheek, but her forehead is creased tight. She darts another glance at me, then grabs Scott's hand and pulls him away, bewildered, down the hall.

Heath grunts. "As if they didn't have enough to say about us already."

15

Rob

His fingers drum against the table, each one dropping like a hammer on the wood. Rob stares bullets across the library. His eyes narrow, but it's not because of the hideous orange carpet or the graffiti carved into the bookshelves.

"What the hell does he see in her?"

He watches Ash flick back her wavy hair, before she traces a finger along Matt's shoulder. It makes Rob want to hurl. Matt just smiles at her like a dumbass. Rob wants Matt to find his someone special, of course he does... even just get lucky for once, but with *her?*

"She's not even that hot," Rob mutters.

Phillip glances at him, a dark eyebrow raising over his pale forehead. He doesn't say anything, but Phillip rarely has to.

"All right, fine, she's attractive," Rob admits. "But she still moved in on Matt awfully quick."

Ash caresses Matt's shoulder a little more. The other kids who are scattered throughout the room steal glances at them, in between whispering gossip to each other and pretending to study.

"*Love at first sight,*" Tess says from across the table. Rob wonders if she means it as an observation or a question; with her talking through her phone, it's hard to tell.

"Oh, really?" Rob says. "You don't strike me as the romantic type, Tess."

She shrugs.

"Matt's been one of our crew for how many years? And then she swoops in and he scurries right off. Hell, it's not even just her. It's that whole circus with her."

That big lug Heath sits sulking next to them—he doesn't look thrilled about Ash's interest in Matt, either. The ghost of a girl Leah is across the table from them with a book laid in front of her, but she hasn't turned a page in a good ten minutes. Not that Rob's been watching them for ten minutes.

It's been more like fifteen.

Heath's finally disgusted enough by their PDA and pushes himself up from the table. He stomps out, each step landing hard against the thin layer of hideous carpet. Leah glances up like she's thinking about going with him, then her eyes flick toward Ash, and she hunches back over her book again. She still hasn't turned that page.

"There's something off about all three of them," Rob says.

"Something off about us too, isn't there?" Phillip says.

"Whose side are you on?"

Phillip shrugs. "Just saying."

"Look, I just mean they're different. Matt's kind of different."

"Seriously?"

"What? They said so themselves."

"*They did say so*," Tess says.

"See?" Rob drums his fingers a few more times on the table. "I just think we need to find out what they can do."

"We already know that," Phillip says.

"Do we?"

Phillip tugs at the strings on his hoodie. "Should we really be talking about them like this?"

"They stole our friend," Rob says firmly. "Don't you want to know what Matt's gotten himself into?"

Phillip's mouth creases, and then he nods. "Okay, well, Heath can hear stuff. Uncanny stuff."

"Yeah, but exactly *how much* can he hear?"

Phillip shrugs. "Dunno. It's probably good he left... or he'd be listening in on us right now."

"No joke." Rob roughs up his hair. "Well, we know Leah's magic trick is like Matt's, right?"

"*Telekinetic*," Tess says.

Rob shakes his head. "You're gonna have to use shorter words with us, Tess. And, anyway, we need to know more about her, too. I mean, Matt can't move anything big, but what about her? Is she gonna get pissed off and throw a car at us or something?"

"For once, you've got a point," Phillip admits. "Maybe I could... find out some stuff."

"They're not going to just tell you."

"They don't have to. People say and do a lot of stuff when they don't know I'm around."

"Does that really work?" Rob says. "I mean, I know you're stealthy and all, but—"

"You'd be surprised. Like, some guys might get a mother-son pedicure when they think no one is watching."

Rob glares daggers at him. Tess lets out a giggle.

"Don't change the subject," Rob huffs. "We need to know more about them. Hell, we don't know much of anything about Ash."

"You're right about that," Phillip says. "Apparently she's got some sort of Ability too."

"Yeah, but what? Has she even given us a clue about it?"

"I don't know. But I am concerned about Matt with her. Ash seems... manipulative. Is that harsh to say?"

"Hell no. I'd say a few other things a lot harsher than that."

Phillip tugs some more at his hoodie strings. "Maybe we should lay off. I mean, I want Matt to be happy."

"So do I, but shouldn't we make sure she's not up to no good?"

"Is that really our job?" Phillip asks.

"Someone should. Look, she just showed up here, from God knows where, on her own. How weird is that?"

"*Emancipated minor*," Tess says.

"She could have come from a really bad situation," Phillip says.

"My gut's telling me there's more to it than that," Rob says. "I want to know where they came from."

His phone buzzes. He shoves his hand in his pocket to drag it out and glances at the screen. "Tess, this is from you? What is this?"

"*Where they came from*," Tess says. "*I think*," she adds.

Rob scrolls through the text, then sits straight up in his chair. "Whoa, this is a police report!"

"They were arrested?" Phillip asks.

He shakes his head. "Doesn't look like anybody got arrested. And it's nothing big anyway. Somebody swiped the cash from the register at a gas station in Pittsburg. But it wasn't even a stickup or anything. It looks like the clerk just got distracted or duped or something. What's this about, Tess?"

"*Keep reading,*" she says.

"Hold up—okay, this is interesting. There were three adolescents in the place right before the cash went missing. Two girls and one big bald guy."

Phillip perks up, but he hesitates for a second before saying, "We shouldn't jump to conclusions. That could be a lot of people."

"Yeah, but we all know who it was, right?"

"Well... it means they came from Pittsburg," Phillip says.

"That's what you're taking away from this? Dude, they robbed the place!"

"We don't know that." Phillip's phone buzzes, and he glances at it. "Hey, here's another police report! How do you find these, Tess?"

"Is that in Pittsburg too?" Rob asks.

"No, this one's in Boston. A little jewelry store reported half a dozen watches missing."

"Let me guess," Rob quips. "The suspects look a lot like our favorite people over there."

Phillip squirms. "The description could match a lot of people."

"That's a yes."

"It's not fair to judge them without all the—wait, they thought the guy in this one was wearing a hearing aid." Phillip grimaces. "Okay, that's a big coincidence."

"No joke," Rob says. "And that was in Boston? Wait, Tess just sent me another one. They walked out with the tip jar at some diner. And this one's in Philadelphia! The little punks get around."

"We don't *know* anything yet," Phillip says.

"You keep telling yourself that."

Tess stops tapping on her phone and turns the screen around.

"What'd you find now, Tess?" Rob asks, leaning in. "Oh, dude... this one's from *here*. From yesterday!"

"It's in Chaplain?" Phillip asks, his face washing out even more than usual. "Where?"

"The pawn shop." Rob's mouth tightens. "And there were *four* adolescents this time—two guys, two girls."

The silence at the table says plenty.

"Matt wouldn't do that," Phillip finally says.

"I sure hope not. Petty theft may not be a big deal for some people, but for Matt?" Rob glares across the room at Matt, who's sitting way too close to Ash. Is he flirting with her now? Is that what he thinks is flirting? God, Matt's terrible at that. He'll need to show him how it's done... wait, he can't *help* him get with her! Rob looks away, disgusted. "Either way, Matt saw what they did, and he's still over there making googly eyes at her right now."

"*I don't want Matt to get hurt,*" Tess says.

"You said it, Tess," Rob answers.

"I don't want that either," Phillip says. "But remember, they're *different*, like Matt. Maybe he can't walk away from that."

"Maybe *we* should walk him away," Rob mutters.

"How do you think that would go?"

Rob frowns and smolders inside, because he knows the answer to that.

16

Rob

He ambles down the hallway, his steps slow and easy. Katie Parkson rushes past, knocking into Rob's shoulder with her stack of books; she glances at him like a nervous squirrel, stutters a barely audible apology, and then scurries off with her books into the math room. Rob chuckles and strides on his way, not in a hurry to get to class himself. He passes a cluster of girls chatting about something. Lisa Schroder glances at him and he flashes a grin at her, making sure his dimples pop—girls love the dimples. She smiles back shyly for a second, then goes back to chatting. Then Rob looks past Lisa, and his smile drops.

Heath.

He leans against the lockers, his arms folded over the bulk of his chest, the fluorescent light glaring harshly off his bald scalp. His eyes are narrow slits as he glares at everyone like he's better than them. Prick. Rob looks back to Lisa and the girls. They're giggling about something now, and then Lisa sneaks a look—at Heath—before giggling again. Heath's scowl tightens a little more.

A bunch of football players herd their way through next, shoving and fist-bumping each other. When they pass Heath, Beefy Brett makes a big grin with his crooked teeth, points a fat finger toward Heath, specifically toward the gray plastic circle on Heath's scalp, and then he laughs a deep dumb chuckle. He and the rest of the jocks stampede their way out.

Rob shuffles his feet to a stop, watching Heath from across the hall. Heath's scowl stays passive, no reaction on his face. It doesn't matter. The popular kids are awful to everyone around here. Besides, he's the one trying to pull Matt away from his real friends, telling him he's not like them, so he deserves it if everyone treats him like...

Damn.

Rob reluctantly plods toward him. Heath turns his scowl to Rob as he slides up.

"Uh, hey," Rob forces out.

Heath grunts.

"Those idiots can be pretty harsh, huh?"

No reaction.

"Don't take it personal," Rob says. "There's nothing to do around here, so they don't have anything else to talk about. You don't have to listen to them."

"Don't listen?" Heath points to the plastic behind his ear. "That's the best advice you've got, genius?"

"I'm just trying to say," Rob snaps back, "that people suck sometimes."

"I noticed."

They stand there as a bunch of guys shuffle past on their way to the metal shop.

"So now what?" Heath says, unmoved from his position leaned back against the locker. "Were you expecting us to hold hands or something?"

"Dude, I was trying to be nice."

"So you say. But I've been kicked around everywhere I've been through, so I'm not in the mood to get all touchy-feely with anyone."

Rob feels his nostrils flare. "Hey, don't get all pissy with me. You're the one trying to butt in and steal my friend."

With a low rumble in his chest, Heath laughs. "You think *I'm* the one trying to do that?"

"Ash sure as hell is."

"You think I have any say in what Ash does?"

"Well, you should try harder to convince her," Rob pushes back. "I don't like her sticking her claws into Matt like this."

"And I don't like hanging around this pathetic town, waiting for something bad to happen."

"What makes you so sure something bad's going to happen?"

"Just wait. You'll see."

"Whatever," Rob says in a huff. "Just make sure whatever trouble you dig up, you don't drag Matt down with you."

Heath eyes him up and down. "You remind me of Brian," he says, then looks away. "Or how Brian used to be."

"Brian?"

"My brother." Heath shifts on his feet, glancing at the handful of kids still in the hall, like his eyes aren't sure what to land on.

"What happened with Brian?" Rob asks.

"What makes you think something happened?"

"I'm not an idiot. I'm guessing you haven't talked to Brian for a while."

Heath's jaw clenches. "It was good that I found out who he really was when I did. And that I found someone who loyalty means something to."

"Don't tell me you mean Ash," Rob snips.

Heath darts a narrow glance at him. "What's that supposed to mean?"

"I mean you're awfully loyal to someone who walks all over you."

"You don't know anything," Heath says, slow and firm. "She had my back when the shit hit the fan. I owe her."

"So that's it," Rob says. "Does Leah owe her, too?"

Heath narrows his eyes at him. "Leah's my sister. She's the replacement for the brother I thought I had but didn't. I'm here to protect her, like my brother was supposed to do with me. Anyone who wants to hurt Leah has to come through me."

"Whoa, whoa," Rob shoots back, "who said anything about wanting to hurt Leah?"

"I'm just saying."

"You sure got defensive real quick."

Heath looks him over carefully. "You got a sister?"

Rob's mind suddenly goes to Addie and her pigtails flipping around on the swing set, and Cassie drawing the charcoal sketch of their house that he has hanging on his bedroom wall. His scowl softens a little. "Two," he says.

"So you know."

"Yeah, well, Leah's not really your sister, is she?"

"Matt's not really your brother."

"Maybe not," Rob says firmly, "but I'm still not going to let him get hurt."

"Same thing goes for my sister."

"You talking about Leah or Ash?"

"Take your pick."

They stand there in thick silence, the last of the other students disappearing into classrooms, until the bell rings overhead.

"Don't you have somewhere to be?" Heath says.

"Don't you?"

Heath shrugs, unmoving.

"Fine," Rob says, turning to walk away. He gets to the end of the hall, glancing back to see Heath still leaning against the lockers in the distance. "Last time I try to be nice," Rob mutters under his breath.

"Last time for me, too," Heath calls after him.

Rob shoots a surprised look back down the hall. Heath points to the gray plastic behind his ear.

They both hold the stare for a moment, eyes narrow, then Rob scowls and turns to storm away.

17

Matt

I step through the school hallway. It feels odd without Rob or Phillip beside me. Not that I never go anywhere without them, it's just... I don't know. I need to get out of my own head. Like how right now, as I walk past the groups of kids that I've walked past so many times before without a second thought, suddenly I feel so *different* from all of them. I don't know what's changed now, since it's not like I fit in before either. But I can't shake the image of my kitchen, pulling that saltshaker, and Dad's face full of shock. Maybe I am that different.

A flash of red hair in my vision pulls me out of my trance. Emily slides through the crowd toward me, hovering a moment like she's not sure if she's going to stop or keep on walking. She stops.

"Hey, Matt," Emily says. "I, uh, haven't seen you around as much lately."

She shifts awkwardly on her legs, the way she used to do back when those legs were all spindly. I can't help but notice that for the first time I can remember when I've been around Emily, I don't shift on mine.

"Sorry," I say, although saying it makes me realize I'm not. "I've been, you know, busy lately."

"Yeah."

The lockers clank on either side of us. A couple girls giggle about some joke.

"I just don't want us to drift apart," Emily says.

I avoid her eyes. "Well, it happens sometimes. You're with Scott now, right?"

"Yeah, but... what about everyone else? You've been ditching them too. You're not going to walk away from them because you made some... new friends, are you?"

I look at her, and I feel my eyes narrow slightly. "Funny, I recall telling you the same thing a while back, when you started dating one of the cool kids."

She looks down. "I know, and you were right."

"So what are you saying?"

Emily shifts on her legs some more. "Just take your own advice, okay?"

We stand there for a moment. My eyes trace over her cheeks, her eyes, her hair, almost out of habit. Somehow it doesn't have the same effect on me as it did before.

I'm startled by another figure sliding up beside me. "Take your own advice about what?" Ash says.

Emily takes half a step back. "Just... advice about his friends."

"Friends? You mean like me?" Ash makes a long, slow motion of putting her arm around me, her eyes locked on Emily the whole time.

"I, uh, actually meant his *other* friends," Emily says.

"Really?"

"Yeah. We've been his friends a long time."

"Have you now?" Ash doesn't blink.

Emily's mouth tightens, crimping her red lipstick. "You don't think I have? I mean, *we* have?"

"Oh, I didn't say that."

I glance back and forth between them. "She—*they* have been really good friends."

"Sure," Ash says with a half-smile.

Pete flies past us on his skateboard, with Principal Stokes yelling after him about no skateboarding in the hall; the two girls are too locked in their staring match to even notice.

"I just don't want Matt to lose what he has," Emily says.

"Hmmm." Ash makes a show of rubbing her chin. "Well, sometimes what you have isn't what you thought it was. Sometimes it takes a new perspective to see that."

"A new perspective?" Emily says, hiding a chuckle. "That's you?"

"Maybe," Ash says. "I can bring a certain... clarity. Don't you think, Matt?"

I glance at her, then at Emily, feeling my eyes bulge wide open.

Ash laughs. "Oh, don't freak out. You don't have to say anything to impress me. See, Amy?"

"Emily."

"Right... anyway, I'm not asking Matt to do anything he doesn't want to. I'm just helping him see himself for what he is."

"And what's that?"

I glance at Ash, wondering the answer to that question myself.

Ash's lips curl up subtly at the edges. "I think he's still figuring that out."

Emily hovers there like she can't decide if she wants to run away or slap Ash in the face.

"I'll, uh, still see you around," I cut in with an awkward smile. Then I'm quick to add, "All you guys."

Emily looks at me, but I don't see the same life behind those green eyes that I usually do. "Sure," she says.

Emily darts one more look at Ash, then turns and walks away slowly. Part of me wants to go after her.

Ash squeezes my arm a little tighter. "Is that your ex?"

"What? No."

She nods. "So you just *wanted* to get with her."

I sputter for a second before saying, "She's just a friend."

"If you say so." Ash starts down the hall, pulling me by the shirtsleeve behind her. I don't even fight back.

18

Matt

I push through the crowd in the hallway, more aware than I've been in a long time of the looks people are giving me. I've always been a reject, but it's different now. Probably because the new girl in town kissed me in front of everyone, and she's an even bigger reject. Either way, I keep getting those looks.

But I'm not the only one people are looking at funny. Leah hunches in the corner, her dark hair hanging limp over her shoulders, her eyes never moving from a chip in the floor tiles. The other kids are doing more than just looking at her—bumping into her with their shoulders, snickering as they walk by.

"Leah," I call out, working my way through the hallway to her. "You okay?"

She nods, slowly swishing her hair, but she won't look up at me.

I finally make it through the crowd to her. "You don't look okay. Hey, uh, why don't we go somewhere and talk?"

Her eyes flick toward mine for just a moment. "I've got math this period. No... geography."

I put a hand on her shoulder. "Does it really matter? Let's get some air. I've been wanting to talk to you anyway."

Leah darts a glance down the hallway. "Ash wouldn't want—"

"Why would Ash care if we talk? What, because she kissed me?"

Leah hunches further down. I can't tell if that's a yes or if there's something else she's scared of.

"Hey, I'm not trying to hit on you. I just want to talk." As I say that, Pete the skateboarder strolls by, glances at my hand on Leah's shoulder, and gives me a wink and a thumbs up. I pull my hand away. "I, uh, think we could both use a talk. Don't you?"

Leah hesitates, studying that chip in the floor from all angles. Finally, she looks up and nods.

"Come on." I smile at her and step toward the back door, making sure Leah follows me. It takes her a second, but she does. I push the door open for her just as the bell rings for class, and the remaining students in the hall slip into their classrooms. I step outside into the sunlight. When Leah finally steps through herself, I shut the door, closing all those jerks inside.

I wander over to the retaining wall which is doing its best to hold back the dirt, failing a little more each year. I sit down on the wall and pat the chipped concrete beside me. Leah shuffles over and gingerly sits down.

"I never thought I'd find someone else like me, you know," I say. "I didn't think anyone else like me existed out there."

Leah glances at me with a faint smile but doesn't say anything.

"Have you ever met anyone else like you—like us?" I correct myself, never thinking I'd be able to say that. "Anyone else who can move things?"

She hesitates, then shakes her head.

I see a crunched-up soda can on the sidewalk. I reach out my hand and let my palm tingle, and the can drags along the sidewalk, then floats its way up toward me. I release before it gets to my hand, and it drops by my feet.

"I can pull things in a straight line," I say. "I can't control it much, though... or get things to hover. Not like you did with those pebbles in the park. It's pretty cool how you can do that."

Leah still doesn't say anything. I keep talking, hoping I can break through her shell. "I can't move anything big. Not much bigger than that can, actually, if I want to get it off the ground. I can go a little bigger if I drag it, like..." I look over at the trash can, hoping it's not as heavy as it looks or this could be embarrassing. My hand tingles and the trash can shudders a little but stays put. I let the tingle rage to a burn, and the can finally jerks an inch toward me. At least it's enough for me to save face.

"That, uh, kind of hurts." I rub my hand. "Or maybe that's the wrong word. It just feels weird, you know? Like when your hand wakes up after falling asleep. Or like a bunch of needles are pricking your skin at the same time."

I glance at her, desperate for her to say something. I didn't realize until now how much I've needed to talk to someone about this, ever since... that day my Ability first came out.

"And when I'm trying to move something heavy, my skin burns," I go on. "But it doesn't feel hot. Isn't that weird? It burns, but it doesn't feel hot?" Leah still doesn't react. I look away with a sigh. "I don't know. Never mind."

"It feels numb," Leah says quietly.

I turn toward her. "What?"

"My fingers feel numb when I move things. Then the feeling sort of prickles when it comes back."

She looks at me and smiles, the green specks in her eyes glimmering a little brighter against the brown.

I smile back. "Can you feel things out there, without touching them? In your mind, I mean?" I look down, suddenly self-conscious. Even with someone else with an Ability, it feels weird to talk about this. "I don't know, I can just *feel* everything out there, like..."

"...like a hazy outline," she finishes for me.

I lock eyes with her. "Yes. *Yes!* Oh my God, I can't believe..." I have to fight back the tears quivering in my eyes. To have someone else actually share this with me, to *understand*, to feel the same things...

Everyone else takes that for granted. It's only the different ones like us who never get to share that. Until now.

"You're actually like me," I say, unable to hide the giddiness in my voice. "I mean, really... well, not quite, I guess. You can make stuff hover. I've always wanted to do that, but I can't."

Leah shrugs. "Don't know how. I just do it."

"Exactly! It's not like it came with an instruction manual, did it?" I rub my hands together. "What's the biggest thing you can move?"

She doesn't answer, but she twitches her fingers. Suddenly, I feel my whole body jerk, and my butt slides an inch across the concrete of the retaining wall.

"Holy crap!" I yelp. "You just moved *me!*"

She smirks, subtle but it's there.

"That's incredible!" I say. "I could never move anything as big as a person. I mean, wow…"

"I can only move big things a few inches," Leah says. "Actually, anything bigger than that—" Her fingers twitch again, and a rusty bottle cap floats up off the sidewalk before dropping again. "I can move little stuff like that all over the place. And I can move a lot of them at once, like those pebbles at the park. Big stuff… I tried for a long time to move them farther, but a couple inches is all I can do."

"Still impressive," I say. "Could you move, like, a car?"

Leah shakes her head. "I tried that. I really tried. Ash wanted me to, but I couldn't."

There's a subtle hint of hurt or defensiveness in her voice, but I'm so excited I ignore it.

"It's just so great to talk to someone else about this," I say. "Someone else who's actually felt it, done it. I thought I'd never have that."

I look at her and I feel like I'm seeing a long-lost sister. I smile, and she smiles back, a tiny splash of color flooding into her cheeks.

"Me neither," she says.

"I missed the chance to do this with my mom. She knew about my Ability… she's actually the one I got it from. She gave me some advice, tried to protect me. But she died before I ever found out that she had the Ability too."

Leah's face pales again and she looks away.

"Don't worry, it's okay," I tell her. "That was a while ago, and I've dealt with it. As much as anyone can deal with losing their mom. It's just… it would've been nice to know, before she died. To know what we shared."

Leah still won't look at me. I wonder if I went too heavy with this.

"It's okay, really. I don't blame her for not telling me. The first time my Ability came out, I was five, and it was a lot to deal with at that age. It was all she could do to keep me from showing everyone. If I'd known my mom could do it too? I don't think I would've been able to shut up about it. And, well, telling people probably wouldn't have led to anything good."

"No," Leah says, her voice hollow. "It wouldn't have."

"Yeah. You get it, right? Parents are just trying to look out for you."

She stares off, not saying anything.

"And then she died a few years later, before I knew she had the Ability too. I pieced it together eventually, but it took a while. Probably longer than it should have. But even though she's gone, and I can't talk to her about it, it's still nice to know. I think... I hope she'd be proud of me."

Leah lets a laugh slip out. Only it doesn't sound like a laugh, it feels cold, agonizing.

"I'm sorry, I didn't mean to bum you out by talking about my dead mom." I fumble to change the subject. "When, uh, did your Ability start? I was five—I told you that, right? On my couch at home. The remote control moved. What a time saver, huh? Never have to get up to grab that again." I laugh nervously. "What about you?"

"Seven," Leah says, her gaze still far off. "Jelly beans."

"Your first time was with jelly beans? That sounds fun."

"Fun?" She shakes her head, not just once but over and over, then her body starts rocking. She holds her hands up over her ears, gripping them tight, rocking faster and faster. "We pray this demon out of her... we pray this demon out of her... we pray—"

"Hey," I say, grabbing her shoulder. "It's okay. It's okay."

116

Leah stops rocking and looks at me, and I can see the shadow of a cold, dark pit hiding behind her eyes. She takes in a long breath, but I wonder how much of her is still in that pit.

"Not all mothers are proud," she says.

I stare at her with my mouth open as a dog howls somewhere in the distance. I try to make myself say something, anything, but I can't. Leah's eyes lock with mine until the fear in them drains away, and then they flash with shame and anger and she looks away. She darts up from her seat and scurries toward the building.

"Leah, wait—" That's as far as I get before she disappears inside. Maybe it's just as well, because I still have no idea what to say.

I push myself up and kick the crumpled can by my feet. Why does the world have to suck? I stand there with my emotions churning, when I startle to see a skinny figure standing by the corner of the building. Mr. Plask watches me through his thick glasses.

"Plask?" I sputter. "How long have you been standing there?" My voice comes out more accusatory than I'd planned.

He roughs his hand nervously through the scruffs of his hair. "Not long."

"You didn't see Leah when she was—" *Did he see what she can do?* I study Plask's eyes, but they're warped through his glasses and I can't get a read on them.

"When she was what?" he asks.

He sounds sincerely in the dark. I can't decide if I believe him or not. It's enough that he knows about me, but Leah's secret is too much. It's not my secret to tell. And after what she just spilled to me, I can't let that out.

"Sorry," I exhale. "I didn't mean to snap at you. It's just... there's a lot right now."

"You want to talk about it?" Plask shuffles toward me slowly, like he's trying not to spook me. Or maybe not to spook himself.

"Is the world always out to get people who are different?" I ask.

"Are you talking about yourself?"

I falter. "I, uh... a lot of people are different."

Plask nods. "People think I'm different, too, you know. Because I look weird and don't have good people skills."

"Oh, I wouldn't say you—"

He holds his hand up. "We both know it's true. It's okay. But I'm guessing that's not the kind of different that you're talking about."

"No. No, it's not." I clench and unclench my fist, staring at my palm. "I've always known my Ability makes me different, but lately I've felt *so*... I mean, my own dad won't..."

"I'm sorry," Plask says. "That must be hard."

I stare off at the door where Leah disappeared. "No. Some people have it a lot harder."

I try to imagine what Leah was describing and what she went through, but I can't picture it. Or maybe I don't want to.

"Are you thinking of someone specific?" Plask asks.

"What?" I shake myself out of my stupor.

"You said some people have it harder. Who did you mean?"

My mind fills with questions about Ash... even Heath. What did they go through? Was it like what Leah went through? Was it worse?

I forcibly shake my head. "No one. Just... life in general."

Plask looks at me for a long time. Finally, he nods. "Life in general can be hard."

I nod back, careful to keep my face even.

19

Phillip

The bell rings, and the students pour out of the school doors into the sunshine. They chat about TV shows and the test they just flunked and who made out with who at the party last Friday night. None of them notice the shadow hovering in the corner. But the shadow doesn't mind.

Phillip leans back against the wall, his hood pulled down low. All the kids stroll by, right past him, without even realizing he's there. It used to bother him, everyone carrying on around him, making plans for dates or parties, never asking him if he wants to do anything. Never saying anything to him at all. Like he's not even there.

Okay... so maybe it does bother him sometimes. It would be nice to be noticed once in a while, let alone included. But you can get to know people pretty well by watching, even if they don't know you exist. You can be a sort of silent, invisible friend.

Matt and Ash walk out the doors toward him. They don't see Phillip either and walk right on past without so much as a glance in his direction. Matt's too busy looking at Ash. Phillip watches them from the shadow.

Ash keeps touching Matt in subtle ways and smiling whenever she looks at him... but not when she looks away. She's good-looking. People think Phillip doesn't notice or care about stuff like that, but he does. But there's something about her he can't put his finger on. Something he doesn't like. Matt doesn't seem to see it, though, the way he's looking at her.

Heath and Leah walk out behind them. Heath looks Phillip's way, but Phillip knows how to stay unnoticed when he wants to. He keeps his body still, but being a shadow is more than that; it's important to look relaxed. Seeing a guy standing stiff as a board and staring at you is just creepy, but a small, nondescript guy not worth noticing... nothing to see here...

Heath stares right through him and keeps walking.

Heath and Leah join Matt and Ash by the curb and hang there, talking. Ash does most of that. Matt says something, and Heath narrows his eyes at him. Heath doesn't like Matt—or he doesn't trust him, anyway. It doesn't take a master of observation to see that. But Leah, she keeps darting glances toward Matt, never looking at him straight on. And while Matt's mostly looking at Ash, he flicks a couple glances toward Leah too. It's not a look of attraction between them; it feels more like siblings.

Kyle Draughton and his football buddies shove their way out the school doors and past Phillip's spot. Kyle points toward Heath and

Leah. "There's those new freaks!" Kyle yells. "Pine was already a weirdo, he must've attracted them. But the new guys are *really* off."

Phillip cringes inside. Not that it's a surprise. Kyle has always been a jerkwad. But what sucks is, most of the other kids are probably thinking the same thing. They just don't say it out loud.

He looks over to see Tess walking out, her head down and looking at her phone like always. A few kids give her sideways glances, but whatever they're thinking about her, at least they keep it to themselves. Tess keeps walking. Her dad stands at the curb, tapping his foot in khakis and a polo shirt. His eyes are fixed on her through his hipster glasses in between irritated glances at his watch. "You're late, Tess," he snaps at her.

"*I was finishing an assignment,*" she replies.

"Sometimes I wonder how much you even pick up in there," he says, as if he didn't even hear her. "Come on, we need to get you home."

"*I have friends here, Dad.*"

He pulls the car door open and shuffles her inside. Tess slides into the seat without another word and without looking up at him.

Phillip isn't one to swear much, but right now he's considering it. Tess's own dad, and he doesn't see her for who she is, much less realize what she can do. Phillip looks back at Matt and Ash. For just a moment, he wonders if Ash is right. All these "normal" people... they don't understand them. Any of them. Maybe they never will.

But then he remembers the police reports that Tess found. Phillip sets his face firmly again. Someone needs to figure out what they're really about.

Ash takes Matt's arm and leads him off toward her beat-up car. Phillip thinks about following them, but spying on Matt is a big step. He'll start with the other two. Leah watches them go, still not looking at Matt directly; Heath grumbles something under his breath. The two of them stand at the curb awkwardly for a minute, and then Heath trudges off down the sidewalk. Leah scurries after him with small, hurried steps.

Phillip follows. His head down, he falls in step with a cluster of other students and immediately becomes a faceless, invisible member of the crowd. Phillip keeps his expression bland and keeps pace with them as they obliviously continue with their conversation around him, until they veer left and Heath and Leah veer right. Phillip breaks off and steps up behind a parked car on the curb.

He doesn't crouch down behind it; that would look suspicious, rookie mistake. He just loiters behind the car while Heath and Leah continue on down the sidewalk. Then he makes his way up to a light post, then a trash can. His steps are quick when he moves, but not hurried enough to attract attention. Head still down, body still relaxed. Eyes always on his persons of interest.

Heath leads them to the Jiffy Mart. Phillip hovers back as they walk under the rusted cover above the gas pumps, and then he ducks behind a pickup truck with oversized tires. A dog eyes Phillip through the truck window and pants happily. Phillip smiles at him. Animals are the only ones that pay him any attention. The dog gives him a friendly bark, but Phillip has work to do. He watches Heath and Leah step through the squeaky front door of the Jiffy Mart. He doesn't go running in after them—another rookie mistake—he waits for a big guy in overalls to open the door and slips in behind him like his shadow. The overalls guy trudges over to the hot dogs, and Phillip slides behind the cases of motor oil.

Heath is rooting through the protein bars. He makes a glance to see if the clerk is watching—she's not, Jackie Burkson isn't about to expend more than minimum effort for minimum wage—and he stuffs a couple bars in his pocket. Leah absently runs her finger over the tabloid covers. Heath moves past her to the beef jerky.

Phillip is beginning to wonder what he's doing here, spying on them when there isn't even anything worth seeing... when Heath suddenly straightens up.

"What's wrong?" Leah asks in her quiet voice.

Heath darts a glance through the front windows to the faded blue van that just pulled up to the gas pumps. "It's the pawn shop owner," he says.

"You sure? I can't see her."

"I recognize her voice. Signing along with the radio."

Phillip's thoughts spin with two things. First, he's seriously impressed if Heath can hear Mrs. Blake all the way out there in her van. And second—they *did* rob the pawn shop. He can only hope that the fourth person with them wasn't Matt.

Mrs. Blake climbs out of her van. She reaches for the gas pump and then makes a quick glance toward the store.

"Shit," Heath mutters.

"What now?" Leah asks.

"She saw me."

"You sure?"

"She muttered something about the big bald guy."

Mrs. Blake starts toward the building, her frown and her steps fierce.

Heath backs away. "Is there a back door to this place?"

Leah darts glances around, and shakes her head. "The emergency exit has an alarm."

Heath grabs her arm and pulls her toward the back of the store. Mrs. Blake stomps inside, glancing around. Before she can get a good look at

Heath, Leah's fingers twitch and the light switch on the far wall flicks, plunging the store into darkness. The sunlight tries to fight its way in through the front windows, but it's not enough to keep everyone from stumbling while their eyes adjust.

"What the hell?" the guy in overalls rumbles, dropping one of his hot dogs.

Jackie at the counter mumbles something about not getting paid enough for this and starts fumbling her way toward the light switch, bumping her knee into the magazine rack and letting out a yelp.

Heath and Leah huddle in the back, with Phillip's shadow a few feet away. "We need to get out of here without her seeing us," Heath says. "Is there anything out there you can use?"

Leah scans the dark room quietly. "Everything's too big."

Mrs. Blake's silhouette stands in the middle of the room, hands on her hips. Then she starts in their direction.

Heath swears under his breath. He grabs a bag of candy off the shelf, tears it open, and holds it out toward Leah. She nods with a mutual understanding and then twitches her fingers.

The candy pieces hover up out of the bag, then launch themselves forward in a massive volley. Mrs. Blake yelps as they pelt against her, and flinches back. The rest of the candies ping off the shelves and the floor, making a racket like a jumble of marbles. Heath grabs Leah's arm and they quickly move to the side, skirting around Mrs. Blake.

Jackie finds the light switch and the *click* echoes when she flips it on. Light pours down from the ceiling and everyone falters again, squinting against the sudden glare. Phillip blinks through the light to see Heath emerging from one of the shelves, trying to duck down, his massive frame not making it easy. Mrs. Blake turns and spots him.

"Hey!" she yells. "I know it's you!"

Heath and Leah still have about thirty feet to get to the door, and Mrs. Blake makes a dash to cut them off. She's pretty quick for her age, too. Just as she reaches the end of the potato chip aisle, Leah glances back and twitches her fingers. The end of the shelf jerks itself across the floor with a screech. Phillip sucks in a breath, watching Leah move the whole shelf like that—that's got to be heavy—but it only shifts a few inches, well short of knocking into Mrs. Blake. She clears the shelf, and she'll be on top of them before they can make it to the door.

Phillip watches it in slow motion. He could just let it happen. But he sees the panic on Leah's face, and something twinges inside him. He grits his teeth, knowing he's going to regret this later... then slips in front of Mrs. Blake and sticks out his foot. Her leg catches on it, and she goes down hard on the floor. Phillip has already slipped away again before she even realizes what hit her. Heath and Leah bolt out the door, and it squeaks shut behind them.

The overalls guy scratches his thick jowls. "What was all that about?"

Jackie shrugs, indifferent to the whole thing.

But Phillip is already out the door, dashing across the parking lot. He spots Heath and Leah half a block away in a dead sprint. Well, Heath is. Leah is desperately trying to keep up. Phillip takes off after them.

They cut through an alley, down a side street. Leah is barely able to manage the frantic pace, and Phillip isn't doing much better, sucking in air as his chest heaves with deep breaths. The street and the buildings bounce up and down with each step. He's starting to wonder how much longer he can keep this up, when Heath finally decides they've lost Mrs. Blake and skids to a stop. Leah almost falls over herself and drops to her knees.

"Are you okay?" Heath asks her.

She nods, panting.

Heath squats on the sidewalk and wipes sweat off his forehead, adjusting the plastic disc clinging to it. "That was too close. I told Ash we should've left town by now."

"We can't leave without Matt." Leah's eyes flick to the ground. "I mean, Ash doesn't want to leave Matt."

Heath looks at her closely. "I know how Ash feels about him. And I know how *you* feel about him."

Leah hunches down.

Heath sighs and pats her shoulder. "It's okay. I know finding someone like you doesn't happen very often. But either way, it's dangerous for us to stick around here for too long."

Phillip's lungs burn with another deep breath. He's trying to process what he saw Leah do back there. She threw all those candies at once, and it seemed like she could control them better than Matt can. But that shelf... she moved the whole shelf. Matt's never moved anything that big. Except she only moved it a few inches, was that as far as she could move it? He hopes so, or else she'll be hard to stop. If it comes to that.

He really hopes it won't come to that.

Heath suddenly perks up, and darts glances around.

"Do you hear something?" Leah asks him.

"A heartbeat. It's racing."

"You sure it's not yours?" Leah asks with another wheezing breath. "Or mine?"

Heath shakes his head and keeps scanning.

Phillip puts his hand over his chest and feels his own heart thumping. Damn, if Heath can hear that from fifty feet away... he slides back into a corner and closes his eyes to calm himself. He feels his heartbeat slow.

Heath takes Leah's arm and pulls her up. "Come on. Let's get out of here."

Phillip stays huddled in his shadow and watches them walk away.

Heath was right. They *are* different.

20

Heath

His steps pound down the hallway. Heath is used to tuning those out, but the echo off the hard floor and the lockers is like a jackhammer going off inside his head. Then a scrawny little nerd at the end of the hall drops his stack of books, and they hit the floor like a cannon blast. Heath grinds his teeth and keeps walking. In the classroom to the right, through the wall, he hears every wheezing breath of that old-as-dirt math teacher. And every squeak of his marker against the whiteboard, every tick of the clock on the wall, and the constant hum of the fan on his laptop. The classroom on the left is more of all that, overlapping and muddying itself together. The echoed *boom, boom* of Heath's footsteps pulse underneath that. And if all that isn't enough, there are fifty conversations chattering at him from everywhere. It doesn't matter if they whisper it or if they're four rooms down the hall, they're all just *there*.

"Do you think Brad likes me?"

"Psst—what's the answer to number three?"

"I don't know why you're so mad, I only kissed her."

"God, the kids here get dumber every year..."

He needs a break. Heath reaches up to his cochlear implant to switch it off, but his hand hesitates and he chews his lower lip. Ash will tear him a new one for turning it off. He's supposed to be ready, something could happen anytime that he needs to hear, blah, blah, blah. Maybe she's right. But she doesn't know what it's like living with this.

Well, maybe she does know. It can't be easy to digest the pain of everyone she touches.

But why are they hanging around this pathetic school? Heath doesn't like schools, or anywhere with a lot of people. People suck. They're too damn loud. And Ash has never bothered with school at any of the other places they've been. But now, they're mucking around this school, around this town, all because of a *boy*. Heath snorts. It doesn't matter what Matt can do. Sticking around here is dangerous.

A deafening clang erupts behind him as someone slams a locker. Might as well have jabbed a screwdriver straight through his ear. Heath rubs his temple and takes a deep breath to center himself. Leah taught him that. Well, she tried... It isn't working. He needs quiet. He plods through the barrage of sounds until he finds the library. Libraries are quiet, right? He pushes through the door.

Heath's shoulders relax slightly. He releases a long, hissing breath. There are only a few students in here, and they have the good sense to shut the hell up. Then he hears the *bang-bang-bang* of someone tapping their pencil, and the squeaking wheel of a library cart being pushed across the God-awful carpet, and—

Screw it. Heath flips his implant off and closes his eyes, and everything plunges to dark, calm silence. He breathes in and out, feeling the rush of air vibrate through his lungs. He can still hear the library cart—not literally, of course, but he feels the shudder in the floor as the wheels wobble along. He places his hand on the bookshelf beside him, and he feels the tremble when someone pulls a book off the shelf.

Heath opens his eyes and sees the librarian glaring at him over her reading glasses as she pushes her cart. He briefly considers giving her the finger before deciding to just make himself look busy so she'll leave him alone. He grabs a book from the nearest shelf without even bothering to read the title, and glances around for a place to sit where he can pretend to read it.

His eyes fall on a table in the corner with a girl sitting alone. It's one of Matt's friends, the girl who always stares at her phone and doesn't say much. He likes the not saying much part. He makes his way to her table and hovers there awkwardly. She doesn't look up. The glare from her phone washes over her face and makes her eyes look glossy. Her fingers flurry over the screen.

"You're, uh, Tess, right?" Heath says, the vibrations of his voice flowing soundlessly through his throat.

She nods. At least he thinks she does; it's a slow, fluid motion, sending her sandy blond hair rustling. He waits for her to say something. She doesn't.

"I'm Heath, in case you don't remember. I'm with Ash. Well, not *with* Ash, just... you know." He shuffles his feet. "You, uh, mind if I sit down?"

Tess shakes her head. He hesitates another moment, then pulls a chair back, feeling the vibrations as it grates against the rough carpet. He drops into it, sending a reverberation up through his body.

Tess's fingers keep pecking at the screen. Heath waits for her mouth to open, but it never moves.

"Oh... right," he says, mentally face-palming himself. "You talk through your phone. I, uh, turned my implant off to give myself a break, so if you just said a bunch of stuff, I didn't hear it."

He reaches up to switch his implant back on, but before he gets there, his phone buzzes in his pocket. He pulls it out to see a text message.

TESS—*I just explained the meaning of life. Too bad you missed it.*

He looks up to see her mouth curl in the slightest hint of a smirk, and he can't help but chuckle himself. Another text message pops up below that.

TESS—*There's more than one way to talk. I should know.*

"Thanks," Heath says. Then he blurts out, "Wait a minute, how the hell did you get my phone number?" That came out too loud, he can tell by the way it reverberated through his chest. He looks over at the librarian to see her stick a bony finger in front of her lips.

TESS—*You can find a lot of things if you know where to look.*

"Oh, yeah? Like what?"

She thinks for a moment.

TESS—*You don't like Mrs. Clayborne, do you?*

"Who?"

TESS—*The librarian*

Heath chuckles. "No, I guess I don't like her much."

An image of a court document pops up on his screen. He does a double-take, and then his eyes pop open. "That stuck-up librarian's got unpaid parking tickets? A *lot* of unpaid parking tickets! I'll be sure to mention that if she tries to stick me with an overdue book fine. Man, I can't believe you found that. I figured you were just playing games on that thing."

TESS—Most people do.

Heath bites into his lip until it hurts. "People can be a bitch sometimes."

TESS—Some of them aren't so bad.

"Not many. People like me have to be careful who we talk to."

TESS—That sounds lonely.

The shock of that word kicks him in the chest. "Are you kidding? I'm not—"

TESS—It just makes you human.

He fights off an angry chuckle. "Me, human? That's rich."

Tess doesn't react. Heath looks closer at her, at the waves in her hair, her small rounded nose, the pink in her cheeks. She's kind of pretty, actually, if anyone would pay attention to her long enough to notice. "I'm guessing you get lonely too, huh?"

TESS—Sometimes.

He rubs his hands together. "You know, it's nice talking to you. I didn't realize you could have a real, you know... conversation."

Her facial expression never changes.

TESS—Most people don't.

"Sorry."

TESS—I'm used to it.

"You shouldn't have to be used to it. But that's how people are. All they see about me is this." Heath jabs a finger at the grey plastic sitting above his ear.

TESS—Cochlear implant. Audio Logistics model 1128.

He shakes his head. "There you go again. How do you find all that stuff?"

TESS—It's what I'm good at. Like you're good at hearing things.

TESS—At least when you have that turned on.

Heath stifles an ironic chuckle. He closes his eyes, relaxing in the silence. He feels the slight tremor in the floor when the heating system kicks on.

"I wasn't always like this, you know." The words surprise him when they come out. He should shut up now... but it's been a long time since he's had more than small talk with anyone other than Leah or Ash. What the hell. "I was born hearing. But just normal hearing, not like a freak. I was normal... until I was ten." Heath leans back and rubs his temple. "Doctors had a long name for it, way too long for a ten-year-old to remember. It didn't matter. It just meant my hearing faded out a little more every day. Until one day, it switched off completely."

TESS—That must have been hard.

Heath glances up at her. Her face is passive like always, but somehow she does look sorry.

"Thanks. The silence wasn't so bad, actually. It was peaceful. It did make it hard to talk to people, though. I could talk to them, obviously, but for them to talk back... everyone just assumed I could read their lips. It's not as easy as you think."

TESS—A common misconception for deaf people

"Yeah." Heath chuckles, his chest shaking slightly and pulsing the tremor up through his shoulders. "I learned sign language. Me and my family. Well... my brother and my mom did. My dad tried, or said he did, but he never learned much. Too inconvenient for him." Heath grinds his teeth, feeling the vibrations through his jaw. "Most of the kids at school didn't bother to learn either. I could catch a few words here and there with lip reading, but it was like watching my life through ten feet of glass. Didn't matter, people suck anyway. I took care of myself. And I had... Brian."

TESS—Your brother?

Heath hesitates, then he nods. "Brian still hung out with me. He was about the only one who did. The rest of them were all ass-wipes. I didn't need them." He exhales, feeling the air rush from his lungs to his throat and out his nostrils. "My mom said I was too isolated. My dad did one better and said I was holding Brian back, that he needed to have 'normal' friends. My parents wanted to fix me so things would be normal again, or they could pretend they were at least. They said they were getting me a cochlear implant."

TESS—You didn't want that, did you?

Heath glances at her gray-blue eyes staring off at her phone. "Observant, aren't you? No, I didn't want it. I'd gotten used to the silence. Getting the implant was about adapting me to them. I didn't want to be adapted, I just wanted them to appreciate me for who I was and who I was supposed to be. So I told my dad I didn't want it. Besides, I had Brian. He was all I needed."

TESS—But something happened with your brother, didn't it?

"We were in middle school by then," Heath says, his stare fixed on a scratch on the table. "You know how kids are at that age, especially when you're different. Brian had always stood up for me, he said he was my wingman and nothing could change that. But one day, I saw him laughing with some other kids. I don't know what they said exactly, but I caught enough from their lips to get the gist. And Brian kept laughing with them. At me." He clenches his fists tight. "He tried to play it off like nothing happened, but when I looked at him, we both knew. He wasn't my wingman anymore. That night, I told my dad he could give me the damn implant."

Heath absently traces his finger over the plastic shell above his ear. "I remember sitting on the exam table, the doctor talking and the sign language interpreter signing for me, explaining what would happen when they turned the implant on. Saying not to get my hopes too high, I might hear a few things but never at a normal level; that it would take a few months to fully develop. Then they turned it on."

He grimaces and shakes his head.

"It was like a bomb went off. My mom asked if I could hear her, but her voice came screaming at me and I nearly fell off the exam table. And a jet engine roared right there in the room. I figured out later that it was the air conditioner. And the *thump-thump* of a giant drum, that was my own damn heartbeat. And the cricket in the air duct, and the squeaking brakes of the car at the intersection outside…"

Heath holds his head in his hands, reliving the memory.

TESS—The implant shouldn't have operated that way.

"That's exactly what the doctor said. That the implant wouldn't even bring me to a normal hearing level, let alone super hearing. That what I was describing was impossible. But the frenzy of sound kept assaulting me. The whole car ride home, it felt like I was in the middle of a speedway, engines revving all around me. So I turned the thing off." Heath's neck tightens. "My dad didn't like that. He said the whole point of the implant was so people could talk to me. I said he could use sign language… he told me to turn the implant back on. Finally I did, and I tried to just get used to the sound."

TESS—Not something you can get used to, is it?

Heath laughs, but there's a coldness to it. "No, it's not. For a month, I'd still jump every time someone would close a door, drop a pencil, or just breathe too loud. My parents told me it couldn't be that loud, I just needed to calm down. They were... understanding, in that impatient way, like they love you because they *have* to but you'd better get yourself together pretty quick. So I did. Or I pretended to." He clenches his jaw tight until it hurts. "I forced myself to stop jumping at every sound, but it would take a lot more than that to fix me. Whatever *this* is," he says, jabbing a finger at his implant, "whatever mutation this thing activated inside me, isn't natural. People aren't supposed to be like this. We're not supposed to hear *everything*. I heard the guy next door make a call to a hooker. I heard the lady across the street make bets with her bookie. And I heard my dad make plans with a friend to go to a strip club, when he told my mom he was working late."

TESS—*Did you tell your parents what you heard?*

He nods. "They didn't believe me. They took me back to the doctor, they ran tests. They said the implant was operating normally, that my auditory nerves were behaving normally. They said I was making it all up to get attention. When my mom found out my dad really did go to the strip club, they had a screaming fight. Then my dad grabbed me by the neck and growled at me, asking how the hell I could've known about that, saying I must've followed him to the club. Christ's sake, I was twelve! The crazy thing is, I think he would have accepted it better if I had followed him. As ridiculous as that would've been, it was still close enough to 'normal.' But I wasn't normal... not anymore."

TESS—*People don't think I'm normal either.*

Heath gives her a long look. "Yeah, I guess not. Sucks, doesn't it?"

Tess shrugs.

"After that, my parents barely spoke to me at all. And my brother, well... I didn't have to wonder what he was saying about me anymore, because I could hear every word of it. Now I was just a freak. People don't like freaks. Things got... bad after that." He rubs his hands together roughly. "That's when Ash found me."

TESS—Ash took you away from your family?

"Family? Those pricks aren't my family. I don't belong with them. *Normal* people... you can't trust people like that."

Heath's eyes suddenly narrow at Tess. He shouldn't have run his mouth and told her all of that. She's normal enough to be dangerous.

TESS—Is that what Ash told you?

He hesitates a moment. "I could see it on my own."

TESS—After she told you.

He bangs his fist on the table, feeling the silent reverberation of the wood. "The point is, you're all the same."

TESS—Me? You think I'm like other people?

Heath points to her phone. "Maybe your voice, your mind, work different than most people. But that's a *normal* kind of different. The kind of different you're allowed to be. What I am... is something else."

TESS—I can still understand what you're going through.

He stares at her, almost wondering for a second if that could be true. Then he shakes himself out of it. "No, you can't." He pushes his chair back. "This was a mistake. Freaks like me have to be careful who we open up to."

TESS—Did Ash tell you that too?

He gives her a silent glare, then he storms out.

21

Matt

I amble along the sidewalk downtown, past the same faded storefronts that haven't changed since I was five. Well, okay, that check-cashing place with the way-too-bright neon sign is new, but Chaplain is just so predictable. A few other people are walking around, all of whom I've seen before, including that old lady I saved from getting run over the other day, who's stumbling out of the liquor store with a fresh case of hard lemonade. I shake my head and notice a car up ahead with out-of-state license plates, and the only reason I notice it is because I can't remember the last time I've seen one of those around here. The car disappears around the corner, as if it knows it doesn't belong.

"What are you thinking about?" Ash asks beside me.

"Not much," I lie, glancing at her, my eyes tracing over the freckles on her cheeks. I pull my eyes away before she notices. "Are you, uh, getting to like Chaplain?"

She gives me a sideways look. "I can't stay here, Matt."

"Why not?"

"You know why."

I kick an empty can on the sidewalk. "The pawn shop? Look, it's not great, but I'm sure we can clear that up."

"That's just the start of it, Matt."

"You haven't robbed anyplace else, have you?"

She gives me a look that says *not yet*.

"Look," I say, "you don't have to keep doing stuff like that. Stealing stuff. Maybe that's who you were before, but you can start over here."

"You don't get it, Matt. Life's not that easy for some of us."

"Why can't it be?"

Ash laughs, but it doesn't sound happy. "I guess I just forgot where I parked my unicorn with the pot of gold strapped to it."

"Ash—"

"What's holding *you* back?" She turns toward me. "Why won't you come with us?"

I squirm under her stare. "I told you, I can't just leave."

"Those friends you keep talking about?" A subtle edge creeps into Ash's voice. "You really want to stay here because of *them?* To see what happens when they turn on you?"

I stare out over the street with the stores and the people I've all seen a hundred times before. "Look, maybe you can cut ties with everyone and everything you've ever known and never look back, but I can't do that."

"Is it your parents?"

The question jabs me like a sharp stick. "Things with my dad are... complicated."

Ash gives me a penetrating look. "That's interesting."

"I'm glad my family drama amuses you," I mutter.

"I mean, it's interesting that you didn't mention your mom."

My mouth sputters, trying to find words, trying to keep my eyes from watering. "My mom's, uh..."

"I have an easier way." Ash reaches her hand toward me, then pulls it back. "Is it okay?"

I glance at her outstretched hand. "You want to read me or whatever? That thing where you feel people's pain?"

"I could feel what's really going on inside you. What's holding you back."

"I'm guessing you don't usually ask people before you do that."

"No," she says. "But you're different. Look, I'm trying here."

I look into her eyes, not sure what I see in there. I hesitate, then nod.

Ash reaches her hands up and places them gently against the sides of my face. Her palms feel strangely cool. She closes her eyes. I hear her breathing, slow and even. She steps in closer until her body is pressed against me. I feel a heartbeat; I'm not sure if it's hers or mine.

Ash

The skin of his cheeks is warm under her hands. She presses her body into him, hoping she'll get a reaction; she's surprised at how comforting his breathing feels against her. She focuses on the tingle in her fingers as the Pain comes through.

140

It's slow at first. She feels Matt reaching for his dad as if he's on the other side of a canyon, and Matt's straining uselessly to grab hold of him. *Why doesn't he just walk away?* There's an invisible tug there, a cord holding him, but it's getting weaker. Their last conversation took a hacksaw to it, and it's holding on by a thread now. It wouldn't take much for someone to cut that for good. Ash is just thinking about how to do that when she's hit by the flash of fire.

It startles her, and she staggers back half a step. She forces herself to maintain the connection, and she moves back into him. She focuses on the warmth of his skin on her hands, but it's not just his skin that's warm; it's almost as if she can feel heat radiating through her palms. More than the heat, she can feel the fear, not hers but his, because of who's inside the fire.

Mom...

She can feel Matt's determination, even through the fear, the resolution to save her... and then it breaks. The determination is gone and the fire dies to a cold darkness, and his mother is falling into a hole with no end and he's just watching her fall, endlessly, helplessly, and above it all, the void is screaming at him, over and over and over and over—

YOU SHOULD HAVE BEEN ABLE TO SAVE HER!

Ash's eyes snap open and she pulls her hands away. She stares at Matt's face as if for the first time, tracing his pale eyes, his too-small nose, his cheeks. She can still feel each of his breaths. She smiles.

Matt

I watch as she opens her eyes again. There's a flicker of something there now, something different than a minute ago.

"You okay?" I ask her.

Ash nods. "I felt... everything."

I swallow, suddenly feeling naked in front of her. "How much everything?"

She looks at me for a long time, long enough for my eyes to trace lines between all her freckles and back again. "It's not your fault your mom died, Matt."

I wince when she says that, even though it's what I've been telling myself, trying to force myself to believe, every second of every day since the night I watched the house burn with my mom inside.

"How do you know that?" I ask, choking back the tears I don't want her to see me shed.

"Maybe it's time for you to move on."

I look into the steel blue of her eyes, and when she draws in a breath, I do the same, as if we're connected now.

"I... don't know if I'm ready," I say.

"I can't wait for you forever, Matt." Ash sighs. "There was something else in there, too, you know. Something you've been hiding from me."

"What?" My mind whirls, trying to figure out what it is. "I don't—"

Then she smirks and points at my foot. "You stubbed your toe this morning."

We both laugh, as if it erupts spontaneously in us at the same time. As the laughter dies out, I lean forward. Just as I'm about to kiss her... her eyes bug out. I jerk backward.

"I'm, uh, sorry," I sputter. "I was just—" But then I realize she's not staring at me. It's something behind me.

I spin around to see the car with the out-of-state plates, and it's heading toward us.

"Damn it," Ash mutters. "Damn, damn, damn..."

"What is it?"

"He found me." She starts backing away with stumbling steps, like she can barely hold herself up. Her face blanches ghostly white.

"Who found you?" I turn to look at the car. A middle-aged guy hunches forward at the steering wheel, his eyes scanning the street. Then he sees Ash, and a look of recognition spreads over his face.

Ash grabs me by the shirt and yanks me forward. She takes off at a sprint, screaming, *"RUN!"*

22

Matt

My frantic steps pound the sidewalk as Ash drags me along, almost ripping my shirt right off of me as I try to keep up. Her strides are frenzied and uneven. She darts quick glances back at the pursuing car as we run.

"Who is that?" I ask, already fighting for breath. "Who are we running from?"

She doesn't answer and pulls me along faster, shoving a lady in jogging tights out of the way. The car accelerates toward us. Ash glances back at it, her usual confidence and swagger faded to fear.

The car's almost on top of us. I glance at the alley beside us, and tug Ash toward it. "This way!" I yell, and manage to wrangle her into the alley and around the dumpster sitting there. The car whizzes past us.

I catch a glimpse of the driver as he goes past, and there's a hate in his glare that makes me miss a step.

Ash keeps running, her eyes staring wildly ahead like she doesn't even register that I'm here. Her foot catches on the broken storm grate and she stumbles, but she keeps careening ahead, ready to wipe out any second.

"*Ash!*" I scream at her, grabbing her arm and jerking her back.

She finally stops. She shakes her head vigorously, her eyes searching, until they focus on me. She draws in a long, shaky breath.

"Are you okay?" I ask her.

"Dandy," Ash snaps. She bolts off running again, her steps more even now.

"Wait for me!" I huff in a breath to take off after her. "Are you gonna tell me who we're running from now?"

"No." Ash fumbles to grab a chain hanging around her neck and pulls it out from under her shirt. A short, skinny whistle dangles from it. Still at a sprint, she puts it to her mouth and gives a hard blow—nothing comes out.

"What the hell is that?" I ask her. "I don't even hear anything."

"Heath will."

"Heath? He's gotta be blocks from here!"

"Trust me."

We cut behind the pizza place when I trip over a case of empty sauce cans, and my knees hit the concrete with a sting. Ash keeps going without even glancing back to see if I'm okay. I grunt and push myself up, rushing to catch up with her. We get to the end of the alley and turn onto the side street, and Ash screams.

The car is rounding the corner half a block ahead to come back toward us. Ash's face blanches white again and she spins and bolts the other direction, with me right behind her. The car revs and picks up speed. I pump my legs faster, my lungs heaving. My shins twinge with pain at each step. Then the car jumps the curb and barrels onto the sidewalk and straight for us.

I gulp in another labored breath and my feet hit the concrete like hammers. A guy ahead of us walking his dog dives out of the way, and the dog dashes off, dragging its leash behind it. The car engine growls behind me and I can hear the gap closing, and just when I'm about to give up, I hear a thud and the sound of tearing metal.

I look back to see the car wrenched to a stop on top of a trash can, the metal enclosure collapsed forward and a spew of bottles and cans and fast-food wrappers tumbling out. Ahead of me, Ash steals a glance back, and there's a momentary relief on her face, right until she trips and goes down hard. She hits the concrete with a painful grunt that sends all the air out of her. I stagger the last few steps to her and grab her arm to pull her up, but her body has gone limp and her eyes are off in a frantic, distant stare.

The door of the wrecked car bursts open and the guy steps out. His eyes are set hard as stone under the lines in his brow. His greying hair is cropped short, and I'm just praying that haircut isn't a souvenir from a career in the military.

"Ash," I plead as he storms toward us, "I need to know who we're dealing with here."

She doesn't answer. Instead she reaches a limp arm forward, trying to crawl away.

"You bitch!" the guy yells. "You think you can run from what you did?"

"Look, uh, sir," I say, "whatever she did, I'm sure we can—"

"You think it's that easy?" he barks.

Another few steps and he'll be on top of us, and there's no break in his anger. I look behind him and see a bottle rolling away from the fallen trash can. I reach out my hand and feel the tingle in my palm, and the bottle shoots up like a fastball toward his head. My aim's off and it misses, but it knicks his ear on the way past.

"What the hell?" He grabs his ear and looks back to see who threw that, except there's no one there.

I glance through the rest of the trash and see a beer can, and my hand tingles again. It launches toward him, but the can is empty and has no weight behind it. He knocks it away and marches toward me.

"Are you another freak like her?" he demands.

When he says that, my fear hardens to anger. "Watch what you call us," I spit back at him.

"So you *are* a freak. Whose life did you ruin, huh?"

I clench my fists together and stand my ground as he storms the final steps toward me. I brace for a punch, but he shoves me to the side and keeps going toward Ash. I trip and slam shoulder-first onto the sidewalk with a sting of pain.

Ash is still trying to crawl, disoriented like she doesn't even know where she is right now. The guy grabs her by the shoulders and drags her up. She flails her arms against him and screams. I push myself up off the sidewalk and dash toward him, my fist pulled back—

I don't even see his punch coming. It thuds into my jaw with an explosion of pain and my head cocks to the side. I tumble back to the ground.

I watch in a daze as the guy slams Ash down to the concrete, and a muffled yelp escapes from her lungs.

"You're going to suffer like *she* did," he hisses at her.

"You're just pissed she finally left you," Ash responds in a daze. "We both know she should've left a long time ago."

He picks her up and slams her down again. "This isn't about me! This is about the thoughts *you* put in her head! You made her try to... to..."

"I didn't make her do anything. That mess was in her head already."

"That's your *mother* you're talking about!"

That word forces its way through the haze of pain in my head.

Mother.

"You're her... father?" I hear myself asking.

He doesn't answer me. He pulls back his fist, ready to pound Ash right in the mouth. I reach out my hand and release the energy. I can't move him, but I focus on just his fist and I pull. His punch goes wide, and his knuckles smash into the concrete.

"Damn it!" he screams at her. "Before freaks like you... before you started using your *deformity* on us... we were happy!"

"*She* never was," Ash rasps at him. "She was only pretending."

His face erupts with rage and he grapples her throat like he really is going to kill her. I struggle to push myself up but my head's still swimming and I stumble back to the concrete again. Then I hear a yell from down the block, and look up to see a big guy running toward us. A big guy with dark skin and a bald head.

Heath.

He's still thirty feet away but running hard. "Back again, Steve?" he yells.

Her dad glares at Heath, then tightens his grip on Ash. She reaches her hands up—at first I think she's trying to pull his hands off of her, but she reaches past them to his face. Steve's eyes bug out and he flinches back.

"Don't do that to me, not again!" he shouts wildly. He releases his grip and reaches to grab her wrists to stop her. He manages to grab both her wrists, but not before she brushes her finger against his cheek. Her eyes flutter closed for an instant.

"Left hip!" Ash yells.

Heath pounds up to them and draws back his arm, his bicep bulging through his shirt, and then he lets loose into Steve's hip like a sledgehammer. Steve grunts and his whole body collapses. He hits the sidewalk and rolls around, writhing in pain.

I finally manage to get up and stagger over to Ash. "You okay?"

She doesn't respond. Her eyes are a million miles away. I'm about to try again when I notice a lady across the street staring at us and talking frantically into her cell phone, and then I hear a siren approaching.

"Shit," Heath says. "We've got to go."

Heath grabs Ash, still delirious, and pulls her along. I glance back at Ash's dad. He tries to pick himself up, then reaches for his hip and collapses again.

"Come on already!" Heath barks at me.

I see the squad car round the corner and I take off behind him and Ash.

No matter how hard I try, I can't fight off the image of Ash's dad trying to strangle her—except in the image, he has my dad's face.

23

Matt

"Wait up!" I yell between breaths, trying to keep up.

"Can't wait," Ash wheezes.

"Unless you want to get arrested. Or punched again." Heath chuckles. "Man, I heard that two blocks away."

The siren dies away behind us as we duck around another corner. I keep pumping my legs and drag in another breath. We make one more cut into an alley and then finally slow to a jog. I fight at another breath. Heath's breathing is still annoyingly steady.

"Did he get away this time?" Ash asks, panting.

Heath pauses for a second, then shakes his head. "Nope. Cops are cuffing him right now."

"Wait a minute," I ask. "What do you mean *this* time? He's done this before?"

Ash purses her lips and keeps running.

Heath's mouth is a tight line. "Ash's daddy has been pretty relentless in tracking her down. Last time was in Chicago, wasn't it?"

"Detroit," Ash mumbles.

"Right," Heath says. "But that thing with his hip is new."

"For Christ's sake," I exclaim, "that was your *dad* trying to kill you!"

"Like your dad's never hurt you?" Ash snaps.

I shudder with the image I can't get out of my head. "Not... not like that."

"Give it time."

"Damn it, Ash, why would he do that to you?"

She keeps her stare fixed ahead. "He can't stand that I showed him the truth about himself. Like he can blame *me* for that."

"What kind of truth?"

Heath glares at me. "Don't go there."

I ignore him and turn back toward Ash. "What happened to make him hate you?"

"Nothing happened," Ash says in a cold tone. "He hates me for who I *am*. First, it was just because I wasn't a boy. Then he couldn't stand that I knew that about him, that I could feel every weakness in him. But what really set him over the edge was what happened with Mom."

"She left him?"

"He had that coming."

"And she tried to... do something?" I ask, fighting the tremble in my voice. "Did you have anything to do with that?"

Ash turns her head toward me, whipping her hair like a kite. "It's not my fault Mom didn't like things about herself. All I did was point them out."

I swallow. "What did your mom do, Ash?"

"She took half a bottle of sleeping pills one night."

"Oh my God..."

"Don't get overdramatic. She's fine. He found her in time and got her to the hospital." Ash's jaw clenches. "And then he hit me so hard he broke my collarbone."

I don't even know how to process all that. "I'm... sorry."

"Whatever. He tried to blame me for what Mom did, but her pain was already there. And what do you think it's like to *feel* that pain, huh?" Ash says, her voice raw. "To feel what your dad *really* thinks of you, deep down, the feelings there aren't even words for?"

I watch her face, and I don't need her Ability to feel her anger.

"What did you feel in him?" I whisper.

She shakes her head. "The closest word for it is *abomination.*"

Heath glares at me with an *I told you not to go there* look. "Makes you wonder what your dad thinks about *you,* huh?"

I shudder, trying to push the thought away. "But... you only feel pain, right? You only feel the negative—"

"Who thinks about their daughter that way?" Ash snaps. "What kind of dad takes those feelings and beats the hell out of her with them?"

She turns and storms away. I start after her when Heath grabs my arm.

"We've been trying to tell you," he says. "Everyone you *think* cares about you, it's just a matter of time."

24

Matt

"Dad?" I call out as I push through the front door. I cringe as I wait for a response; I can't decide if I actually want one.

"Matt? Uh, in here."

Damn. Silence would have been so much easier. But, no, I need to do this. I need to find out what he really feels about me.

I plod slowly into the kitchen. He's pulling a couple of microwave dinners out of the freezer, wiping the frost off the boxes. I guess any motivation to cook real food died the other day, when...

"Dad, can I talk to you?"

He fumbles with the frozen dinners, almost dropping them. His face washes out to gray. "Talk? A-About what?" He darts a quick glance at me before his eyes go back to the floor.

I'll admit, I'm finding a spot on the floor pretty interesting myself right now. I have to force the words out. "You know. *It*. We need to talk about it."

He glances anxiously at the dinner boxes, avoiding my eyes. "I, uh, thought we'd try the Salisbury steak this time. We haven't had that one before."

"We need to talk about the thing I can do." I get another flash of the image of Ash's dad trying to strangle her, and I search my dad's face, looking for any of that anger hidden underneath. "Do you hate me for it?"

He won't look at me. Keeps shuffling the dinner boxes in his hands. "We have some rolls in the pantry to go with these, I think, and there's some ice cream—"

"*Listen* to me, Dad!"

He looks up at me, but his eyes are lifeless. "I can't do this, Matt."

"You can, and you will." I take a step toward him, my face firm. "I've been tiptoeing around this my whole life with you. I know I have to hide it from most people, and I can deal with that, but you're not most people. You should be able to accept me the way I am."

A swallow bulges down his throat. "It's not that easy, Matt."

"God damn it, yes, it is! I'm your son, aren't I? What if I'd been born blind?" I suddenly think of Heath. "Or deaf?"

"That's different."

"No, it's not! This is how I am. Am I really that repulsive this way?" Another flash of the image; this time, it's my dad's face leering, his hands around my throat. "How long until that turns into real hate?"

"I don't—"

"Is that how you felt about Mom, too?"

Shock washes over his face, and he bites his lip. "I loved your mother."

"She was like me, Dad. That's where I got it from. You knew that, right?"

"I... we didn't talk about it."

I pound my fist on the counter, the bang echoing hollowly through the room. "I know you didn't talk about it, that's the point! I'm asking you, did you hate her for it?" I stare at him through watery eyes. "Do you hate *me* for it?"

"Matt, I—I don't know how to deal with this. It's not natural."

I grind my teeth. "Yeah, I've heard that one before. Well, it's natural for *me*."

"But it shouldn't be! It's not—" Dad roughs his hand through his hair where the gray is coming through. "I can't do this! I need... I need..." He hunches down under the sink and throws open the cabinet doors, flails his arm inside, knocking over the bleach and the ant spray, until he pulls out a bottle of scotch.

"You've been hiding alcohol?" I yell.

"This is the least of our problems right now." He rips the cap off and chugs straight from the bottle. He comes up for air, then lifts the bottle for another gulp when he stops himself. His hand jerks the bottle toward his mouth, then away. Finally, he grits his teeth. "Damn it!" He hurls the bottle across the room, and it shatters against the wall in a spray of glass and alcohol.

"Good for you, Dad," I mutter at him. "Showing some real growth there."

"Do you know how hard it was not to drain that whole thing? Do you know how hard it was to... to..." He glares at me, and there it is. The hate. "*You* drove me to that! Before you went and brought this up, I was happy!"

My mouth sputters with hurt and rage. The doorbell rings before I can say something I'll regret. More than I already have. I turn and storm away, feeling the smoke fume out of me with each step. I grab the doorknob and pull the front door open so hard it slams into the wall.

Ash stands there. The waves of her hair cascade over her crimson shirt, the red, brown, and gold of her hair mixing into it. She looks me up and down. "Looks like you're having a bad day."

"What are you doing here?" I demand.

"Nice to see you, too."

"Look, I'm sorry, it's just—"

"I get it. Bad day. Look, we have to leave."

"Leave where?"

"Leave town." Ash points to her car behind her. Heath and Leah are inside. "We're going now."

"Like right now?"

"Yes, *right now.* We shouldn't have stayed this long, and this thing with my dad showing up made it a hundred times worse."

"But can't you at least stay long enough to—"

Ash holds up her hand. "No, Matt. I'm getting in that car, and we're putting this town behind us. I thought I'd give you one more chance to come with us."

I bite my lip. "I can't just leave."

"Why the hell not?" She jerks her head toward the house. "What's in there that's so good it's worth staying for?"

I look back. I don't see my dad, just the broken remains of his scotch bottle. That pretty much sums it up for him anyway. And my mom... she's just a picture in a frame.

"You know what? You're right." I step out the door and slam it with a bang. "Let's go."

"Wow. Seriously?"

I know it's just my anger pushing me. I know if I let it cool, I'll rethink this. But right now, I don't want it to cool. I don't want to wait for my dad to really turn on me—the way Ash and Heath keep saying he will. I squeeze my eyes shut to keep the tears from spilling out. "I said let's go."

25

Matt

The faded street signs roll by through the window as Ash's car carries us along. Past the same houses that have been here forever; the corner of Mrs. Spitz's fence that's been crooked since I was in third grade; the half-painted side of Mr. Jorgenson's house that he's been saying he'll finish for the past three years. The memories start to crowd out whatever resolve I have, and I look away.

Leah reaches her hand over, although she doesn't quite touch me. "You okay?" she asks in a quiet voice.

"Yeah," I say, except I'm not. What the hell am I doing? I can't just run away. But I get one more image of my dad trying to strangle me, and I clench my jaw tight.

Heath chuckles. "So who pissed you off enough to make you change your mind about leaving?"

I shoot him a look that says *don't ask,* and he shrugs.

"Where are we headed?" Heath asks Ash.

"Does it matter?" she says.

None of us respond, because no, it doesn't.

We reach the outskirts of town where the trees get thicker and the houses get farther apart. Mostly older houses that look like they could really use an episode on one of those fixer-up TV shows. After a grove of trees, we pass along a wrought-iron fence. It stands in stark contrast to all the neighboring houses, but I barely pay it any mind until Heath whistles.

"Who does *that* belong to?" he asks.

The fence is commandingly tall, at least eight feet, and the black paint gleams fresh on every bar. It stretches on and on, up to the gate at the driveway ahead.

"That's Crossman's place," I mumble. "But he's, uh, not staying there at the moment."

Heath turns around in his seat. "You're gonna have to give us more than that. We're not from around here, remember?"

"Crossman owns the auto parts factory, which pretty much means he owns the town. Or he used to."

Heath chuckles. "If he's that much of a big shot, I'm surprised he lives out here with these other riffraff."

"He doesn't live here, really. He's got a penthouse up in the city somewhere. This is just where he stays when he drops by to check on things."

We keep coasting along the fence until the house looms into view through the bars. Three stories of brick, copper, and the finest materials money can buy.

"Damn," Heath says. "This is just the place where he crashes once in a while?"

Leah leans over to stare at the house. "He has a house like that, and he's not even living there? He's at his... penthouse?"

"Not exactly," I say.

Ash jerks the car to a stop. "Okay, so where exactly *is* this dude right now? And what do you mean he 'used to' own the factory?"

"He's, uh, in the county lockup, awaiting trial."

"Really?" Heath chuckles. "The richest guy in a small town like this got busted? That's gotta start some gossip."

"Little bit, yeah."

"So what did he do?"

I scratch my neck. "He killed some people trying to cover up a defective product. But he got caught, and the factory is getting bought out by someone else."

Ash taps her fingers on the steering wheel. "And no one's in that big, expensive house?"

"Not no one." I point to the gate up ahead. A booth sits by the gate with a security guard in a gray uniform, eyeing us through the window. "In case you were thinking about a quick smash-and-grab," I add.

Ash turns around to give me a look. "Don't tell me what I should be thinking about. And by the way, I don't have to touch you to tell that you know more than you're letting on about this Crossman guy's trial."

I look down and hope my cheeks aren't blushing as red hot as they feel.

"Matt's right, for once," Heath says. "That job would be bigger than anything we've tried before."

"I didn't ask you," Ash snaps. She chews her lip, staring at the guard booth. "It's just a rent-a-cop."

Leah clears her throat, though it's barely audible. "There's probably more security than that."

"Exactly," I say. "Besides, I thought you were getting out of town?"

She glares at me in the rear-view mirror. "I thought *you* were getting out, too?"

I look away, my resolve fading.

Ash stares at the house, and I can tell she's mentally calculating what kind of stuff she could pawn in there. Finally she lets out a sigh ripe with frustration. "Fine." She throws the car in gear, then lurches us to a stop again. "Wait, what's that?"

A truck pulls around from the back of the house and starts down the drive toward the gate. The guard in the booth gives us another look.

"Maybe we should get out of here," I say.

"Maybe you need to chill out," Ash snaps. "You see what that is?"

I squint as the truck pulls closer. It's big, gray, and boxy. When it gets close to the gate, I can see the rivets in the steel and the reinforced windows.

"That's an armored car," Heath says.

"Exactly," Ash says. "And you don't call one of those things to pick up anything cheap."

Heath scratches his scalp. "Yeah, but it means more security. Which means this is *way* bigger than anything we've hit before."

Ash keeps the car idling, watching through the windshield. When the armored car stops at the guard booth, she slaps Heath in the arm. "What do they have in there?" she demands.

Heath squints, concentrating. "Didn't say."

"Did they pick something up or drop something off?"

"Didn't say that either."

The armored car pulls away and down the street.

"Damn." Ash chews her lip, then glares at Heath. "Wait... you're holding out on me! They did say something, didn't they?"

Heath hesitates, then nods. "They're coming back again on Wednesday."

I cringe as I see the wheels turning in Ash's head.

"Which means," she says, "whatever they dropped off, there's more coming. Or whatever they picked up, there's more left."

Leah fidgets in the seat next to me. "You want to break in there? Are you sure?"

"No, she's not," Heath says firmly. "I told you, we've never hit anything that big before."

"That's the point," Ash says. "We've been pulling small jobs, barely scraping by. We can't even afford a decent car. Maybe we need to up our game and finally take what we deserve." She looks at me in the rearview mirror. "Plus, now we have *him*."

I'm about to tell her I'm not some master thief and this definitely isn't what I signed up for when I got in the car, when my phone buzzes. I pull it out and see a text.

PHILLIP—u doing ok? i know you've had a lot to think about lately, just want 2 make sure u know i'm here for you. we all are.

That cuts through my shell of anger, and I know I can't leave. Even if my dad does hate me, even if I'll never fix that, I still have friends.

"Uh, guys..."

Ash and Heath's voices are loud and heated now, but they're talking over each other and I can't catch what they're saying.

"Guys!" I yell. They stop arguing and pivot to look at me. "I can't do this," I say.

Heath grins. "You owe me five bucks," he tells Ash.

"Shut up," she says. "You can't do what?"

I glance at Phillip's text again. "I can't leave."

Leah's mouth quivers, and she turns toward the window.

"Fine," Ash says. "For now. Because we're staying too."

Heath glares at her. "What?"

"We're staying." Her eyes are locked on Crossman's house.

"We were leaving town for a *reason*," Heath says.

"It can wait."

I raise an eyebrow at Ash. "You're not really thinking about robbing the place, are you?"

"Don't worry your little head about that," she says snidely. "We're just going to stay in town a while longer. Until you get a little more perspective."

Ash finally pulls the car away from the curb, and I watch Crossman's house slowly disappear behind us. But something tells me I'm going to be seeing it again sooner than I'd like.

26

Matt

I push my way out the school doors into the cool air. A cluster of guys knock into me as they shove past, chuckling about a dirty joke. On the other side of the sidewalk, Tom Hackett tries to wrangle his tuba case, which is nearly as big as he is. Though with Tom, that's not saying much. I wander past without giving any of them much thought.

Then... I see Rob and Phillip. My steps drag to a stop.

My guilt kicks me in the gut, and I look down at a glob of gum stuck to the sidewalk. I almost left town yesterday, almost left my friends behind without looking back. I don't know... if I'm honest, maybe I was never really going to go through with it. But still, I got in the car.

Rob looks the other way, pretending he doesn't see me. I think about doing the same, then swear at myself and drag my feet forward toward them.

"Hey, guys," I say, forcing a casualness to my voice. Damn it, I shouldn't have to force anything with them.

"Hey," Rob says stiffly, still not looking at me. His skin seems a little darker today somehow, and there's no hint of his usual smile.

Phillip manages a smile on his pale cheeks, but it's strained.

I kick at an empty soda can on the sidewalk. "What's up with you guys lately?"

"You wouldn't know, would you?" Rob snaps.

"What's that supposed to mean?"

"He, uh, means we haven't seen you much," Phillip says.

I'm finding a lot of interest in the label on that can on the sidewalk. The word "sorry" starts to weasel its way up my throat, but I gulp it back down. "I've been busy," I say instead.

"Sure you have. With your other friends," Rob says.

Phillip awkwardly adjusts his hoodie. "What he means is we miss seeing you around."

"What I *mean*," Rob says, "is you're being an ass, ditching us for a bunch of bigger asses."

"They're not bad once you get to know them," I insist.

"Why would I want to get to know them?"

"Come on, give them a chance. If you'd just follow them around for a while, you might actually like them."

Phillip coughs and looks down.

"What's the matter, Phillip?" I ask him.

Phillip avoids eye contact with me and looks up toward the school doors. "Hey, Tess, how are you?"

Tess steps through the doors, managing to weave between a couple volleyball players even though she has her eyes down on her phone.

"*Hi, Matt,*" she says as she steps up to us. "*Haven't seen you much lately.*"

"Exactly," Rob quips.

"So, uh, Tess," I say, giving Rob a look, "how've you been? Win any more chess games?"

"*A few,*" she says.

An awkward silence stretches out after the words from her phone fade out.

Phillip reaches into his hoodie to scratch his neck. "So, uh, how are your folks handling the factory buyout? My mom won't really talk about it."

Rob shrugs. "My dad seems okay with it. It's not like he ever cared much for Crossman."

Phillip looks at me. "What about your dad, Matt?"

Suddenly, the smoldering lump in my gut starts to heat up again. "What about him?"

"Well, is he stressed or anything?"

I grit my teeth. "Something like that."

"Something like what?"

I swallow down the answer and stare past him.

A car pulls up to the curb and Tess's dad steps out, glancing at his watch with a huff. "Come on, Tess," he calls out.

Rob jabs me in the shoulder. "Dude, Phillip asked you a question. What's up with your dad?"

I shake my head stiffly. "You don't want to hear the answer to that."

"Why not?"

"*What did your dad do, Matt?*" Tess asks.

I squeeze my jaw tighter until it hurts. "I said you don't want to know."

"Tess!" her dad yells. "Come on!"

"*You can talk to us, Matt,*" Tess says.

"He could, back in the day," Rob says. "But it's getting harder, isn't it?"

"Don't start with me, Rob, I'm not in the mood," I snap at him.

"I'm just saying. You haven't been around much."

"He's still our friend," Phillip says.

Rob shrugs. "I hope so."

"Tess!" Her dad storms up, his steps brisk enough to wrinkle the pleats out of his pants. "You can play games on your phone later! Let's go!"

He grabs her by the shoulder and starts to pull her away, and I feel the heat ignite in my face.

"What gives you the nerve to treat her like that?" I snap.

He jolts to a full stop like I just punched him in the throat. "Excuse me?"

"You drag Tess around like she's an invalid, like she can't walk forty feet to your car on her own!"

Rob stares at me like he's watching a car wreck. Phillip coughs nervously.

Her dad glares at me through his glasses. "I think I know what my daughter needs."

"The hell you do! You don't know her at all. You think she's just playing games on that phone? Do you have any idea how smart she is?"

His face flushes furiously red. "Who the hell are you to talk to me like that?"

"I'm someone who actually knows her." I step forward and jab a finger into his chest. "Maybe if you paid attention to who your child *is* instead of who you *want* her to be, you wouldn't make her feel ashamed. What kind of dad does that, huh?"

His jaw shakes with tension. He looks like he's about to let loose on me, and I'm just preparing for another volley myself when Phillip grabs my arm.

"Let's, uh, let him get Tess home, Matt," Phillip says quietly.

I stare bullets at him. "I'm not letting this bastard take her anywhere."

"He's her dad, Matt."

"Like that gives him the right?"

Phillip tugs on my arm. I fight him at first, then finally give in and let him pull me away, but I keep my eyes trained like lasers on Tess's dad. He stews for a minute longer, then grabs Tess's arm and storms toward his car.

Phillip spins me around to look me in the eye. "What's gotten into you?" he asks.

"I'm just tired of assholes like him."

"Look, he is a... one of those... but where did all this come from?" Phillip's soft green eyes probe me. "Did something happen?"

"Why would something have to happen for me to stand up?" I snap at him.

"Because this isn't like you, Matt."

Something inside me hardens until it cracks. "Maybe it should be."

27

Heath

Every rustle of the dry leaves in the trees erupts in a wash of sound like static, like a million candy wrappers crinkling at the same time. And the gusts of breeze make their own sound too, whistling like a gale in a hurricane. Heath's steps plod along the sidewalk, the rubber soles of his shoes squishing a soft squeak with each step. He reaches out his hand and absently drags his fingers along the bars of the iron fence, but that only lets loose a hum of vibrating metal as if he'd struck a tuning fork. He winces and keeps his focus on the guard booth around the corner, fifty yards away, concentrating to tune out the jumbled mess of background noise.

There's a clinking of metal on ceramic as the guard stirs the coffee in his mug, but that's the most excitement from the booth in the last half hour except for some sighing. The dude does a lot of sighing. He's probably as bored as Heath is right now. Heath plods a few more steps forward, then sighs himself and turns to backtrack the other way. It would make this more entertaining if he could at least do a full lap of the property, but it would be stupid to walk past the guard booth and draw attention to himself. So he keeps pacing the same stretch of sidewalk, back and forth, over and over. He glances through the bars of the fence at the monstrosity of a house hidden behind the trees.

Ash is overreaching on this one. Sure, anyone who has a house like that has got to have some expensive shit to steal, but expensive shit breeds security. Not to mention, they should've left town already anyway, with or without her new boy toy. But when she'd told Heath to spy on the place to find out what that armored car was carrying, they both knew it wasn't a request. So he's been out here all damn afternoon, trudging back and forth over the same damn sidewalk, waiting for something interesting to happen.

Wait, there it is—the guard sneezed. He'll be sure to report back on that one.

The rumble and whine of an engine cuts through the other mess and quickly grows as the car speeds toward him from down the street. A sorry-looking thing with chips in the blue paint and one fender that doesn't match. A series of pops accompanies the whine of the engine—it's misfiring on one of the cylinders—as it revs it up. Both the driver and the dude riding shotgun are wearing blue letter jackets from this town's excuse for a high school. They whiz by, the tires scuffing against the rough asphalt, and the passenger flips him off. The dude says something unflattering that most people wouldn't hear, the sound muffled inside the car's cab, but Heath hears it just fine. He grits his teeth and keeps his eyes on Crossman's house until the sound of the engine fades. Another gust of wind sends the leaves in the trees crinkling again.

"This is ridiculous," Heath mutters to himself. "What am I even doing here?"

He turns and strides away from the house, not even caring what Ash will say about him leaving, when a ringing suddenly echoes from inside the guard booth. Heath stops in his tracks, all his senses directed at the sounds in the booth.

The clank and sloshing of liquid as the guard sets down his coffee mug.

The deep exhale of another sigh.

The clatter as the guard fumbles for the telephone receiver. "Hello? Yeah, I told you, Wednesday. No, there's one more pickup after that."

The armored car service, it has to be. Heath strains to hear what the caller is saying, but that side of the conversation is out of his frequency range. Ash always thinks he can hear *everything,* but it doesn't work that way.

"I know you could get it all in one trip. That's not the point," the guard says. "Mr. Crossman wants it split up."

There's a rough sound as the guard scratches his chin. Sounds like he could use a shave.

"Because he doesn't want all that cash in one truck, waiting for some idiot to steal it."

Heath can't help but perk up at that, even if this whole thing is a bad idea.

"Well, Mr. Crossman doesn't trust your security that much. Hey, don't take it personal, he doesn't trust me either."

The voice on the other end of the line sounds irritated, even if Heath can't make out the words.

"Yeah, I know it's a drive to get out here from the city, but what do you care? Crossman's paying you, isn't he? Just be here on time."

The guard hangs up the receiver with a reverberating clunk, and then there's a scrape of ceramic as he picks up his coffee mug again. A long, messy *slurp*.

Heath turns and walks off, satisfied that the show's over for now. A dry leaf crunches under his shoe making an awful crinkling racket, but he barely notices. His mind is too busy with everything else.

He thinks about not telling Ash about this at all. Nothing happened, it was a boring afternoon. The guard said the armored car was carrying his dead mother's ashes or something stupid like that. But he only thinks about that for a second, because he knows sooner or later she'll find out, and he owes her. More than that, he owes Leah. He'd march straight into hell if it would help Leah. And besides, as much as he tells himself not to, he can't help but feel an itch when he thinks about how much money must still be sitting in that house. However much was there to start with, there are still two more loads to pick up. Loads big enough to send an armored car. If they could even just grab a handful of that...

But damn, this is a bad idea.

Phillip

One more shadow stands among the trees, still and silent. The breeze rustles against Phillip's hoodie, just like it rustles the leaves around him. His head and body never move, but his eyes do, watching across the street, following Heath as he plods back and forth across the sidewalk.

Heath has been pacing that same stretch for over an hour. If he was anywhere else, Phillip would figure he was just bored or had something on his mind. But here—Phillip's eyes track up, past the iron bars of the fence, to Crossman's house—there's a reason he's here. You don't hang around the house of the richest guy in town unless you're up to something. Heath is casing the joint for a job. Tess found those police reports, so this wouldn't be the first time Heath and the others have stolen something. But all of those were small, petty theft stuff, what they could grab and carry out quick. Or were the small jobs the only ones Tess was able to find?

A car engine revs, a clunky blue compact with two guys from the football B-squad crammed into it. The car whizzes by as fast as the beat-up engine will carry it, and Ryan, in the passenger seat, flips Heath off before the car disappears down the street. Heath keeps his head down and keeps trudging along.

Phillip feels his conviction waver, looking at Heath's face. It's not easy being a reject. What Phillip's had to deal with is one thing; people just overlook him. But Heath, and Ash, and Leah... and Matt, if people really knew about him... that's something else. Maybe he shouldn't be out here spying on Heath like this. Besides, it looks like he's leaving.

But then Heath stops dead, his face laser-focused. Does he hear something? Phillip follows Heath's eyes to the guard booth. It looks like the guard's on the phone. Can Heath hear what the guy's saying all the way from there? He's got to be fifty yards away.

The guard hangs up the phone, and Heath turns and strides off. Whatever he was lurking around here for, he got it. Phillip follows him, the only shadow among the trees that moves.

28

Rob

The taco casserole smells greasier than usual today. Rob jams a fork into it and pulls out a long string of cheese that refuses to break. He slaps the fork back down.

Phillip slides noiselessly into the seat across from him. "Where's Matt?"

"Hell if I know," Rob says. "Although I'm pretty sure I know who he's with."

Tess taps at her phone at the end of the table. *"He's been spending most of his time with her."* Her eyes almost look sad, although with Tess, it's always hard to tell. *"With them,"* she adds.

"No joke," Rob says.

Phillip shrugs. "Hopefully she makes him happy."

"She's doing a lot more than that. She's rubbing off on him in all the wrong ways. Or maybe it's that Heath dude, I don't know. Either way, *something's* sure gotten into him."

"You're talking about yesterday after school, aren't you?" Phillip darts a hesitant glance at Tess.

"You bet I am. He laid into Tess's dad something fierce. Have you ever heard him go off like that before?"

Phillip shakes his head. "No. Sorry about that, Tess. I'm sure Matt was trying to help, but it was out of line."

"*It's okay,*" she says.

"Is it really, though?" Phillip asks.

Her fingers tap methodically over the phone for a moment. "*My dad doesn't understand me. It sucks sometimes. Sounds like Matt's dad doesn't understand him either.*"

"No, I don't think he does."

"*Matt was trying to help. And he wasn't wrong about the things he said. But he just made my dad angrier.*"

"Sorry about that." Rob hesitates, dragging his fork through the casserole. "Uh, how angry was your dad, though? He doesn't, like, hit you or anything, does he?"

"*Of course not.*"

"Good." Rob nods repeatedly. "That's good. I, uh... sorry, I shouldn't have asked that."

"*You were trying to help.*"

"I still can't believe Matt yelled like that," Phillip says.

Rob exhales, glad to change the subject. "Yeah. I mean, he'd finally gotten some confidence in him when we went storming the factory... but this is different. And you know why that is, don't you?"

Phillip tugs on the strings of his hoodie. "Sounds like he's been going through some stuff with his dad."

"Are you kidding? It's Ash and her crew. They're a bad influence on him."

"They're not all bad."

"From where I'm sitting, I don't see a lot of good," Rob says. "They're up to something. I just wish I knew what it was."

Phillip looks down at his plate and fumbles with his fork.

"Wait, you know something, don't you?"

Phillip shrugs. "Not sure yet."

"But you know *something*."

"Okay, yeah. I've been... following them around."

"You've been *spying* on them? Man, Phillip! Didn't think you had it in you."

"I wasn't spying, I was just... okay, yeah, I was."

"You were trying to help," Tess says.

Phillip shifts in his seat. "Thanks, Tess, but it doesn't make me feel better about it."

"Will you get to it already?" Rob says. "What'd you find out?"

"I've been following Heath mostly. He can hear way more than you think. You wouldn't believe—"

"Come on, get to the good stuff."

Phillip exhales. "He was hanging around outside Crossman's house."

"That big-ass place outside of town?"

"221 Oak Street," Tess says.

Phillip nods. "He was there for over an hour, pacing back and forth along the fence."

"What, like he was casing the joint?"

"I don't know, but he was definitely up to something." Phillip grimaces. "Sorry, that's mean to say."

"It's not mean if it's true."

"But what if it's not?"

"Why else would he act like a stalker outside the biggest house in town?"

"*Is he planning to rob it?*" Tess asks.

Phillip shakes his head. "I don't know. It was like he was waiting for something. He kept looking at the guard booth. Then the guard made a phone call, and Heath left right after that."

"Why would Heath want to watch the guard make a phone call?" Rob asks. "Not much to see."

"I think he could hear it."

"He could hear what the dude said all the way inside the booth?"

"I'm telling you, his ears are incredible."

Rob taps his fork against the tray. "It doesn't make sense. I thought that implant thing he has is for deaf people, so how is his hearing *better* than everyone else's?"

"*Doctor couldn't explain it,*" Tess says. "*Didn't even believe him.*"

Rob stares at her. "How do you know that?"

"*He told me.*"

"He told you that? He sure doesn't like talking to me."

"You don't have the most, um, cuddly personality." Phillip ignores the look Rob shoots him. "Look, let's focus here. What do you think Heath was doing at Crossman's house? He left right after the guard hung up the phone... like he'd heard whatever he was waiting for."

"Where'd he go after that?" Rob asks.

"Just back to the motel."

"So not much to go on."

Phillip rubs his neck. "I shouldn't have spied on him like that."

"If you hadn't, we wouldn't know the dude's up to something."

"If he *is* up to something," Phillip says.

Rob raises an eyebrow.

"Okay, fine," Phillip admits. "I know he is. I just... I was hoping he wasn't. For Matt."

"For Matt," Rob echoes. "Man, I hope he doesn't get roped into this. I told you, that crowd is a bad influence."

"*Do you think Ash is involved too?*" Tess asks.

"Are you kidding?" Rob says. "She's the one pulling everyone's strings."

"Even Matt's?" Phillip asks.

Rob bites his lip. He knows what the answer is... but maybe he can ignore it for a little while longer.

29

Ash

Her fingers drum on the steering wheel and she glances for the hundredth time through the smudged windshield at the guard booth. The glow of light from inside has grown more pronounced against the darkening sky, but other than that, nothing's happened. The guard takes another drink of coffee. Ash holds up the binoculars to get a better view. His eyes seem tired... or maybe just bored. He's got crow's feet starting to form around them, although it's hard to tell because his shaggy should-have-been-cut-a-week-ago hair hangs down over his forehead. But she's not here just to watch him sit in the booth. Ash drums a little harder on the steering wheel.

Her eyes pan across the fence to the giant house. There has to be some impressive stuff in there worth stealing, even without whatever the armored car was there for. Heath is right—they've never hit anything this big before—but that's the point. They need to go bigger. They deserve it. She glances at the guard booth again.

A car pulls up. The guard waves at the driver in recognition. The gate slides open, smooth and silent. The car parks and then the driver gets out—he's wearing a gray security guard uniform too. The guy in the booth gets up and stands impatiently in the doorway as the driver walks up. They talk for a minute; could be work stuff, the game last night, or griping about their girlfriends. Heath could tell her every word, but it doesn't matter. He'd just get in the way for what's coming next.

The guard leaves his replacement in the booth and gets in his car with a hollow slam of the door. Ash turns her key, grimacing at the sad sputter of the engine—but maybe they're finally going to be able to do something about that. The guard's car pulls away from the curb and Ash follows, her headlights off.

She doesn't have to follow him very far. The dude goes straight to a bar. Ash parks and steps out of her car, up the uneven front step, and under the flickering neon sign to the door. She straightens herself up and pushes her way in.

The light is dim inside, and cigarette smoke trails up to the ceiling from half a dozen tables, where overweight losers sit hunched over their beers and look like they've been there for a while. The twang of some God-awful country song plays in the background.

The guard sits at the bar, alone, a bottle of something already in front of him. His tie is off and his hair a little more mussed, but he hasn't bothered to change his uniform. He turns when Ash opens the door, and he keeps looking at her. Every other sleazy loser in the place watches her, too, and she can feel them undressing her from here. She wouldn't mind giving every last one of them a kick in the balls, but she's here for a reason. She keeps walking.

Ash makes sure not to look straight at her target; she ambles to the bar, wearing an indifferent half-smile, and slides onto a stool two seats over from the guard.

The bartender looms over her, a tall, rough-looking dude with a tattoo scrawled across his thick neck. He eyes Ash skeptically.

"Light beer, please," Ash says.

"We don't serve minors here, little lady," he says with a gravelly voice.

Ash laughs. "Oh, I know I don't look my age." She pulls out her fake ID, thinking how it had better be worth what she paid for it. "I can only hope that's still true when I'm pushing forty, am I right?"

The bartender casts scrutinizing glances between the ID and Ash's face. She turns her smile up to three-quarters. Finally, he grunts and slaps the ID back on the bar, followed by a bottle.

Ash grasps the bottle, feeling the cool condensation on her fingers, and takes a slow sip. She watches the guard out of the corner of her eye, waiting. She feels all the fat guys at the tables still gawking at her. The bartender continues to eye her as he stacks glasses. Finally, the guard reaches for the bowl of nuts. Ash darts her hand out toward the bowl too. But she doesn't care about the nuts.

Her fingers brush his, and her eyes blink shut.

Longing for approval... not from his father, this is from someone younger, someone...

Daughter.

Perfect.

Her eyes flutter open again and she lets out a calculated nervous giggle.

"Sorry," she says. "Didn't mean to bump into you like that."

"No worries." He goes back to his drink, not taking the bait yet.

"You don't mind if I chat with you, do you?" Ash is careful to keep her voice friendly but not flirty. "I'm just a little homesick, and... you sort of remind me of my dad."

He coughs on his beer at that. She's getting somewhere.

"I, uh, guess I'll take that as a compliment," he says.

"You should. My dad's a great guy." Her insides curdle when she says that, but she manages to maintain her perfect smile.

The guard stares off and brushes his hair out of his eyes. "You know, I've got a daughter about your age."

"You do?" Ash says with practiced surprise. She points to his uniform. "She must be proud of you, doing such an important job."

His face sours, the crow's feet etching themselves deeper. "Not so much."

"Oh?" She dials the surprise up. "Why shouldn't she be? My dad's a security guard, and I'm proud as hell of him." She swallows a little bile down her throat at saying "dad" and "proud" in the same sentence.

He grunts a sarcastic chuckle. "Why? Wouldn't you rather he was a real cop?"

"Of course not. My dad protects some important stuff." Ash gives one last tug on the hook to set it. "I'll bet you protect some important stuff, too."

He straightens himself up on his stool, the hunch in his shoulders suddenly disappearing.

Bingo.

"You know what?" he says. "I do protect important stuff."

Ash smiles, and treats herself to a long gulp of her beer. "So how much help do you have to guard that stuff? Or are you good enough that you handle it all on your own?"

30

Matt

I glance at Ash beside me as we walk through the school hallway, lockers clanging around us. A bunch of kids hustle toward the band room, and the herd pushes me closer to Ash as they squeeze by. I don't mind, and Ash doesn't seem to mind either. I think about reaching out to hold her hand, but I'm not sure we have that kind of relationship; though, truth be told, I have no idea what kind of relationship this is. I just know she understands me in a way not many people can.

And, okay, I like the way the freckles pop against her cheeks and sort of match her hair, and... yeah, she's kinda hot. So sue me.

"Something on your mind?" she asks me, flashing those steel-blue eyes.

"W-What?" I stammer. "Nothing."

"Why, Matt, you're not hiding something from me, are you?"

"Why do you bother asking? You could find out just by touching me."

Ash gives me her best naughty smile. "Any particular place you had in mind?"

My cheeks light on fire and I sputter to change the subject. "I'm, uh, surprised you haven't left town yet."

She shrugs. "You didn't leave either."

"Well, yeah, but I have reasons to stay."

"That's debatable. But now I have a reason to stay, too."

I turn to look at her. "Crossman's house?"

"Whose house?" she says in mock surprise.

I raise an eyebrow at her.

"Oh, you mean the gigantic mansion with no one in it?" she says.

"You're not really thinking about robbing the place, are you?"

She opens her mouth to answer, then glances past me. "Shit."

"What?"

I follow her stare across the lobby to the front doors. There's a man standing on the other side of the glass, arguing with Mrs. Spitz, the receptionist. He keeps pointing at the door and yelling like he wants her to buzz him in, but she shakes her head. Then he looks this way, and I get a look at his face—hard lines on his brow, under short-cropped graying hair—the same face that was nose-to-nose with me the other day when he punched me in the jaw.

Steve. Also known as Ash's dad.

"What's he doing here?" I mutter.

"What do you think, genius?" Ash snaps.

"I mean, shouldn't he be in jail? He assaulted you, not to mention me!"

"Well, when *we* didn't stick around to press charges, they wouldn't have been able to hold him very long."

Steve continues glaring through the glass until Mrs. Spitz barks something at him. His scowl deepens, but finally he turns and skulks away.

"He doesn't give up easy, does he?" I say.

"Doesn't matter," Ash says. "I only need a few more days."

I shoot her a look. "To rob Crossman's house?"

"Why do you care? That rich bastard's got it coming."

"Do you really believe that?"

"Don't you?" She glares right through me. "What, you think Crossman is such a stand-up guy?"

I match her stare for as long as I can, then look down. "Fine. Crossman is an asshole. But that doesn't give you the right to—"

"Yes, it *does!* For God's sake, people like him are out to get people like us. They *all* are! Aren't you tired of letting them take everything from you? For once, don't you want to take something back?"

I turn and look away because I don't want to admit she might be right. It *would* be nice to take something back, do something for myself for once. I glance at everyone milling through the lobby, and try to push that thought out of my head. Principal Stokes gripes at a cluster of cheerleaders, telling them it's time to get to class. A delivery guy pushes a dolly full of printer paper up to the front door across the lobby. Mrs. Spitz buzzes him in. But through all of that, I still feel Ash's eyes burrowing into the back of my neck.

"I asked you a question," she says.

"Look, I'm not going to say it wouldn't feel good to take something. But it's not right to—"

I stop dead, because Steve comes sprinting back to the doors with a crazed determination in his eyes. He shoves the delivery guy out of the open doorway, hurdles the dolly and the boxes of paper, and lands firmly on his feet in the lobby. Ash lets out a whimper and goes white. I grab her arm and start backing us into the hallway.

The students in the lobby stop and stare at Steve, trying to figure out what the hell is going on. Principal Stokes bounds up, his gut bouncing, yelling that he can't barge in here like that and what's his reason for being here? Steve doesn't even acknowledge him. Instead, he strides forward, darting glances around.

"I know you're here!" Steve yells, his eyes searching. "Did you think I was going to stop coming for you? I've got nothing left to lose!"

Ash takes one more faltering step back, then she spins and breaks into a run. Two steps later she face-plants right into Beefy Brett's letter jacket. Brett barely moves, but Ash bounces backward and goes down hard with a yelp.

Steve shoots his look in our direction, and he locks eyes with me. His mouth breaks into an angry smile and he starts toward us. I pull Ash up off the floor and run, dragging her behind me.

"What's going on?" Katie Schmidt asks up ahead.

I dodge around her and her clarinet case, squeezing through a cluster of other kids. Ash pulls her arm out of my grip, finds her footing, and runs alongside me. I glance back to see Steve tearing after us, shoving kids out of the way. Fortunately he runs into Beefy Brett too, who slows him down a little. We round the corner just as Mrs. Spitz's voice blasts frantically over the intercom: *Lockdown! Lockdown!*

Everyone in the hallway glances around, but no one moves. "What is this, another stupid drill?" Tommy Watson says. Ash shoves him out of the way.

"*This is NOT a drill!*" Mrs. Spitz yells, full of static.

That finally throws everyone into a panic, and the crowd scatters. Everyone dashes in different directions, darting into the nearest classrooms. Doors slam shut. Ash keeps running past all of them and past me too, straight down the hall. I huff to keep up with her.

"Ash!" I yell, but she doesn't even look back. Damn it, I have to get her out of this hallway or Steve will see us. I reach for Ash but she's a step ahead of me. My legs burn as I strain forward, and I finally catch hold of the back of her shirt. I clench my fist around the fabric and dart to the side, jerking her with me, and we go careening through the doorway to the teachers' lounge.

"We have to keep going!" she yells, her eyes wild.

"No, we need to hide!"

She tries to push past me. I shove her back into the lounge, knocking over the flimsy table and one of the folding chairs, and push her back against the fridge. She starts to yell at me again and I clap my hand over her mouth to shut her up.

I can hear Steve's footsteps pounding in the hallway now. I look back at the door and reach my hand out. My palm tingles, and the doorstop slides away, and the door swings shut. I watch through the narrow strip of glass in the door; I can feel Ash's heartbeat kicking into my chest. Or maybe that's just my own heart.

I see Steve blur past, and I let out a breath.

Then the door flies open. I tense up, but it's Mr. Plask. He rushes in, glances anxiously at the toppled table, and then at us. "Matt? What are you doing in here?"

"Shut the door!" I hiss at him.

"What's going on out there?" he says anxiously and way too loud. "Why are we in lockdown?"

Ash waves her arms at him. "Shut up, moron! He'll find us!"

"He's looking for you?" Plask says.

I try to shush both of them, but it's too late. Steve bursts into the doorway, out of breath and eyes like fire.

Plask jumps like a startled hamster. "Who're you? Y-You can't be in here!"

Steve shoves him out of the way, and Plask goes staggering into the hallway. Steve starts toward us. I frantically look for options because he's blocking the door. I reach for one of the chairs and my hand tingles as it slides in front of him. He trips over it but keeps coming. My eyes go to the coffee pot. My hand tingles, then burns, and the pot jerks itself into the air. Half of the coffee sloshes out, and then the pot clocks Steve right in the back of the head. He grunts and drops to his knees, and the coffee pot falls to the floor, shattering and gushing everywhere. Ash sees her chance and dashes around him. I hurry after her, slipping on the spilled coffee, and grab the doorframe for support. I make it out into the hallway to find Mr. Plask dashing back toward me, holding one of the chemical bottles from the science room. I'm about to tell him to get the hell out of here when I turn and see Steve staggering his way out of the lounge door.

"Hold your breath!" Plask yells.

Before I have time to ask him what he's talking about, he hurls the bottle past me. It hits the floor next to Steve with a crack, and a thick gray smoke comes hissing out of it. Steve coughs as the cloud envelopes him.

I run past Plask, managing to get out a "thanks." He gives me a quick nod and scurries off in the other direction. I glance back to see the hallway full of smoke, and still no sign of Steve. I keep running and catch up with Ash.

"Now do you see?" she hisses at me between breaths as we run. "That's what the normal people do to people like us. It's time for you to get your head out of your ass and accept that, and take what's yours."

I don't say anything back, because I'm out of breath and I don't know what to say anyway. We push through the exit doors just as a chorus of sirens shriek their way into the parking lot. I keep running, trying to put them as far behind me as I can.

31

Matt

My steps amble along the sidewalk downtown. The storefronts seem cold beside me. I don't know where Ash is. She needed some time alone after her dad tried to assault her again. I can't blame her. Steve got arrested back at the school, at least I hope he did. Me, I just wander. Other people hurry by around me, intent on their errands, their schedules. All the "normal" people. I walk alone, and they ignore me. That sums up most of my life. But if they knew what I really am? What would they do then?

My mind flashes with the crazed look Steve had in his eyes. Will my dad ever look at me like that? Will my friends? Ash's voice keeps digging deeper and deeper into my head. Maybe I can't count on any of them. Maybe I do need to take care of myself.

A chilly breeze gusts by. It wouldn't be so bad, except I've been walking out here for a while now and the cold is starting to get to me. I decide to step inside to warm up for a minute. I push through the door of the little menswear store, leaving the cold breeze behind me. The shuffle of my feet on the scuffed hardwood floor is the only sound, since I'm the only one in here. The lanky sales clerk gives me a bored look through his thin-rimmed glasses. I shuffle on through the racks of suits, trying to pretend I'm interested in buying something. The suits aren't anything fancy—this is Chaplain, after all—but for a second, I still imagine wearing one of those, with a good job someday as some kind of executive. The image doesn't last very long.

I walk past the ties, the watches, and the bottles of cologne—there's a mix of musky, outdoorsy smells that I guess are supposed to smell like *men*. Finally I get to the wallets, and I linger. I'm not really one for jewelry or fancy clothes, but a nice wallet would be one status symbol I could go for. I scan the rack, and one catches my eye. Hand-stitched with a glossy finish, and I can smell the leather.

The sales clerk wanders over and looks me up and down, clearly mentally calculating that I don't have enough money to buy whatever I'm looking at. Which is accurate, but still annoys me. "Can I help you with anything?" he asks me, his tone sounding more like *"buy something or leave."*

"I'm, uh, just looking, thanks," I reply.

He folds his arms, as much as he can with all the starch in his shirt, and stays put. I glance at the wallet one more time, then decide it's not worth having this guy glare at me. I turn and walk toward the door.

But with each step, an ugly ball of resentment builds in me. Who does he think he is, looking down on me? I'm not some freak who's beneath him. In fact, I'm *better* than him. I can do something no one else can do, and what do I have to show for it?

Ash's voice rings in my head. *Take what's yours.*

I keep walking, but I reach my hand out, subtle. I search for the watch case sitting on the counter—I don't even have to turn around, I can feel it in my mind without even looking. That's right, I'm *special*, damn it. My hand tingles and the case scoots toward the edge of the counter, and then gravity takes over.

The crash echoes through the empty store and the clerk goes scampering over to it. I smirk, but I keep walking. When I reach the door, I turn back. The clerk is busy picking up the watches. He's not paying attention to me, because why should he? No one could swipe any of his precious merchandise from here.

No one but me.

My eyes lock on that hand-stitched leather wallet. I reach out my hand and let the energy release, and the wallet lifts off the rack and flies in a straight line through the air to my hand. I close my fingers around it, savoring the smooth feel of the leather, and cast one more look at the oblivious clerk as I step out the door with a satisfied smirk.

My strides are longer as I walk away from the store, and my shoulders are taller. I don't even mind the chill of the breeze now. I take a long whiff of the leather and slide the wallet into my jacket pocket. That's mine now. It was mine, and I took it.

There's a nagging voice in the back of my head that sounds a lot like my mom, telling me that what I just did was wrong. I shove that voice down and rub my fingers over the leather again. I deserve this. I keep telling myself that, trying to reinforce it. I notice my shoulders have hunched again; I force them back up.

"Matt?"

"What? I didn't—" I jolt to a stop and my heart thuds like a cannon. "Oh... Phillip. What're you doing here?"

He looks at me from under the shadow of his hoodie. His eyes seem more focused than usual. "What're *you* doing?"

"Just walking," I say quickly.

Phillip's eyes uncomfortably search my face. "Are you okay?"

"Of course I'm okay. Why wouldn't I be?"

He glances at my jacket pocket. He doesn't say anything, but he doesn't have to.

"You were *spying* on me?" I blurt out.

"I've been worried about you."

"I don't need you to worry about me."

"This isn't like you, Matt."

I feel my cheeks burn, but push back. "How would you know what's like me?"

"We've been friends a long time, Matt."

"That doesn't mean you know me. I'm not like you. I'm not like anybody."

"This is about Ash, isn't it?"

"So what if it is?" I snap. "She understands me."

"Does she?"

His eyes are so honest, it makes it hard to get mad at him. But I still manage it.

"Damn it, Phillip, you spied on me! Friends don't spy on their friends."

He looks down. "I'm just worried about you."

"Well, don't be. I'm seeing things clearer than I have in a long time."

I storm off before he can say anything else that will burrow under my skin. I rub the leather wallet in my pocket again, but it doesn't feel as smooth as it did a minute ago.

Ash

The motel door squeaks as she swings it open, and the overhead light flickers. Ash steps onto the frayed carpet, the multi-colored pattern trying to hide the built-up collection of stains.

Heath is laid out on the bed, taking up most of it. He frowns at her without bothering to get up. "Interesting day at school?"

"You know how it is." Ash shuts the door with another squeak.

"So we're not going to talk about it?"

Leah shifts in her chair in the corner, rubbing her hands over the scuffed armrests. "I was scared."

"Scared of what?" Ash says.

"For God's sake," Heath barks, "the school locked down! A crazy guy shoved his way in, shouting about finding someone."

Ash shrugs. "There are a lot of unhinged people out there."

"Cut the shit, Ash. Your dad came back again."

"It was no big deal," Ash says firmly. "We took care of him."

" 'We'?"

"Matt helped."

Heath rolls his eyes. "You should've called me."

"I said we took care of it. Matt was surprisingly resourceful."

Leah looks up. "He was?"

Heath scoffs.

"He was *good,*" Ash says. "That's why we need him."

"Whatever," Heath says. "The point is, Steve's still a problem. How long do you think the cops will hold him this time?"

Ash shrugs. "Hopefully a few days."

"And what happens then? This town is too small for us to hide in."

Leah wrings her hands together. "What if he really hurts you? Or Heath?"

Ash takes a couple of slow steps toward her. "That's why we need to stick together. Because if we're alone, people like him could hurt one of us."

Leah hunches over, the message landing home. Heath leans toward her and pats her shoulder. He signs something to her with his hands, and she forces a faint smile.

"You two need to stop using signs I don't know," Ash says.

Heath looks at her over his shoulder. "You could always learn them."

Ash flips him off. "What does this one mean again? I can never remember."

"Don't change the subject," Heath says. "We need to leave town. We already had the pawn shop bitch to worry about, and now Steve?"

"We can't help it. We're not ready for the job yet."

"The job is a bad idea."

"It's worth it. You know that as well as I do."

Heath grates his teeth together. "It's a *bad—*"

"We're your family," Ash says, cutting him off. "Remember? Remember what we did—what *I* did—to become your family? We're doing this."

He stares hard back at her. Ash looks back and forth between Heath and Leah; finally she relaxes her shoulders and lets out a long breath. "This job is for all of us. You know that, right?"

After a long moment, Heath nods. Leah won't look up, but she nods too.

32

Matt

I walk reluctantly through the school hallway, weaving through everyone still talking about the lockdown yesterday. I hear at least a dozen theories about it.

...The guy was a serial killer who's killed students at five different high schools and was looking for his next victim.

...He was an acting scout who was trying to track down someone he'd bumped into earlier to make them the next big star.

...He was a CIA agent come to stop someone who'd stolen nuclear launch codes.

"How the hell would a high school student get their hands on nuclear launch codes?" I ask Tom.

"Hey, it could happen," he says. "I saw a movie about that last month."

I brush him off and plod on my way, but truth be told, I was grateful for the distraction from where I'm going. I glance at my phone, to the text I got from Phillip this morning—*really need 2 talk 2 u at lunch.*

I can't believe he had to send me that, had to ask. It used to go without saying that I'd have lunch with them. It was just assumed. Until Ash.

Damn it, I shouldn't have to feel bad about that. People move on sometimes. Emily started dating Scott, and now she eats at the cool table most of the time.

But even I know this is different.

I force myself on toward the lunchroom, knowing I can't put this off any longer. And I shouldn't want to put this off anyway. They're my friends. At least I hope they still are.

"Matt?"

I turn to see Mr. Plask shuffling beside me down the hallway.

"Oh... hey."

"Are you all right?" Plask asks anxiously, adjusting the bulky glasses on his face.

"Never better."

"What was that with the lockdown?"

Shit. Another topic I don't want to talk about. "Nothing. Just a... misunderstanding."

"That man attacked you!"

"Yeah, well, it turned out okay." I keep moving down the hall, keeping my eyes ahead of me. "I, uh, guess I never said thank you for coming back to help like that. What was that bottle you threw at him?"

"Chemistry is my superpower," Plask says. "But why was he coming after you? Or was he after that girl with you, the new student?"

"Don't worry about it." My voice comes out way more dismissive than it should be.

Plask keeps shuffling beside me. "Are you in trouble, Matt?"

"I'm fine. Thanks for your help and your concern, but—"

"Matt, you can talk to me. About anything. You know that, right?"

I stop and look at him. "Yeah. Yeah, I know. Thanks. I, uh... have to be somewhere."

I turn and step quickly away, trying my best to force the guilt away as I leave Plask standing behind me.

I get to the lunchroom and see the group sitting across the room as I walk in. Phillip gives me a subtle wave. Tess won't look at me; that's normal for her, but Rob makes a point of not looking at me. I walk slowly to the table and hesitate before pulling my chair out, almost like I should ask permission first. But I shouldn't, so I don't. I slide myself into it.

"Hey, guys," I say, trying to force a casualness to my voice, like I haven't been completely ignoring them lately.

"Hey," Phillip says.

I nod to Rob, but he still won't look up. We sit there for a moment, the clatter of trays and murmur of conversations carrying on around us.

Phillip clears his throat. "Crazy about yesterday. The lockdown."

"Yeah, crazy." I look back and forth between them, trying to read their faces. "Do you, uh... know what happened?"

"The guy got arrested," Tess says.

When no one else says anything, I let out an exhale, hoping that's all they know. "Good."

"The same guy got arrested a few days ago," Tess adds.

My stomach tenses up. "Really?"

"*Tried to strangle an adolescent girl downtown.*"

"Oh," I say, hoping I sound surprised enough. "That's, uh—"

"*A tall, bald, adolescent male broke up the fight.*"

I swallow. "That could be a lot of people."

Rob finally looks up at me. "We're not that stupid, dude."

"Is Ash okay?" Phillip asks quietly.

I hesitate, then nod. "Yeah. Thanks."

Rob shoots Phillip a look. "That wasn't my first question."

"But we do care that she's okay," Phillip says. "Heath and Leah too."

"Look," Rob says forcefully, "your new friends have brought trouble with them. Did they drag you into their mess?"

"They didn't drag me into anything," I insist.

"But you *are* in the middle of their mess now, right?"

"What Rob's trying to say," Phillip says, "is that we're worried about you."

"Why?" I snap. "Because they've got some baggage? Everyone does."

"You wanna talk baggage?" Rob leans forward. "What did Ash do to that guy that made him want to kill her?"

I glower and stare at the table. "It's personal."

"Personal to her, or to you?"

"Maybe it's both."

"Dude—" Rob starts in hot, then takes a breath. "Look, man, we're just saying you haven't known Ash and her crew for very long, and they're already turning you into someone else."

"Who are they turning me into?"

His dark brown eyes stare into me. "You tell me."

"There's nothing different about me, Rob."

"*It took an invitation to talk to you,*" Tess says.

I cringe at that but try to hide it. "People drift apart sometimes."

"It's more than that, Matt," Phillip says. "We miss you and all, but we're really concerned about what they've done to your... morals."

I turn to him, fuming. "You told them about the wallet?"

"He didn't have to," Tess says. *"I saw the store's security video."*

My jaw drops.

"I erased it for you," she says.

I feel a wall of shame wash over me. I think I tell her thanks; I'm not even sure.

"The point is," Rob says, "Ash is a bad influence on you."

A fire ignites inside me and pushes the shame away. "Who I spend my time with is my own damn business."

"She's changing you, Matt. You have to see that."

"So freaking what?" I pound my fist into the table, sending the lunch trays clattering. "Maybe she's making me better."

"Do you feel better?" Phillip asks. His tone is sincere, but it only pisses me off more.

"You don't know anything about this," I snap.

"I know you always used to do the right thing," Phillip says. "Even when it was hard."

Rob nods. "He's right. You're the one who got us all to stand up to Crossman, even though it was completely stupid. Because it was *right*."

"Because it was right," I echo cynically. "Well, maybe right and wrong isn't as clear as I thought it was. Not for people like me."

"You don't mean that, Matt," Phillip says.

"How should you know? You're not like me."

His eyes cloud with hurt. "I still care about you."

"So does Ash," I snap back.

"Are you sure?" Rob asks. "I mean, really, really sure?"

202

"Of course I'm sure!" I yell, my voice strained to breaking. "Why else would she have stayed here to be with me?"

Phillip won't quite look at me. "It seems like maybe she wants something from you. Like she's... maybe using you."

I shoot fire at him with my eyes. "Using me for what?"

"I don't know. But they're up to something. Heath has been—"

"You've been spying on him too? Jesus, Phillip, what's your problem? Can't you mind your own business for once?"

"Hey." Rob raises his hands, motioning for calm. "He's trying to look out for you. We all are."

"*Trying to help,*" Tess says.

"Really?" I say, not bothering to hide the disgust in my voice. "You guys have a piss-poor way of showing it."

I push up from the table and turn to leave. Rob grabs my arm.

"Come on, man," he says. "Don't walk away like this."

"Get your hand off me," I growl at him.

"Matt, seriously—"

I reach with my other hand and the energy releases like fire, burning as hot as my rage. Phillip's soda can flies up straight into Rob's face. It smacks him in the cheek. He flinches back and lets go of my arm. The can drops to the floor, spraying liquid on the way down.

Rob's speechless for once. Phillip jolts back in shock. Tess's fingers flurry anxiously.

I walk away without looking back. I hear Phillip's voice calling behind me, but I don't stop to hear what he's trying to say. I get to the hallway without breaking stride.

My phone buzzes, and I pull it out to see a text.

TESS—This isn't like you, Matt.

A glimmer of regret almost makes it through; then I grit my teeth, shove the phone back in my pocket, and keep walking. I keep going all the way down the hall to the back exit door, and slam into it with my shoulder to let out some of my rage. It doesn't help, and now my shoulder hurts. The door flies open and hits the wall with a bang.

"Whoa there," comes a smooth female voice outside. Ash leans against the side of the building and smiles at me. "What did that door do to you? Geez, I come out here to ditch class and get some peace and quiet, and you show up making all this racket."

Without a thought, I take two long strides to her, grab her by the shoulders, pull her in, and kiss her. I put my hand behind her neck and press myself into her tighter, feeling her silky hair and warm skin under my fingers, feeling her lips squish against mine. She leans in and kisses me back, and it ignites something inside me. With my eyes closed, everything else in the world is shut out. Finally, I come up for air and pull back.

"Wow," she says with a devilish smile. Then the smile fades slowly. "I'm sorry about your friends coming after you like that."

I swallow. "You felt that?"

"I've been trying to tell you, Matt. Those people aren't like us."

"I didn't want to admit it, but you were right." My mouth tightens to a thin line. "They don't understand me. They never will."

Ash squeezes my hand. "But I do."

My phone buzzes again. I shut it off without even looking at it. I don't have anything else to say to any of them.

"Did you stay in town because of me?" I ask Ash. "Or because of whatever you're planning at Crossman's house?"

She smiles. "Can't it be both?"

"Look, we both know you should've left by now. I'm glad you're still here, but why are you?"

The ice blue of her eyes warms just a little. "I'll be honest, Matt, if we hadn't seen that armored car at Crossman's house, I probably would've left without you. But that would have been a mistake, and I would have regretted that for a long time."

"So you did stay just to rob Crossman's house," I say, my face dropping.

"I stayed to do that *with you.*"

"But you knew I don't agree with stealing."

"I also knew you'd come around. It's time to take what's yours. What's *ours.*"

I chew my lip until I'm about to draw blood. Ash puts both of her hands around mine and looks me in the eye.

"We're doing this for Leah and Heath too," she says. "They need you."

"What exactly are you planning to steal?"

"That's what we're working on." Ash senses my hesitation and adds, "It's Crossman, Matt. You said yourself he deserves it."

"I said he's an asshole. That's not the same thing."

"He's one of *them,* Matt. For once, let's take what belongs to us."

I try to find my conviction for what's right. I really do. But maybe I've lost that... or maybe I never had it to begin with.

"Okay," I say, forcing a firmness to my voice to cover the tremor of guilt. "I'm in."

33

Heath

The library door squeaks as he opens it. Well, squeaks isn't the right word, but normal people don't have a word for what it sounds like to him, so it'll have to do. Just a long, slow rub of the hinges like steel sandpaper. All the other morons here are oblivious to it.

Heath's shoes scuff across the hideous carpet, the sound almost as loud as the orange color. The path by the door is smooth, worn down by the trample of feet. It's not that he can feel it, but he can hear it. It gets rougher and louder as he steps off the path toward the study tables. The librarian looks up from the stack of books she's reshelving and eyes him suspiciously over her glasses. Her breath has a faint wheeze to it, like she's about to come down with bronchitis. Heath gives her a wide berth. He didn't come in here to talk to her anyway.

The taps of Tess's fingers on her phone screen carry across the room like an old typewriter. She sits alone, her face washed out by the glow of the screen. Heath takes a deep breath, the sound of rushing air flowing through him. He walks slowly to the table, focusing on the scuffing of his shoes on the carpet.

"Hey," he says. "Mind if I sit here?"

TESS—Go ahead

Heath glances at the text on his phone. "Thanks, but, uh, my implant is on. We can just talk normal today, if you want."

"*Fair enough,*" Tess says, her fingers tapping against the screen. "*But I thought Ash didn't want you opening up to people like me.*"

He grinds his teeth; sounds like chewing gravel. "Sorry about that. I didn't mean anything by it."

"*You don't have to mean anything for it to hurt.*"

Damn. This is going to suck more than he thought. "Sorry," he repeats. He hovers for an awkward moment, then slides into a chair. It has a bad leg that makes a subtle creak when he sets his weight into it.

"*What do you know about the lockdown?*" Tess asks.

His neck tenses. "What lockdown?"

"*No way you don't know about that.*"

"Okay, fine. Some guy shoved his way in here trying to find somebody. So what?"

"*The same guy was arrested a few days earlier. Attacked someone downtown.*"

Heath fights to keep his eyebrows from raising. He's surprised she knows about that. "Really?"

"*Seems like he really wants to hurt someone.*"

"I, uh, don't know. Maybe he just wants to talk."

"*Sure.*" Her face is blank; is she being sarcastic?

"Well, we'll deal with him if we have to, I guess," Heath says.

"*Because you dealt with him the first time, right?*"

He tries to hide his shock. "What?"

"*Someone broke up the fight. Tall, adolescent male, bald.*"

This girl is good. "What, you think that was me?"

She keeps tapping, a flurry of hammer blows, but no words come out.

Heath scratches his cheek. "I know this is a small town, but I can't be the only guy like that around here."

"*Sure.*"

Man, she's hard to read.

"Anyway," Heath says. "Speaking of this being a small town, there's not much worth seeing around here. All the houses look the same... except this one big-ass house on the edge of town. You, uh, know anything about that?"

"*Why do you want to know?*"

He shrugs, making a show of it. "I don't. Just bored, and it's a cool house."

"*221 Oak Street. Seth Crossman's house.*"

"That's the one," he says, careful not to sound too eager. "That Crossman dude owns a factory around here, doesn't he?"

"*He did.*"

"A guy like that must have some pretty expensive stuff stashed in their house."

Tess keeps tapping, her face blank.

"You ever wonder what he's got in there?"

"*Not really.*"

Heath crosses his arms and taps his thumb against his arm. Someone sneezes two doors down the hall.

"I wonder," he says.

"*About what?*"

"About what he's got in there. Probably got a bunch of paintings by famous dead guys, maybe a stuffed tiger or something like that?"

No reaction on her face.

"Maybe he's even got a vault," Heath says. "You know, a big safe? To keep his cash, or gold bricks, or... whatever..."

He watches her closely. The librarian taps her pencil on her desk, a deep *thump-thump-thump* in his ears.

Still no reaction. He's going to have to push.

"You know... I saw an armored car pull out of there the other day."

Tess's fingers pause for half a second, hovering over the phone, then flurry at it with a vengeance.

Got her.

"Makes you wonder what an armored car would be picking up there. Or dropping off?" Heath edges forward, trying to steal a glance at her phone, but she's got it too close to her face. "Maybe something for that vault of his? You know, if he has a vault."

"*If he has a vault,*" Tess says. Her fingers are a blur now.

Heath rocks in his chair. The right front leg creaks like it's ready to splinter any second. "Anything interesting in all those tabs you have open?"

She shakes her head, but there's a hesitation to it. Her fingers keep pounding.

Heath lets out a long, hissing exhale; sounds like a king cobra inside his head. Damn. He was hoping he wouldn't have to do this the hard way.

"Sorry," he says.

"*For what?*"

"This."

He lurches forward and grabs her phone. Her fingers claw around it, surprisingly strong, but another yank and he jerks it free. His eyes scour the screen.

"Holy shit..."

He rifles through the browser tabs. A *lot* of tabs. She'd found everything he needed and more.

A twinge of pain pings in his shoulder as Tess pounds a fist into him with a deep thud. She doesn't say anything; she can't. He stole her voice. He chews his lip and avoids looking at her. He doesn't have time for guilt, he has work to do. He keeps his eyes on the screen.

The Crossman dude *does* have a vault. Iron Fortress model 627A, she found a schematic and everything... and there's the log of the armored car pickups. And there's another armored car log from ten years ago, but why did she pull that up? Wait, that was right after Crossman had the vault delivered, and right after a withdrawal from his bank for—

"Oh my freaking God, twenty million dollars!"

The librarian shushes him from across the room, sounding like a leaf blower on steroids, but Heath tunes it out. His gears are spinning like mad. There have been how many armored car pickups, and how many left? And that means Crossman has got how much still in there? And where are they taking the money *to?* Heath keeps swiping the screen, looking for—

A hiss erupts from Tess's mouth. Then it shrieks into an upper frequency like a dog whistle that most people can't even hear, but it jabs through Heath's ears like a railroad spike. His hand darts toward his implant, but before he gets there, he loses his grip on the phone. It clatters to the table. Heath reaches for it but Tess purses her lips and whistles again. He cringes and forgets the phone, finally manages to

210

switch his implant off, and plunges the room into silence. Tess tucks the phone tight against her chest. Heath thinks for a second about wrestling it away from her again, but he feels vibrations in the floor and glances up to see that librarian bitch stomping toward him. He kicks his chair back and pushes himself up. He almost tells Tess he's sorry one more time, but it would be an empty word now. He showed her who he really is. He strides to the door before the librarian can get to him. He pushes through the door with a soundless thud against his shoulder.

The students flow past him in the hallway, a silent stream of bodies. He pays no attention, his mind spinning. Ash is going to flip when she hears about this, twenty million—

Heath stops dead and flattens himself against the lockers. Through the crowd, at the end of the hall, a woman in a dark blue uniform stands talking to the dumbass principal. The other kids throw curious glances toward her, their mouths twitching with gossip about what a cop is doing here, but Heath knows exactly why she's here. He turns and moves the other way, his head down, falling in with some guys from the basketball team who are hopefully tall enough to hide him. He switches on his implant.

"... about the man who pushed his way in here and triggered the lockdown," the officer is saying.

Heath keeps his steps quick, hopefully not quick enough to get him noticed.

"The same suspect was arrested a few days prior for assaulting three adolescents downtown," the officer says. "Didn't get much description on two of them..."

Heath grits his teeth, knowing what's coming next.

"... one male was tall, dark-skinned, bald, appeared to be wearing a hearing aid."

Heath shoves the basketball player in front of him and hurries forward.

"What the hell, buddy?" the guy blurts out.

Heath doesn't even bother a reply. He quickens his steps.

"I know who that is," the principal says behind him. "New student."

Heath whips out his phone and pounds out a text to Ash and Leah as he keeps moving—*get out of the school NOW.*

"A male adolescent of similar description is a person of interest regarding a reported incident at the pawn shop," the officer says.

Heath rounds the corner and breaks into a run. His heart rate accelerates and amplifies, beating in his ears. Each breath whooshes through his lungs. Another fifty feet and he'll be out of here—

A door handle clicks ahead of him like a gun bolt. The classroom door swings open and a tall woman steps out, hard sole shoes clacking against the floor. Heath skids to a stop with a screech of rubber. The teacher turns to look at him and narrows her eyes. "No running in the hall."

"Sorry. I'll slow down." Heath steps toward the exit, but the teacher slides in front to block him.

"Where are you going? Get back to class."

He chews his lip, and strains his ears.

"This way, Officer," the principal says. Two sets of footsteps pound in his direction.

Heath takes a step backward. "I was just going to the bathroom."

"The bathroom is that way," the teacher says, pointing with a stiff finger.

His phone goes off in his pocket like a hive of bees. He yanks it out to see a text from Leah—*what's wrong?*

He huffs and shoots back—*out! NOW!!!!*

Heath looks back up to see the teacher glaring at him. "Are you even listening to me? Do I need to take your phone?" She holds out a bony hand.

He clenches his teeth. The officer's footsteps are getting closer.

Then another door swings open and Ash steps out. She glances at him and glares. "Heath? What the hell is going on?"

The teacher throws her hands up. "Now where are *you* going? Seriously, you two need to—"

"Screw it." Heath shoves the woman into the lockers with a clang of reverberating metal, grabs Ash by the wrist, and runs for the exit, dragging her behind him. He bursts through the door with a thud, out into the whistle of the breeze.

"We're done at this school," Heath says.

Ash shoots him a look that says he'd better explain later. "Fine. We already got what we came for anyway."

34

Matt

The door chime dings above me as I step into the diner. I say "the" diner because it's the only one in town—unless you count the snack bar at the Jiffy Mart, which I don't. That's the advantage of a small town. When Ash texted *meet me at the diner*, I didn't have to ask any follow-up questions.

I scan over the room, which hasn't changed as long as I can remember. The cliché-looking tables with red padded chairs that could use some reupholstering; the black-and-white tile floor that's all scuffed up. There are a couple truckers on the bar stools, and the old retired guy who spends half his time in here drinking coffee and flirting with the waitress. Apparently the flirting hasn't gotten him a date yet because he's still here. The waitress chews her nicotine gum and looks at me over her thick-rimmed glasses before going back to topping off the truckers' glasses of water.

Ash is in the corner booth, her eyes drilling into me. Heath is beside her, leaned back into the bench, his face a tight mask; Leah is there too, hunched over. I cross the room toward them. They all watch me, but I don't get any other reaction from them.

"What's up with you guys?" I ask. "You tell me to meet you here, urgent, and now you all look like your cat died."

"Cat?" Heath grunts.

"What, are you a dog person?"

Ash leans forward, her eyes narrow and unblinking. "Let's get serious. This town is closing in on us."

I glance around the diner. The waitress scratches at her frizzy hair. One of the truckers lets out a belch and scratches at his gut. "The situation doesn't look too dire from here."

"A cop showed up at the school looking for us," Heath says.

I spin to look at him. "Why? The pawn shop?"

"Among other things. The real problem is Ash's dad. He sped up the clock on the time bomb."

"They're trying to find out who he's after," Ash says, "since the idiot got arrested twice in one week for assaulting someone, but they don't know who it was. The cops here have nothing better to do than to dig their heels in. And since Baldy here has such a... shall we say unique look, they pegged him as one of the ones at the pawn shop too."

"We can't go back to that school," Heath says. "They'd be waiting for us."

Ash shrugs. "No big loss."

"Does this mean you're leaving town now?" I ask.

"We should," Heath says.

"No," Ash says firmly. "We're hitting Crossman's house first."

My conscience tries again to tell me we should forget the breaking and entering thing, but somehow instead I say, "Then we do it tonight."

I'm glad there are no mirrors around because I don't think I can look at myself right now.

Heath shakes his head. "There's another armored car pickup tonight. They'll be on edge."

"Then we wait until tomorrow night," Ash says.

Leah shifts in her seat, her eyes down at the table. "Risky to wait. They already came for us at school."

"She's right," Heath says. "We're running out of places to hide."

Ash bangs her fist on the table. "We're doing this, okay? I'm so damn tired of just scraping by. We *deserve* it. You see that, don't you?"

I clear my throat, trying to peel back the awkwardness. "Are you sure the job is even worth it? I mean, I know the guy's loaded, but what would he have just lying around—"

"Twenty million bucks."

As I struggle to prop my jaw back up, the waitress finally shuffles over. "What'll ya have?" she asks, in between smacks on her gum.

"Uh, nothing, thanks," I finally stammer out.

She glances back and forth between us. "You kids gotta order something if you want to sit here."

"Just give us a minute," I say. When she fixes her glare on me, I add, "Please."

She shuffles off, taking one last look over her shoulder.

I turn to Ash. "Are you freaking serious? You want to steal twenty *million* dollars?"

"Not quite," she says. "Tell him, Heath."

He shifts in his seat. Ash jabs him with her elbow.

216

"He had twenty million in there to start with," Heath says. "The armored cars have been pulling it out in chunks. The one we saw the other day was number one. Tonight's number two. There's one more pickup next week, which means there's still—"

"Almost seven million bucks," I mutter.

He narrows his eyes at me. "I know how to count."

"Okay, but how the hell did you find all that out?"

Heath hesitates, then shrugs. "You can find a lot of things if you know where to look."

I stiffen. "That sounds like something Tess would say."

"Maybe."

I stare him down. "How'd you get her to look that up for you?"

Ash leans in and fixes a cold look on me. "It doesn't matter. *She* doesn't matter. None of them do. Whose side are you on, ours or theirs?"

I take a long breath to calm down. The waitress saunters back over, tapping her pencil on her pad, and clears her throat. But before she can hassle us again about ordering something, the door chime dings and half a dozen cheerleaders pile through. The waitress grumbles and shuffles toward the new arrivals. I'm just about to turn back to Heath to give him a piece of my mind when I see red hair emerge from behind the other girls—Emily.

We lock eyes for a split second before we both look away, pretending we didn't see each other. She follows her girlfriends to a booth on the other side of the room.

"Are you even listening to me?" I catch Ash saying.

"Huh? Yeah. Sure."

She eyes me like she knows I'm full of it. "We need this job, and we're doing what needs to be done."

"Whatever." I give Heath one more glare. "It's just... seven million bucks? That's a big jump from knocking over the pawn shop."

"Don't get all squeamish on me," Ash snaps. "It's the perfect job. I got all the info on the security, and it's pathetic. One guard in the booth watching the cameras, two more milling around the house and the perimeter. That's it."

I raise an eyebrow at her.

"Don't worry, I didn't get that from your little friend. Just focus on the fact that it's the *perfect job.* We'll have the money out of the safe and be gone before they know what hit them."

"It's in a *safe?*" I protest. "What are you planning to do, blow it up?"

"You know where the safe is?" Heath asks, seemingly unfazed.

Ash smiles. "Through the trophy room."

"You know where *that* is?"

"We'll find it."

"It's a big-ass house," Heath says.

"We'll *find* it."

I look across the room. I try to pretend I'm not looking at Emily, but I can't help it. She's chatting with the other girls, laughing... but she makes a quick glance in my direction, then drops her eyes when she sees I'm looking at her.

"Besides," Ash says, "they got the first two pickups off without a hitch, and they're down to the last load of cash. You know the guards are feeling relaxed and cocky. It'll be a cakewalk."

I pull my gaze away from Emily and chew my lip. "You're sure you have the security pegged?"

"Don't worry about it," Ash snips. "Matt, remember who we are. Remember what we can do." She looks back and forth between me,

Heath, and Leah. "We're not like those people. We're *better*. We can do this."

She's right about one thing—we're not like other people. Maybe that's all it takes. Heath nods from where he's leaned back in his seat. I look at Leah; she's still hunched over, but she looks up and her eyes meet mine.

"We can do this," I echo, more to convince myself than anything else. The question whether we *should* do this... I can't make myself say that out loud.

"Tomorrow night," Ash says firmly.

"Look, I'm still not clear on how you plan to—"

The waitress stomps back to us and slaps her hands on the table. "You kids gonna order somethin', or what?"

"For Christ's sake," I yell, "we're in the middle of something! Can't you mind your own business?"

The waitress smacks angrily on her gum. "Do I gotta call the cops?"

I'm about to tell her where she can shove the cops when Leah nudges me.

"We should leave," Leah says quietly.

"No cops," Heath grunts.

Ash stands up. "Our apologies," she says with thinly veiled sarcasm. "Wouldn't want to spoil your nice little town."

The waitress eyes us as we slide out of the booth and toward the door. Ash pulls it open with another ding of the chime. I step through behind her when something tugs on the back of my shirt. I spin around to see Emily's green eyes drilling into me.

"What's gotten into you, Matt?" Her voice doesn't have anger in it; it's more like concern, which is almost worse.

"Nothing," I say, but even I don't believe that. "What are you talking about?"

"You went off on that waitress for no reason. That's not like you, Matt."

Heath and Leah climb into the car in the corner of the parking lot. Ash stands beside it and crosses her arms.

"Sorry," I say. I can't decide if I mean it or not. "I have to go."

"Wait, just—" Emily puts her hand on my arm, then pulls it away and awkwardly shoves it in her pocket. "Matt, I've known you since we were kids. You were always such a good guy. But lately, you've been so distant..."

"I'm right here."

"You know what I mean." Her eyes flick toward Ash. "I feel like she's changing you."

"Maybe she's helping me see who I really am."

"I liked who you were before, Matt," Emily says. "I don't think Ash is... good for you."

"What?" I almost laugh, it shocks me so much.

"I think she's in it for her, not for you."

I take a step to leave. "I have to go."

Emily grabs my hand. "I care about you, Matt."

I look into her eyes, and something inside me hardens. I pull my hand away from hers. "You're telling me this now? What, you finally realized your boyfriend Scott is a loser?"

"Matt, I'm not talking about—"

"You had your chance with me. Hell, you had plenty of chances. It's not my fault that you blew it and waited until it was too late."

"Matt, I'm with Scott."

"You're just jealous of what I have with Ash."

"She's manipulating you!"

"Whatever you need to tell yourself. I'm with her now, and it's way better than anything I could've had with you."

I turn and storm away before my anger has a chance to cool. I wanted to get over Emily, didn't I? That's one way to do it.

35

Matt

The morning sun pries its way through my bedroom curtains. I roll over in bed and squeeze my eyes shut, but the light still finds its way in. It's already halfway through the morning by most people's standards, but I don't have to worry about being late for school. I'm not going. Probably never will again. What do freaks like me need with school anyway? But the sun keeps seeping in, and I can't hide from it forever.

I finally throw off the covers and pull myself up off the bed, throwing some clothes on mechanically. I stumble to the door and swing it open, when suddenly, I startle at the skinny shadow in the hallway.

"Dad?" I sputter. "I, uh, thought you'd left for work already."

"I decided to go in late." He shuffles on his feet and won't look at me straight on. "What about you? Aren't you late for school?"

I don't even hesitate. "I'm not going."

"Not going? Why not?"

"Really, Dad? Seems like we've got bigger things to talk about. Oh, wait—we don't talk."

He exhales. "I know. We've been avoiding each other, since..." He glances down at my hand before his eyes flick away.

"You still can't even say it, can you?"

A guttural sound escapes his mouth, but no words.

"Damn it, Dad! Ash was right about people like you."

"Ash?" He looks at me confused. "Who's Ash?"

"You don't deserve to know. Hell, you don't deserve to know a lot of things about me anymore."

"Matt..."

I step back into my room and slam the door with a bang. I stand there, breathing heavily. I can hear my dad breathing on the other side. I wait for him to leave, but I can still hear him out there.

"Matt, I'm... I'm trying."

"No, you're not!" I spit back at him.

"Okay." Pain cracks in his voice. "Okay, maybe not. But I *want* to. I..."

His words fade out. I'm pretty sure he was trying to say "I love you," but he can't. Because he doesn't.

"Don't worry," I say. "You won't have to try for much longer."

"What does that mean?"

I don't answer.

"Matt, please," he says through the door. "I'm still your dad."

I have to bite my lip to keep from screaming at him. Maybe it would feel good, but that's not how I want to go out. I throw my closet open and start shoving clothes into my backpack. Because after tonight, I won't be coming back here.

"Matt?"

My lungs churn with anger and hurt. I take deep breaths, but it only makes it worse. He'll never understand. People like him never will. I finally hear his breathing fade as he steps away from the door, then his footsteps down the stairs, then the front door closing. Good damn riddance.

I stuff another pile of clothes into my backpack and look around the room for anything else I should take with me. The sad thing is, I can't find anything in here that really matters. Maybe my whole life here never mattered. I turn to leave when my eyes fall on the picture of my mom.

For the first time since I can remember, I can't look at her... but I can't leave here without her. I have to hope that tomorrow or the next day I'll be able to look at her again. That she'll be able to look at me again. I pick up the frame and slip it into my bag. With one last look at the room, I step out the door.

The house is empty and quiet now. For just a second, I wish my dad hadn't left. I wish we could try one more time. But I only think that for a second. Ash was right about him. She was right about all of them. It's time we take something back. I let my anger choke out my conscience completely, and walk down the steps and out the front door.

My steps slow on the front walk. Part of me expects—or maybe hopes—to see Rob's hatchback waiting for me at the curb. But it's not there, because Rob doesn't understand me either. Ash was right. I start down the sidewalk, but not toward the school. There's no point in even walking past there anymore. I head toward the motel.

My phone buzzes and I pull it out, expecting a text from Ash, but it's not.

TESS—*I know what Ash is planning*

I stare at it for a full minute, chewing on my lip. I shove the phone back in my pocket without responding. I keep walking. Then I yank the phone out again, stare at it for a couple more steps, swear under my breath, and then stuff it back in. I do that three times before I finally pound out a reply.

MATT—*so what?*

TESS—*You don't have to help her*

MATT—*who says i am?*

TESS—*Ash is good at getting people to do what she wants*

I feel my whole body heat up at that one.

MATT—*i do what I want*

TESS—*Are you sure? This isn't like you*

MATT—*u keep telling me that*

MATT—*evryone keeps freaking telling me that*

MATT—*how do u know what's like me?*

MATT—*damn it, it's crossman. he deserves whatever we can stick to him*

I stand there fuming as my fingers finally stop pounding the screen.

TESS—*You don't believe that*

MATT—*don't i? u know what he did*

MATT—*u know he's just pulling the $$ for his legal fees*

MATT—*screw him*

I shove the phone back in my pocket along with a knotted ball of anger. It buzzes again, and I yank it out with the urge to hurl it across the street. But my eyes catch on the screen, and I freeze.

It's a list of bank transactions—where Crossman is moving his money to. And it's not going to his worm of a defense lawyer, it's going to...

Crossman Foundation for Emergency Response.

The screen is full of accounts and ledgers, but it all points to the money paying for one thing—Chaplain's own fire station.

My fingers hover over the screen, but my mind is a thousand miles away, trapped in my nine-year-old body, watching our house burn. Waiting for the firefighters to get there. If Chaplain had their own station... I know my mom is never coming back, but if some other kid could keep their mom because of what Crossman is doing...

Is this real? Is it just a publicity stunt where the money slides around through shell corporations and disappears? But I remember Crossman's face that night at the factory. Even after he'd had people killed, even as he held a gun at my head, there was conflict and regret trying to force its way through the cracks in his shell. He had his own demons that dragged him down that path, maybe he didn't do a good job of fighting them off, but maybe he's finally let go of that, maybe now—

I startle as a car revs past me. I look up and it's a police car. It's in a hurry.

And it's headed toward the motel.

I take off running after it, my only thought that I hope Ash isn't going to be in cuffs in the back seat by the time I get there.

36

Matt

My steps falter on the sidewalk as I dash behind the cop car. I huff in breaths as fast as I can, but it's six blocks to the motel and I don't know how long I can keep this up. The car disappears around the corner ahead, no siren but it's clearly on a mission, and I have a sinking feeling of what that mission is.

I fumble with my phone and text Ash—*cops coming, get out!!*

I keep my eyes on the screen as I run, which only makes me trip. I stagger to stay upright, but all I care about is getting a reply that she's okay. Nothing. I text her again—*did u get this? GET OUT!* I keep my eyes glued to my phone for another block. Still nothing. I finally stuff the phone away and make a sprint for it, as much as I can sprint anyway. Three blocks later, I finally stagger up to the motel, a huffing, wheezing mess.

The cop car is parked out front. The officer—a husky Latina who looks like she could kick my ass without breaking a sweat—is talking with the old lady who runs the motel. The officer glances my way, and I duck behind the side of the building. I don't think she saw me. I peek around the corner. They're walking toward Ash's room now. The owner must have ratted them out, damn it. She pulls out a key and opens the door—I can't see inside the room. Is Ash in there? What's happening? The officer's just standing there, not shouting or pulling her gun, but what's she saying? Something flicks against my cheek, and I brush it away, and squint to get a better look. What's she *saying?* Then something hits my cheek again. I turn to see who's throwing stuff at me.

It's Leah. She stands at the back corner of the motel. A handful of pebbles float in front of her, then she drops them with a twitch of her fingers. Ash steps out from behind her. I dash over to them.

"Why didn't you text me back?" I wheeze.

Ash gives me a nonchalant smile. "What, you didn't think we could take care of ourselves?"

"Of course not, it just *(wheeze)* would've been nice to know *(wheeze)* when I was sprinting over here..." I stop before I pass out and suck in a long breath, until I feel like my lungs are finally working again. "How did you know the cops were coming?"

Heath steps out from around the corner. "Old lady was on the phone with one of her gossip buddies. She put together that we're the ones causing a ruckus around town. Plus, she was starting to get wise to the fact that we're never going to pay her for the room. So she called the cops, and we split."

"You should have *texted* me," I hiss.

"Hey, we stuck around for you," Ash says. "And I had Leah get your attention."

Leah looks down. "Sorry about that."

"As much fun as this is," Heath says, "we need to put some distance between us and that cop."

"Fine," Ash says. "I'm hungry anyway."

"Can't go back to that diner," Heath points out.

Ash looks at me. "Any other place to eat in this dump of a town where we haven't worn out our welcome?"

The Jiffy Mart benches aren't exactly comfortable, and the table isn't exactly clean, and the whole place smells like burned meat and cheese from a can—what doesn't already smell like motor oil, that is—but this is Chaplain, and aside from the diner this is about it in the way of food choices. And Jackie Burkson slumped behind the counter is the closest thing to a chef in this place. She barely looks up from her phone as Heath slaps down a couple bills and walks away with a tray full of breakfast burritos, the stale leftover ones that have been sitting under the heat lamp all morning. He drops the tray at our table and Ash looks over the burritos warily. She picks one up and takes a bite; she makes a sour face but keeps chewing. Leah takes a sniff, then slouches back on the bench. Apparently not hungry enough to brave the burritos. I've braved Jiffy Mart burritos before, and running six blocks made me plenty hungry, so I grab one and chow down.

"We make our play tonight," Ash says. "We clearly can't wait much longer, but I want it dark. We all good?"

Heath nods. "I'm good. I'm just wondering about Matt over here. He seems a little preoccupied."

"Hmm?" I mumble. "What?"

Ash grabs my shoulder and gives my body a shake. "Are you with us? You finally gonna break your goody-two-shoes rules and take what's ours?"

I cough down a bite of burrito. "Do you guys, uh, wonder what Crossman is doing with the money? Where he's been moving it to?"

Heath looks at me. "What the hell do I care?"

"It doesn't matter what he was doing with it," Ash says. "He doesn't deserve it."

"But what if... he's actually doing something good with the money?" I ask.

"Something good?" Ash says. "Are you kidding me?"

"I found out he's giving the money to a foundation. To build a new fire station."

Leah shifts beside me. "He's giving it away?"

"No, he's not," Ash snaps. "It's a publicity stunt. Isn't the douche about to go on trial? He's trying to get people to like him so he can get off. Or it's a scam so he can hide the money from the IRS. Either way, at the end of it, there isn't going to be any fire station."

I nod reluctantly. "I've thought about all that, and... yeah, maybe. But what if it's real?"

"He's an asshole," Ash says. "You said that yourself."

"He is. Or... he was. I don't know anymore."

"Matt—"

"Look," I insist. "Crossman did some bad stuff, and he needs to pay for that. But I talked to him when he was going through with it, and for a minute there I thought maybe he wouldn't. I think, deep down, he wanted to do the right thing. Maybe he finally is."

Ash glares at me with hard eyes. "Not people like him. People like *them.*"

"We're not talking about your dad, Ash."

She reaches back and slaps me right across the face. The shock knocks me sideways and I almost fall off the bench. I manage to catch myself, but my backpack tumbles to the floor.

Jackie finally looks up from her boredom behind the counter. Her eyes hold on us for a moment longer than they should.

"Don't you *dare* bring him up!" Ash yells. "And haven't you been paying attention to anything going on? It's us versus them, Matt."

I rub at the sting in my cheek. Maybe she's right. Maybe Crossman, and everyone like him, will never change. Maybe I need to wise up to the way the world is. I reach down to pick up my backpack, and freeze when I see the corner of the picture frame sticking out of it.

"It's time to take back what belongs to us," Ash says. "We're going to take it. Are you with us or not?"

I reach out slowly and grasp my fingers around the frame, and slide it out. My mom's eyes stare back at me through the glass.

"Don't you want to live in a world where people can change?" I say, as much to myself as to them. "Where people can do the right thing?"

Heath lets out an exasperated sigh. "Are you really that naïve? And stupid?"

I keep staring into my mom's eyes. "If there's even a chance that money will help save people, I can't take that away."

He shakes his head. "You *are* that stupid."

"Chaplain needs that fire station," I say. "When my house burned, my mom—"

Ash slaps her palm to her forehead. "Oh my God. That's what all this is about?" She snatches the picture from me, the wood frame scraping roughly across my fingertips. "She's *dead,* Matt."

"Give her back," I demand, grabbing for the picture.

Ash holds it away from me. "You could build ten fire stations and it wouldn't bring her back."

"Do you think I don't know that?" I say, my voice breaking. "Look, that station will save people. Not her, but other people."

Ash glares at me for a long moment, her freckles popping out from her cheeks like fireworks... then she hurls the picture across the room. The shatter of glass and splintering of wood echoes through the store. I bolt up to run after it but Heath shoves me back into my seat.

"Why would I want to save any of those people out there?" Ash says, her eyes burning. "It's still *them.*"

Jackie at the counter is full-on staring at us now. Tina Cooper, standing by the shelves, forgets about the granola bars she was browsing through and scoots to the counter. She whispers something to Jackie.

My phone buzzes in my pocket. My hand fumbles to pull it out, my mind still whirling from the look on Ash's face.

"You get a text from one of your little friends?" Ash snaps. "What do they want with you now?"

I stare at the screen. "It's something Tess found. A report from... the Brookside Juvenile Detention Center."

I notice Leah stiffen beside me, but she doesn't say anything.

"You all did time there together?" I ask.

"Yeah. So?" Ash says dismissively.

"Because of the stuff you stole?"

"We've been over why we do that. Do you know what those people did to *us?* Do you know what happened to Leah while we were there?"

Leah hunches a little further down.

"You broke out of there?" I ask.

"Well, duh," Ash says.

I keep reading, then my mouth tightens. "It says two staff members were injured. *Seriously* injured."

Ash throws her arms up. "So freaking what, Matt? You want to have a pity party for them? Screw them. They were in our way, and they *deserved* it."

I blink at her in disbelief. "Is that what you're planning to do to Crossman's security guards, too?"

"Sure as hell."

"Ash, you can't—"

"You need to get it through your head, Matt. All those people out there hate us. They've been stabbing us in the back our whole lives, and now we finally get the chance to stick the knife in *their* throats."

"Jesus, Ash," I mutter. "Stealing is one thing, but this?"

She reaches out and grabs me by the neck. For a second I think she's going to strangle me, but I see the flicker in her eyes as she stares me down.

"You really are that weak inside," she says, disgusted, and pulls her hand away.

Heath darts another glance at Jackie and Tina. Jackie's making a phone call now, still looking at us. "We need to go," Heath says. He starts to pull Ash away. She shakes him off and storms past him toward the door.

I grab Leah's arm before she can follow them. "Leah, you don't think that, do you? Everyone isn't just out to hurt us. We can—"

I don't get a chance to finish because Heath lunges over and shoves me, like a battering ram hitting my chest. The air puffs out of my lungs and I stumble backward, my hand ripping free from Leah's arm. I slam into one of the shelves, the one with the pathetic excuse for a toy section in here, and the shelf comes down with me as I hit the floor hard. Dolls and plastic dinosaurs go flying. A bag of marbles hits the floor and splits open, and the marbles go scattering.

I look up from the floor to see Leah rubbing her arm where I must have scratched her, her face frozen in horror. Heath stands over me, his face set hard. "If you think the people out there don't hate people like us, you're either blind or freaking stupid. And now you choose them over us? And you hurt my *sister?*"

He takes a step toward me. I flinch back and instinctively reach out my hand. My fingers tingle and I pull at the first thing I see—his cochlear implant. The plastic disc pulls away from his scalp. Heath grunts in surprise and throws his hand up to grab it, and it makes him trip. He goes down on one knee. Leah shrieks. With a spasm of her hand, the marbles on the floor come flying straight toward my face.

I shield my face with my hands, just as the marbles pelt me like a flurry of hailstones. I pull my hands away and stare gaping at her.

"Don't you *dare* hurt him!" Leah screams at me.

"Leah," I plead, "I was just trying to protect myself—"

She flicks her fingers and the marbles fly at me again. I manage to close my eyes before they hit me in my cheek and my neck and my ear, and I fall back to the floor. I open my eyes to see Leah storming out. Heath gives me the finger and follows her.

I look back at the counter and see Jackie and Tina staring at me. I drag myself up and bolt toward the door. I manage to grab the broken frame of my mom's picture off the floor, and then I keep running, on and on, alone.

37

Ash

The leaves rustle against the breeze, shivering in the twilight. Ash peers around the bush at the guard booth half a block away.

"What's going on in there?" she asks Heath.

He squints off into the booth. The glow of security monitors wash over the guard's face, but he's focused on whoever he's talking to on his cell phone. He doesn't look happy, although it's hard to tell from here.

"He's arguing with someone," Heath says.

"Anything we need to worry about?"

He listens, then shakes his head. "Nah. I think it's his daughter. Something about her taking money out of his wallet."

"Then he's distracted. Perfect." Ash slides her hand out of her pocket, a small white capsule pinched between her fingers. "You're up, Leah."

Leah stares at it. "I don't want to hurt him."

"He doesn't matter."

Leah's mouth tightens.

"Fine," Ash says with a sigh. "It'll just give him a nap, all right? We don't need to hurt anyone. Yet."

"But what happens if we—"

"Let's do this, Leah," Ash orders.

Leah hesitates another moment, then flexes her hand. The capsule jumps up out of Ash's fingers and hovers, then slides through the air toward the guard booth.

"I just thought... Matt would be with us," Leah says.

"Well, he's not. He had his chance, and he blew it. Eyes on the job, Leah."

The capsule glides through the open window of the booth. Ash pulls out a pair of binoculars for a closer look.

"A little to the left," Ash says. "*Left,* Leah."

The capsule hovers beside the guard as he pinches his eyes shut and yells something into the phone.

"Matt could've helped me with this," Leah whispers. "Maybe we should give him another chance—"

"Forget him," Heath says. "He's a prick."

Leah presses her lips together. The capsule trembles in the air.

"Further left, Leah," Ash says. "No, right now. No—"

Leah's fingers spasm and the capsule drops. Ash holds her breath and looks at Heath.

"Clattered off the desk and onto the floor," he says.

Ash grinds her teeth. At least the guard is still arguing on the phone.

"Sorry," Leah whimpers.

Ash huffs and slides her hand back in her pocket. She comes out with another capsule. "Let's focus this time, okay?"

Leah stares at the capsule, her eyes glazing over. "He was supposed to be here. He's like me."

"Are you still on that?" Ash snaps.

Heath puts a hand on Leah's shoulder. "I get it. We don't find people like us very often."

"We've been over this," Ash says. "Matt had his chance, and he *blew* it."

Leah swallows. "But what if he—"

"Focus, Leah," Ash says. "Remember what Matt did."

Leah's face tightens. "He chose those people over us. Over me."

"Those people out there hurt you, and Matt wants to help them. But we're not going to let him, are we?"

Leah's eyes burn with conflict. Finally, she nods.

"Okay," Ash says, her voice firm. She holds up the capsule. "Now do your job."

Leah takes a long breath and then flicks her fingers. The capsule floats up out of Ash's hand and toward the booth.

Ash peers through her binoculars. The guard has the phone against his ear, his eyes closed, his mouth tight but not saying anything. His daughter must be going off on him. Good for her. The capsule glides in through the window.

"Not that far, pull it back," Ash says. "One more nudge to the right... and... drop!"

She watches the capsule fall, but even with the binoculars she can't follow it. She looks at Heath.

He smirks. "Splashdown."

Ash looks back at the booth. The guard slams his cell phone on the desk, grabs the coffee mug, and takes a long, angry gulp. Ash smiles and leans back against the fence.

"Now what?" Heath asks.

"We wait until you hear him snore."

38

Matt

I trudge along the sidewalk, determined, my head down. The last remnants of sunlight peer through the trees and through the tall iron bars of the fence guarding Crossman's house. The bars flow past me with each step. The leaves rustle softly, sort of peaceful, except I sure don't feel very peaceful right now. I keep peering through the fence, looking for Ash or Leah or the dome of Heath's head. Because I can't let them get inside that house. I can't let them steal that money. And I damn sure can't let them hurt anyone.

I hate that I'm walking alone. I should have Rob and Phillip and Tess with me, but... well, we all know how I treated them. I thought about talking to them after school; I walked halfway to Rob's house before turning around again, and then I sat staring at my phone for half an hour trying to work up the guts to text Tess. But here I am, walking alone. Because I don't deserve their help. I couldn't apologize that way, not when I'd be asking them in the same breath for them to come here and help clean up my mess.

I will apologize, I owe them that much, but that will come later. Assuming I live through this.

I look back through the fence at the three stories of Crossman's house. The windows are lighted, and I don't see anyone moving around. Hopefully that means Ash and her crew aren't in there yet—

A pair of arms wraps around me out of nowhere, jolting me to a stop. "Get off me!" I yell, flailing around.

"I can't let you do it, Matt!"

"Phillip?" I wrangle out of his hold and turn to look at him, shocked. "What are you doing here?"

"We're not going to let you rob Crossman's house." The green of his eyes is hyperintense, the lines in his pale forehead creased tight under the shadow from his hoodie.

"You think I'm here to steal from Crossman?" I sputter.

"Tess showed us what Ash is planning. But this isn't you, Matt, and if you go through with it, you won't be able to live with yourself."

"But I'm not—"

Phillip grabs me again, squeezing the air out of me with his skinny arms. "We won't let you do it, even if you hate us for it!"

" 'We'?"

I look past him to see Rob running up, with Tess shuffling behind him. Rob's face is set hard, his skin darkened to umber in the dying light. "You can let him go now, Phillip," Rob says. "It's my turn to pound on him."

"Guys," I protest, pulling free from Phillip again, "I'm going to rob the house."

"Damn straight you're not!" Rob strides up, balling his fists. "Matt, when the shit went down with Crossman, *you* were the one who stood up to him. Because it was *right*. And now you let Ash talk you into doing this?"

"I'm not—"

"*I showed them everything*," Tess says, stepping up behind Rob. Her phone screen glows softly against her face.

"You saw the stuff about the foundation, didn't you?" Phillip says. "The fire station? Matt, your mom..."

"I told them it's probably a publicity stunt," Rob says. "And it's not like it brings your mom back. But if there's even a chance of it getting built, Matt, you can't—"

"I didn't come here to rob the place. I came here to stop Ash!" I finally get out.

Rob's face relaxes. "Really?"

"Yeah," I sigh. "You're right, about all of that. Thanks for sending that stuff to me, Tess. And, uh, sorry it took me so long for it to sink in."

"*I knew it would eventually*," she says.

"So you came here to stop Ash," Phillip says, "but you came without us?"

I swallow. "I didn't deserve to ask for your help after the way I treated you guys. I know I hurt you."

The corner of Phillip's mouth twitches. "Yeah, you did."

"I owe you all an apology. A big one. But I couldn't apologize just because I needed something from you."

Rob looks me over carefully. "Well, that's one thing you've gotten right. But you still should've asked us."

"When we stormed the factory with you to stop Crossman," Phillip says, "we didn't just do it because you're our friend. We did it because it was right."

"I thought," Rob says, "that was something we did together, like some stupid bond or something. But then Ash and her clowns waltz into town, and you decide we're not good enough for you. Because we're not 'like' you," he adds, with overly aggressive air quotes. "Apparently, we're only allowed to be your friend if we can move things with our mind or see out the back of our head or something *special* like that."

"I'm sorry," I plead. "I... thought Ash was showing me how the world really is, since she has an Ability like me. But it turns out Ash is looking out for her, and only her. And she doesn't care who she hurts."

Rob gives me a long look, chewing his bottom lip. "Yeah, well, I'm guessing she hurt you, too. So screw her, and let's get out of here."

I shake my head. "I can't let her steal that money."

"So call the cops."

"If the cops show up, someone will get hurt. Tess, did you show them that report about Ash and the others breaking out of juvenile detention? About the staff members that got injured?"

Tess nods.

Rob rolls his eyes. "Don't tell me. You're afraid they'll hurt the cops, so you'd rather we storm in and they hurt *us* instead?"

"They won't hurt us, Rob. Maybe I can still reason with them. With her."

"You sure about that?"

No, I'm not. "Look, this is something I have to do. You don't have to stay, but when Ash gets here, I'm going to—"

I jump out of my skin when Phillip materializes right next to me. "She may have already been here," he says. "I just checked out the guard booth."

I tense up. "What did she do?"

"The gate's open, and the guard's asleep."

"Asleep or drugged?" I swallow. "Or dead?"

I don't wait for his answer. I take off toward the booth.

"Damn it, wait for us!" Rob calls behind me.

My legs stumble in an awkward sprint until I skid to a stop in front of the booth. I peer inside at the guard, who's slumped over the desk. I scan anxiously for blood or bruises but don't see any. Finally, I see his shoulders heave up and down. I let my own breath out.

Rob huffs up beside me. "You've gotta stop taking off on your own like that."

"Sorry. I wanted to make sure Ash didn't do something stupid with him."

Phillip and Tess hurry up behind Rob.

"He okay?" Phillip asks.

"Yeah," I reply.

The guard punctuates this by shifting to the side and letting out a snort.

"Okay," Rob says, "we've established he's just sleeping. Now can we get out of here before he wakes up?"

I shake my head. "I'm going in the house."

"I already told you, call the cops," Rob says.

"It's too late for that. Even if they believed us, and even if they got here in time, cops would just escalate things until someone gets hurt."

"*You really think it's up to us?*" Tess asks.

I nod. "It's up to me. You guys... I can't ask you to come in there with me."

Rob lets out a long, exasperated breath. "Oh, what the hell. If you're going to do something stupid, you know I'll be right behind you."

I smile. "Thanks. I don't deserve that."

"You're right, you don't," Rob says, but he smiles too.

Phillip nods. "I'm in. You know that."

"What about you, Tess?" I ask.

"*Glad you want to do the right thing,*" she says. "*So do I.*"

"Thanks, guys."

The guard snorts again.

"Let's, uh, get moving."

We hurry past the booth and into the grass and the shadows. The house sits about seventy feet away, through the trees.

"Do you have any plan for once we get in there?" Rob asks, running beside me.

Not really, no. "The safe is through the trophy room," I answer, hoping that sounds like a plan.

"Okay, but do you know what the trophy room even looks like?"

"I don't know. Trophies."

Phillip tugs on my jacket. "Do you know how many other guards there are?"

"Uh, no," I answer. "Why?"

Phillip points off to the side of the house, through the trees. A flashlight beam plays along the edge of the fence. "There's one over there."

"Get out of sight!" Rob hisses. He sprints past me. He'll be to the house in a few seconds. Phillip is all but a ghost anyway. As long as I don't give us away...

I see a glow behind me, and turn to see Tess's phone.

"Tess, your phone!" I whisper frantically.

She douses the light with her hand. I put my hand on Tess's shoulder and hurry her along. We get to the front door, and Rob is already there. I glance back at the guard's flashlight beam, still across the yard and thankfully not aimed at us.

"Let's get inside before we get arrested," Rob says. "Door's locked. We need your magic trick to open it."

I step up and raise my hand, feeling my fingers tingle.

"*If the door is locked,*" Tess says, still shielding her phone screen, "*does that mean Ash isn't in the house yet?*"

My thoughts hesitate as I feel the deadbolt click.

"Leah," Phillip says beside me.

I glance at him, my hand turning on the doorknob.

"She could have opened the door the same way you did."

I barely register what he said when the knob twists fully and the door pushes open—and immediately something strong and firm clamps around my neck and drags me inside.

Heath glares at me, shoving me against the wall. "You should know by now that nobody can sneak up on me," he growls in my face.

"It's... just... me," I manage to get out, his hand still on my throat.

"Exactly."

In my peripheral vision I see Rob rush in and take a swing at Heath, only to have Heath shove him to the floor. I'm vaguely aware of the size of the room behind him—the entryway is freaking huge, with a couple hallways, three or four doors, and a stairway, and that's just what I can see around Heath's head—but right now I'm more concerned with Heath's fingers clamped around my windpipe.

"Please don't kill him, Heath," Leah says faintly behind him.

Heath glances back at her. He chews his lip for a second, which feels a lot longer because I'm struggling for air, then he releases his hand.

"Thanks," I breathe. I push myself away from the wall, but he shoves me back.

"She only asked me not to *kill* you," Heath says.

Ash stomps up to me. "What the hell are you doing here?"

"You're a smart girl." Rob hauls himself up from where Heath knocked him to the floor. "You figure it out."

Heath gives him a glare like he wants to shove him again. "And you brought your little friends with you? You think that's gonna make any difference?" His eyes move to Tess, and his scowl tightens. "I thought *you'd* know better than to come here. Maybe I should snap that phone in half." He takes a step toward her when Phillip appears out of nowhere, blocking his path.

"Where'd you come from?" Heath barks.

Phillip smirks. "I guess someone *can* sneak up on you."

Heath takes a step to move around him, but Phillip moves with him and pushes Tess behind himself. "If you want to get to her, you'll have to go through me."

"That's the plan."

"*Enough* already!" Ash shouts. "Matt, did you seriously come here to stop us? How stupid are you?"

"I can't let you steal that money," I say, finally getting a full breath back in me.

"You think this Crossman guy can't spare it? Look around!"

Now that I don't have Heath's fist around my throat, I can see the room is even bigger than I'd thought. The floor is marble, and a massive family crest is etched into it. Most of the walls are covered with hardwood paneling that I'm sure is imported from someplace expensive. The portraits on the walls—half of them of Crossman's own smug face—are in frames an art gallery would salivate over. The chandelier glints with more gold and crystal than any honest person has a right to.

"Look," I say, "I know Crossman is loaded, that's not the point."

"Isn't it?" Ash says.

"That money is for the fire station. For saving lives."

"No, it's not. We've been over this."

"We need that fire station, Ash."

"What about what *we* need?" she hisses through gritted teeth. "What we *deserve?*"

Rob scoffs. "You think you deserve seven million bucks? You must think pretty highly of yourself."

Ash shoots him a look. "You have no idea."

"What matters right now," I say, "is we're not letting you steal the money."

"You think you can stop us?" Heath says.

"You have no idea," Rob quips.

"Damn it, Matt!" Ash yells. "Crossman is one of *them!* And so are the firefighters you're so worried about, and everyone else in this God damn town!"

Rob takes a step toward her. "*I'm* one of 'them' too, you know."

"That's right," Ash says. "So you should've figured out by now that I don't care about stepping on you to get what belongs to me."

I can feel the tension rising to a dangerous level and clear my throat. "Come on, everybody, let's just... calm down, okay?"

Rob takes another step toward Ash. "You really think you're that much better than us?"

Heath steps in to block him. "You really have that much of a problem with people like us? Asshole."

I see the anger ignite in Rob's face, and I know there's no stopping what's about to happen. Rob leans back, getting his weight behind him, and charges like a bull. He hits Heath hard enough that he goes down, with Rob on top of him. They hit the hard marble floor in a tangle of limbs, grappling with each other.

"Stop it, Heath!" Ash yells. "You can beat him up later. We've got work to do!"

Heath keeps tussling without losing a beat. I'd say he didn't hear her, but... well, you know. He rolls over and manages to get on top of Rob, then he pulls his fist back. The punch lands on Rob's cheek, and his face snaps to the side. Heath pulls back for another one.

"*Rob's going to get hurt,*" Tess says.

"Not if I can help it." I reach out my hand toward the back wall, toward one of the smaller portraits of Crossman. With a tingle of my fingers, it flies off the wall, straight into Heath's head. He flinches as the frame cracks against his skull.

Heath shakes off the impact and raises his fist again. I pull at another frame. It comes flying toward him—then it jerks to the right, not much but enough to miss him. It goes flying past him and into the banister, shattering the glass into a pile of shards that fall to the floor. I glance at Leah. Her hand is contorted and tense, and so is her face.

"Don't you dare hurt him," she hisses at me.

"I'm just trying to protect my friend," I tell her.

Rob struggles with Heath on the floor. He starts to push himself up, then Heath slams him back down against the floor. I reach toward another portrait and start to pull. Leah screams and her hand spasms with rage. The scattered glass shards on the floor jump up and come flying at my face.

I throw my hands up just in time. The glass bites into my skin. When the shards fall again, I look up at Leah, hoping to reason with her, but the rage on her face says she's done talking. She raises her hand toward me and I flinch, wondering what she's going to throw at me next, when Phillip appears beside her and grabs her by both wrists. She struggles against him, and he stumbles.

"We have a *job* to do!" Ash yells. "Will you all just—"

Heath suddenly holds his hand up to cut her off. "Stop."

"Now what?"

"Guard's coming." His eyes dart toward one of the hallways.

"How long?" she hisses.

"Any second."

I glare daggers at Ash. "You're not going to hurt that guard."

"Why shouldn't I?" she shoots back.

"Because if you do, there's a bigger chance he'll sound the alarm."

Her eyes glower at me. "I hate that you're right. But if he gets in our way, if anyone does, all bets are off."

The footsteps are getting closer. Phillip makes a determined look toward the hallway, then looks at me. "I'll buy you a little time," he says.

"Don't do anything stu—" I cut myself off because he's already disappeared, and we're way past stupid anyway.

Ash grabs Leah's arm and pulls her toward the stairway. Heath forces himself up to follow, but Rob grabs his collar. Heath wrestles with him and shoves him back down, knocking the wind out of him. Rob rolls over on the floor with a groan.

I'd help him up but I'm bolting after Ash. I get to the base of the stairs a few steps behind her. "You can still stop this," I hiss after her. "Let's all just get out of here!" I reach to grab her arm. But Leah darts a fierce glance back at me and twitches her fingers, and my hand jerks upward on its own, grabbing nothing but air. I stumble backward in surprise as Ash and Leah hurry up the stairs.

Heath starts toward the stairs to follow Ash, but he's got too much distance to cover. His eyes dart back to the hallway and he scowls. He goes the other way to the nearest door and slips through it.

I look back to Rob. He's still on the ground but Tess shuffles to him and reaches down to pull him up, then she steps toward one of the doors. Rob starts after her and then stumbles, still trying to get his breath back. Tess is already slipping through the door when the guard's shadow breaches the mouth of the hallway. Rob's eyes go wide and he ducks the other way through a different door.

I'm dashing up the stairs. I'm almost to the top where I'll be out of the guard's sightline, when I suddenly stop.

The pictures.

I spin around and see the two portraits I pulled off the wall broken on the floor. If the guard sees those, he'll know something's up. I reach out both hands and the frames fly off the floor toward me, but I know I won't be fast enough. I dart a glance toward the hallway, feeling the sweat bead on my forehead.

The guard's shadow stops, and spins around with a startled yelp. Whatever Phillip is doing to distract him is working. Just a few more seconds... the broken frames of the pictures slap into my hands, my fists clench around them, and I bound up the remaining stairs just as I hear footsteps on the marble floor below.

I duck down the hall and lean up against a doorway, trying to catch my breath. That was too close. I think about waiting until the guard leaves and going back down to find Rob or Tess, but in the mess that just happened, I'm not even sure which doors they went through. Best to keep going. I stare down the hallway, scanning for Ash and Leah. I don't see them either.

I hurry along, my steps soft on the thick, expensive, plush carpet. I scan the oak doors on either side, more doors than I care to count.

Damn, this is a big house. I hope the others don't get lost in here.

39

Rob

The breath heaves slowly into Rob's lungs as he leans against the door. That slam Heath gave him against the floor sure took it out of him. The punch to the jaw wasn't fun either. He rubs his cheek, fantasizing about how he's going to kick Heath's ass the next time he sees him.

Static from the guard's radio hisses from the other side of the door. Rob sucks in a breath and holds it.

"Any activity on your end, Carl?" the guard says, his voice muffled through the door. "I could've sworn I heard some voices in the lobby." His footsteps pace back and forth just outside, as the radio crackles with another voice. Rob stays stiff as a board. The guard yawns. "Nah, I checked it out but no one here. Yeah, yeah, I'll keep an eye out."

Rob finally exhales when he hears another door open and the guard's footsteps fade away. He looks around to see where he ended up. A couple couches and chairs sit around the room, looking like they belong in a palace somewhere, daring anyone to sit actually on them. Geez, is Crossman really *that* rich? For just a second, Rob thinks about letting Ash steal Crossman's money... or better yet, stealing it himself. But he kicks himself and pushes the thought away. Matt's idealism must be rubbing off on him.

Either way, there's no safe full of money in this room and no delinquent wanna-be supervillains to stop, so it's best to keep moving until he finds one or the other. He ambles across the room toward the side door; he's about to step around one of the gaudy, overstuffed couches when he changes his mind and plants his foot right on the cushion, and steps up and over the back of the couch. He smirks, hoping he left a nice dirty shoeprint. He grabs the doorknob—yeah, the door is solid oak and feels expensive too—and pushes it open.

A pair of olive-skinned hands immediately grab him by the collar and jerk him into the room. Heath glares down at him.

"Did you *still* think you could sneak up on me?" Heath mutters.

"Who says I wanted to sneak up on you?" Rob shoots back. "I was hoping to have a chance to pay you back for earlier."

Rob leans back, pulling against Heath's grip. Heath hangs on, but all Rob needs is some room. When he forces enough of a gap, he pulls his fist back and lets loose into Heath's face. Heath grunts and releases. Rob stumbles before steadying himself, then readies his fist again.

Heath pulls his own fist back, then stops. "Wait," he says quickly.

"Oh, I'm just getting started."

Rob throws another punch. Heath catches his fist and glances to the door. "*Wait!* Guard's coming again."

"Do you think I'm dumb enough to fall for—" Rob stops when he hears a thump in the next room. "Shit."

Rob moves toward the opposite door, but Heath grabs him and throws him backward, taking off toward the door himself.

"Son of a bitch," Rob mutters, pulling himself up off the carpet. Heath is already at the door. He glances back with a smirk, then twists the knob, but it sticks shut with a click. Locked. Heath loses his smirk. Not getting out that way. Rob's eyes dart back to the only other door, knowing the guard will step through there any second. He quickly scans the rest of the room—it must be for storage; there are a couple of antique trunks and a bunch of file cabinets. Against the side wall is a big wooden cabinet, and Rob is quick to notice it's big enough to hold a person. Namely, him. He bounds over to it and pulls the doors open, relieved to see there isn't much inside except a few sweaters. Rob steps inside and starts to pull the doors closed, only to have them tugged open again.

"Move over," Heath grunts.

"Get your own cabinet!" Rob snaps.

"I'm not happy about this either, but there's nowhere else to hide in here, so piss off and—"

The door cracks open and both their eyes dart to it. For half a second Rob thinks about shoving Heath out, but as satisfying as that would be, it would just get them both caught. Rob smushes over as far as he can, and Heath hurriedly crams himself in. He pulls the cabinet shut just as the guard steps into the room.

Rob squints in the dark. A sliver of light seeps in between the doors. The guard's shadow crosses through the light, and he can hear the faint beat of music coming from the guard's earbuds. Rob stifles a sneeze from the smells—cedar, wool, and dust—and holds his breath. His leg cramps and he shifts his weight, which shoves his elbow into Heath's gut. Heath muffles a grunt, and Rob grinds his elbow in a little more.

Heath shoves his hand into Rob's face and smushes him against the side of the cabinet, the wood scratching at his cheek. Rob has to bite his tongue to hold in a yelp. He peers through the crack between the doors and can still see the guard moving around out there. Heath shoves his hand further into Rob's face, and his thumb jabs him in the eye. Rob winces and bites his lip, grinding his heel over Heath's foot in return.

The smells are getting stifling, including the stink of both their sweat. Heath jabs an elbow against him again, and it's getting harder to keep quiet. Rob squints through the crack, and he doesn't see any movement. He doesn't hear anything, either.

"He's gone, right?" Rob whispers. He looks at Heath, but his face is an unreadable shadow in the dark. Rob pries himself toward the doors.

Heath shoves him back and sticks his finger in front of his mouth. He edges forward far enough to put his ear against the cabinet door and then holds there, listening in tense silence.

Then Heath pulls back and punches him right in the face. "Sucker," Heath gloats, jumping out of the cabinet. He leaves Rob stunned, and bolts across the room, disappearing out the door.

Rob rubs his eye. "That's it. I'm definitely not inviting him to my birthday party now." He struggles out of the cabinet and hustles after him.

40

Heath

It doesn't take long before that wuss Rob's footsteps die out behind him. Heath ducks down a side hallway and through the dining room to lose him. His own footsteps smush against the ridiculously thick carpet, and his pulse thumps through his veins. He slows down and crosses through another hallway—seriously, how big is this place?—and scans over the doors. No sounds coming from any of them, other than the whoosh of air overhead from the heating system. Well, the door at the end of the hall is bigger than the rest, so maybe that's something. He strolls to the end and pushes through the door.

The room on the other side is dimly lit. Heath stops to let his eyes adjust. When they come into focus, he can see the room is huge. He steps forward and then almost trips on the step down, putting his hand out to steady himself. It lands on a plush armrest. He looks over to see a theater seat—two rows of them, complete with recliners and cupholders. Heath turns to see what the seats are all pointed at and sees a projector screen the size of a highway billboard.

"Damn," Heath mutters. "Gotta get me one of those."

He's almost thinking about firing up that bad boy, but there's obviously no safe in here and Ash would smack him around if he gets off mission. He starts to leave when he hears a tapping sound coming from the front of the room.

It's Tess, standing statue still. Aside from her breathing and the taps of her fingers against her phone screen, she doesn't make a peep. Heath steps down through the seats, making his way toward her. "So it's just us, huh?" he says. "You lose your gang too?"

"*Looks like it,*" Tess says.

"You're seriously sold on stopping us from taking that money?"

"*One hundred percent.*"

"Why?" He scoffs. "You really let Matt brainwash you like that?"

"*This isn't about Matt. It's about what's right.*"

"You keep telling yourself that. I'm gonna do what I have to."

"*So will I.*"

Heath's mouth tightens. "You will, huh? How exactly are you gonna stop me?"

The gray-blue of Tess's eyes glimmers. "*You'd be surprised.*"

"So that's how it's gonna be. I figured you of all people would understand." Heath's voice turns hard. "What're you looking at on that phone, huh? Gotta be something I can use." He storms toward her with a moment of hesitation—she's so small. But nothing matters right now except the job. "Sorry about this."

Tess's fingers suddenly flurry faster. "*I'm sorry too.*"

"You're sorry? For what?"

258

"This."

With one last jab of a finger on her phone, a shriek blasts out of the overhead speakers, stabbing through Heath's ears. It only lasts a second, but it jolts him to a painful stop. Tess steps backward, away from him. Heath shakes his head to clear it and takes a stride toward her, reaching for her phone.

Another punch of sound hits him, this time from behind. His hand darts up toward his implant to shut it off, but before he can get there, a thud of bass like a bomb goes off in the speakers to the right. Disoriented, he falls forward, his hands jerking forward to catch himself. He fumbles on all fours on the floor. A shrill whistle screeches from the left, grating like fingernails across his brain.

With a final effort, he manages to get his hand up and switches off his implant. Everything drops away. He crouches, panting on the floor, the dull ache still throbbing in his head. He looks up to see Tess moving away from the front of the room. A punch of vibrations hits him as a silent thud against his chest.

"You're in for it now," Heath mutters. "Your tricks won't work anymore." He pushes himself up and strides toward her.

A blinding flash erupts from the screen, stopping him in his tracks. He squints against the light until his eyes adjust, then he clenches his fists and takes another step forward. But then the light cuts out to complete darkness and he staggers again, knocking his knee against one of the seats. His lungs let loose in a yell that he can feel even though he can't hear it. The light flashes on again and he forces himself forward. He can just make out Tess's small figure up ahead of him through the glare. Then the light strobes in quick bursts and he loses sight of her. Another step forward. Then darkness, then blinding light again before he can react, then more darkness, and he trips and tumbles down the theater steps. His face crushes against the carpet.

He fumbles on the floor in the dark, not even sure which direction to crawl, when the overhead lights finally come on again, normal light, and he looks around in a daze. Tess is nowhere to be seen.

He feels a reverberation in the floor and looks to the back of the room, to see Ash standing there and the door swinging back from where it banged against the wall. Ash is mouthing something, he can't make it all out but it's some version of "what the hell is going on in here?" At least, that's what her face is saying. Heath points to his implant.

Ash's face flushes with a fresh wave of irritation. Her hands whip to sign to him, "*Are you kidding me? Turn it on!*"

He reaches for it, but the ache is still ringing in his head. He signs back, "*I need a minute.*"

Ash's scowl creases tighter. "*Fine. Now what the HELL happened?*"

"*Tess,*" he spells out with his fingers.

"*That tiny little bitch? Is she the reason you're laid out on the floor too?*"

"*Something like that,*" Heath signs back with a grimace.

"*You're three times her size!*" Ash adds a *you're pathetic* facial expression for emphasis.

"*I wasn't expecting her to turn the theater system into a freaking weapon,*" Heath signs.

Ash glares and flails her hands in frustration before signing, "*I don't know those signs! Would you just—*" Her signs devolve into nonsense, although Heath gets the gist. He takes a deep breath and switches his implant on.

His thumping heartbeat floods into his ears, and the rush of air from the heating system, and Ash growling as her hands continue to flail in incoherent signs. The sounds grind at the pang in his head. Heath gets to his feet, but his head throbs and he staggers.

Ash's face softens. She makes her way over to him and looks him over. "Are you okay?"

"I will be in a minute," Heath answers.

She casts an anxious look back to the doors. "We don't have a minute. The guards damn sure heard that, and they'll be on their way."

"Right. Yeah."

Heath takes a step and falters. Ash grabs his arm to steady him, but he shoves her hand away.

"I said I'm fine," he snaps.

"If you're fine, then let's move."

Heath forces one foot in front of the other and they hurry up the steps. The thud of each footstep jostles through the dull ache in his head.

41

Matt

I'm walking through Crossman's home gym when a muffled shriek startles me. At first I think it's a person, hopefully not someone getting murdered, but then I realize it's something else. The shriek stops and then there's a thud and a whistle, but they're all loud as hell, coming from downstairs. I'd passed a staircase a minute ago and I hurry back to it and down, missing a step and almost tumbling to the bottom. I pick myself up and rush toward the direction of the sound.

I'm getting pretty close when the noise stops. I'm trying to decide if that's a good thing or a bad thing for us, and keep going in the same direction. I get to a long hallway; I'm pretty sure the sound was coming from the room at the end of the hall. I'm almost there when the door opens, and the dark gray of a guard's jacket emerges. I frantically throw myself through the nearest doorway and into a dark room.

"*Mark?*" comes a staticky voice from the guard's radio. "*Is something going on in there? I thought I heard something.*"

"All good," the guard responds. "The freaking theater system went haywire. The thing must have a mind of its own. I guess that explains the sounds I've been hearing."

I smirk in the darkness. I'm guessing Tess had something to do with what the theater system was doing. I can only hope that whatever it was, it worked out in our favor.

I hold myself still until I hear the guard walk past, then my hand fumbles along the wall until I find the light switch. I squint as my eyes adjust to the light.

The first thing I see is a fish tank. That barely does it justice. The thing is the size of a small car, with a dozen multi-colored fish flitting around the pea gravel and the not-so-small castle at the bottom. Above that is a giant map of the world full of pins stuck across it, I can only assume marking all the spots Crossman has gone galivanting to spend more of his money. On the opposite wall, rows and rows of mahogany shelves hang, and sitting on those are rows and rows of collectible shot glasses. Probably from all those places with pins on the map. In the middle of the room, in between the shot glasses and the map and the fish tank, are tables and pedestals holding statues and vases and all kinds of other ridiculous crap. A bunch of paintings hang on the walls, along with a mounted rhino head. I'm so busy gawking at all of it that it takes me a second for it to register.

"The trophy room," I whisper under my breath. "That means the safe has to be right through—"

Before I can finish, the side door opens. I stop dead, thinking it's a guard, but the bald head stepping through is unmistakable.

"... right through there, isn't it?" Heath finishes for me, jabbing a finger toward the doorway at the far side of the room.

I take a step toward it, but Heath squares up where he stands between me and the vault room. The olive skin of his cheeks spreads wide in a grin.

Ash steps in through the door behind him. "Matt." She says my name like it's something sticky under her shoe. "You're still trying to stop us?"

"I have to," I answer.

"But you don't have your little friends with you anymore."

Heath takes a step toward me. I'm suddenly aware that I'm very alone.

Another figure comes hurrying in through the side door. For a second I hope it's reinforcements for me, but it's Leah. Her hair stands out starkly black in the light.

"Where have you been?" Ash snaps at her.

"Looking for you." Leah looks over and sees me, and her mouth tightens.

Ash glances back and forth between Leah, me, and the doorway. "Leah, take care of Matt," she orders.

Leah's face only flinches for half a second; then, her eyes set hard.

Heath turns and glares at Ash. "You're setting *her* against him?"

"I need *you* to open the safe," Ash says. "And Leah can handle herself. Right, Leah?"

Leah nods, never taking her eyes off of me.

Heath doesn't move, darting glances between Leah and me, until Ash grabs his shirt and drags him toward the door.

"I'll be right in here if you need me, Leah," Heath says, his eyes shooting bullets at me.

"I won't," Leah answers firmly.

Heath and Ash disappear through the door, and it shuts with a dull thud. I rush to follow them, but I only get three steps into the room. Leah's hand twitches, and a giant vase on the pedestal next to me shifts and tips toward me. I jump back in time for it to miss me, and it smashes to the floor.

Damn, I'll bet that was expensive.

"We can talk about this, Leah," I say, my voice hesitant.

"Nothing to talk about. I have a job to do."

I take a timid step forward, my foot crunching against the broken shards of the vase. Leah's hand twitches, and across the room I see movement in the fish tank. The pea gravel, dozens of tiny pebbles, all rush to the surface of the water and then into the air. The pebbles hover above the tank. I eye them warily.

"You don't have to go through with this." I take a slow, hesitant step. "You can help me stop it."

"I said there's nothing to talk about." Leah's voice is firm and cold. She twitches her fingers.

The hovering pebbles launch toward me. I stop and throw my hands up to block them, gritting my teeth with the pings of pain.

"This isn't what you want, is it?" I say, the rocks coming toward me like a barrage from a machine gun.

"I'm doing this for Heath and Ash."

I try to get a look at her around my hands, but a pebble smacks me in the cheek, barely missing my eye, and I pull back behind my hands. "You can't let Ash control you like that."

"Ash and Heath are my family!"

"Ash is in this for Ash." Even as I say that and know it's true, it hurts, even more than that rock to the face just did. "She's manipulating you."

"Don't say that!" Leah shrieks.

"She was manipulating me, too. It took me a while to see that."

The impacts of the pebbles slow. I risk a glance around my hands and see the resolution breaking in Leah's face. "Stealing that money will hurt people," I say.

"People that aren't like us."

"That's what Ash told you. What do *you* think?"

The pebbles stop coming at me and hold there, hovering. I slowly lower my hands.

"We need that money," Leah says.

I take a step toward her. Her face hardens, the lines sharp against the pale skin. Her hand flinches, and I cringe—but the floating pebbles drop and skitter to the floor. I let out a breath.

"You don't need it," I tell her. "Not like this." I take another hesitant step forward beside the remnant of a pillar that looks like it came from a Greek temple somewhere. "There are other ways for you to—"

Her hand twitches again, and the pillar beside me tips and falls. I jump backward, and it whips right in front of my head and thuds to the floor.

"Don't come any closer," Leah orders.

"I don't want to fight you, but I can't let this happen." I step over the pillar.

"I said *don't* come any closer," Leah snaps.

I hesitate, my body tense. She keeps staring me down. I have to distract her if I'm going to get anywhere. My eyes go to a painting on the far wall. My hand tingles and the painting pulls away from the wall, dropping to the floor with a clatter. Leah turns to look, for just long enough.

I take off across the room at a sprint. Leah's head whips back around toward me. Her eyes narrow and her fingers flinch. A display table shifts, not much, just enough for the leg to catch my foot. I go tumbling to the side, and my gut slams into a desk with a display of old coins. I wince and push myself up. Leah's eyes glare fire from the midst of her pale face. I bite my lip, already regretting this, and take off toward the door again.

Leah's hand twitches, and I feel my whole body shift in mid-step. My foot comes down off balance and I sprawl out across the floor, knocking the wind out of me. I look up, struggling to pull in a breath. "Please stop this, Leah. I'm like you, remember?"

She stares at me intensely for a long moment. "I thought you were, but you're not. You chose the other people over me."

"It can't be us versus them. Everyone deserves a chance."

Her face flinches. "They didn't give *me* a chance."

"I know." I see the pain in her eyes, and it hurts me too. "I know they hurt you. But people can change. My dad hasn't accepted what I can do, but maybe someday he can; and maybe I pushed too hard. Maybe there's still a chance for him to be better. He's my dad, and I still love him. Even your mom—"

"My mother?" Leah's eyes suddenly ignite with fire. "You think there's a chance for *her?*"

I cringe. "I... think there's a chance for everyone..."

"Do you have any idea what she did to me?" Her voice is barely recognizable. "And you want me to *love* her?"

"J-just calm down, Leah," I plead. "You're not acting like yourself right now."

The fire in her eyes erupts with a nuclear-level explosion. "That's what my mom used to say to me. Do you want to pray the demon out of me, like she used to do?"

"That's not what I meant, Leah, I just—"

Her hand spasms violently. I roll over on the floor to pull myself up, realizing too late that just above me is a bronze statue of some warrior, and it's shaking on its pedestal. It tips toward me and I watch it drop in slow motion, and I specifically notice the dude is holding a sword. The tip of it drops straight for my gut. I frantically roll to the side and the sword misses me, but the bronze torso slams down on my legs, and I swallow a yelp of pain.

Leah storms toward me. I pull to get my legs out from under the weight of the statue. I glance at Leah's face but I barely recognize her. I begin to wonder if she's actually going to kill me. I look to the massive shelf on the opposite wall with all the shot glasses, and I reach toward them and pull at one with my invisible grip. The glass flies off the shelf, straight toward Leah, and knocks her in the back of the head. She stumbles for a second, then starts toward me again. I pull at another glass, and another. One hits her in the shoulder, one in the neck. The next strikes her right in the mouth, drawing blood. She staggers to a stop. I manage to push the statue off me and struggle up, but my legs are unsteady.

Leah's fingers flick toward me. I dart glances back and forth, watching for something else about to fall on my head, but the area around me is clear. Then I see a flash of movement, and I look to the giant map on the wall. My mouth drops open in horror.

All the pins from the map pluck themselves out and hover beside it. Leah's fingers keep twitching, back and forth, and the pins turn in the air, one by one—lining up the points toward me.

"Leah," I plead, "please don't. I'm on your side."

"No, you're not."

42

Heath

The *click-click* of the tumblers reverberates through the steel. Heath presses his ear up against it, ignoring the cold of the metal, focusing everything on the clicks, straining his hearing for the distinct hollow echo.

"What's taking so long?" Ash demands behind him.

"Shut up," Heath shoots back. "This is hard enough without you yapping."

A crash of something reverberates through the trophy room behind him, and he cringes. He hasn't heard Leah scream or anything, but he still can't stomach the fact that it's her back there fighting Matt instead of him. By God, if he hurts her...

"What are you waiting for now?" Ash snaps.

"Damn it, I can't deal with these distractions." Heath reaches up and switches his implant off.

Ash's mouth drops open and her eyes shoot bullets at him. He ignores her and closes his eyes, breathing in the silence. He places his palm against the safe, feeling the cool metal, the imperfections in the surface. He turns the dial and feels the clicks reverberate through the metal to his hand.

Matt

I stand paralyzed as the pins hover across the room, the tips glinting ominously at me. I glance at Leah, looking for any crack in her rage, but there is none.

My eyes search the room desperately, and fall on the coin collection on the desk I ran into earlier. My hand tingles, and the coins fly toward Leah. She flicks her hand toward them, and their paths jerk in the air, and they whiz harmlessly past her.

Leah's eyes burn with a fresh burst of fire. She twitches her hand again, and the pins launch toward me like a flurry of arrows.

I frantically reach for a painting on the wall and ignite the tingle in my hand, and it flies off the wall toward me, but not fast enough. I lunge toward the painting to close the distance and grab it with a flailing hand, pulling it in front of me just in time. The pins impale themselves through the canvas, and I'm staring at two dozen silver points staring back at me, an inch from my face. I wince with pain and drop the painting, looking down to see four pins that missed the painting and embedded in my arms.

Leah advances toward me. I shrink back, pulling the pins out of my arm with another jolt of pain. I glance back and forth, looking for anything else I can use to protect myself, when I see Phillip emerge from a shadow behind Leah. He puts a finger to his lips and scurries silently toward her. Before I can say anything or even figure out what's happening, he's on top of her.

Phillip reaches around and grabs both Leah's wrists from behind. Leah's eyes burst wide in shock and she struggles wildly, but Phillip is clamped on tight.

"Let me go, you bastard!" she screams.

"Don't hurt her, Phillip!" I sputter.

Phillip strains to hold on as she flails her arms. Leah's fingers spasm, and I flinch, darting glances for something about to fall on me or on Phillip—but the movement is across the room, a porcelain statue that drops from its pedestal and cracks to the floor.

Phillip grunts with effort. He darts a glance at me, then to the doorway. "I don't know how long I can hold her. You need to stop them." When I hesitate, he adds, "I'll be okay."

I want to tell him to forget about me and get himself out of here, but I know he's right and there's no other option. I clench my jaw and run toward the door. As I pass Leah, she locks her eyes on me with a stare that could burn through steel.

"I see who you really are now," Leah mutters at me through gritted teeth. "You and your *friends* too."

The guilt and regret go down my throat like acid. I wanted things to go so differently with her, to have an ally, a friend, like me. But that's gone now, and it's never coming back.

Sometimes, being a hero means becoming someone's villain.

I force myself not to look back as I charge past her toward the door.

Heath

The final tumbler clicks into place, sending the vibrations resonating silently through the steel into Heath's palm. He opens his eyes, grasps the handle on the safe's door, and pulls.

There's a shudder at the first movement, and then the door swings open with a slow, smooth motion. Ash is mouthing something in the corner of his vision but he can't tell what she's saying and he doesn't care. His eyes are locked on the interior of the safe, the image even more focused in the silence—stacks and stacks and stacks of bills.

Heath reaches his hand in, slowly, barely aware of himself, and grasps one of the bundles. The crisp edges bite against his fingers. He brings it to his nose and smells the thick scent of money. He flips through the stack with his thumb, the bills flapping against the air and creating a silent breeze against his face.

His trance is broken by Ash shoving him. He irritatedly turns to look at her. She's saying something, her mouth moving way too fast for him to follow.

"For God's sake, sign language," he barks at her.

With an added scowl, she grabs him and spins him around to face the door.

That prick Matt is standing there.

43

Matt

When I burst into the room, the first thing I see is the safe. Open. But I don't get a chance to count all that money—and damn, that's a lot of money—because the next thing I see is Heath storming toward me.

"You don't give up easy, do you?" Heath barks at me.

It takes some willpower to stand my ground against him. "You're *not* taking that money."

He scowls and reaches to his cochlear implant. "What did you say?"

"You're, uh, not taking that money," I repeat.

He holds up a fistful of bills. "It sure looks like I am."

"For God's sake, Heath," Ash fumes, "just hit him already so we can pack up and get out of here."

Heath pulls his fist back and I cringe. Then he stops. "Why is Leah screaming out there?"

"I didn't hurt her," I say, my voice a lot thinner than I'd planned.

He takes another step toward me. I involuntarily shrink a step backward. He's pulling his fist back again when Leah bursts in through the door, her face washed red with rage.

"Did he hurt you?" Heath demands.

"He tried," Leah says.

I know there's no point in protesting as Heath looms toward me on one side and Leah moves in on the other. I look past them and see the money in the safe. As I take my last step backward and bump into the wall, I release the energy in my hand. The door of the safe swings toward me. Heath hears the squeak of the hinges and spins around, lunging for it, but he's not fast enough. The door slams shut with a clank.

"Damn it!" Ash yells.

I straighten up. "I told you. You're not taking that money."

Heath grabs me by the collar. "I'd kick your ass for keeping me from that money, but I'll *kill* you for hurting Leah."

He winds up to hit me and I close my eyes. I hear a thud of a fist, but I don't feel anything. I open my eyes to see Rob's fist unloading against Heath's jaw.

Heath staggers back a step. Rob pushes his way into the room.

"I owed you that from earlier," Rob says, a satisfied smirk popping his dimples.

"You never learn, do you?" Heath mutters. "You want to do this? Let's do this."

He's winding up when Tess shuffles in behind Rob.

"*Silent alarm,*" she says.

Heath freezes. "What?"

"*The safe triggered a silent alarm. I shut it off.*"

276

"Uh... thanks," Heath says.

"But I think the guards saw it before I did."

Ash darts a glance at the safe. "You'd better hurry, then."

"Damn it!" Heath barks.

He rushes toward the safe. Rob grabs his arm to pull him away. Heath swings his elbow back and knocks Rob in the mouth, but Rob keeps hanging on. As they continue to tussle, Ash storms up to Rob. She touches his hand and her eyes narrow; then she kicks him in the ankle—right where he sprained it last week playing basketball. Rob winces with the same face he made that day in gym class, and goes down. Heath shakes free from Rob and rushes to the safe. I hurry to help Rob up. Heath plasters his ear against the safe and twists the dial.

Leah twitches her fingers, and my arm jerks just as I'm trying to pull Rob up. My hand slips and he hits the ground again. I'm just looking around for anything I can use against Leah when I see a grey uniform filling the doorframe.

The guard stares at us, disbelief flushed over his narrow face. I dart a nervous glance at Ash.

"Let's, uh, nobody do anything rash," I say, trying to force my voice calm.

Ash's eyes narrow. "All bets are off." She lunges toward the guard.

Shit.

I dive toward Ash and grab her around the waist. She struggles against me, thrashing like a wild animal, her arms flailing for the guard's jacket. He staggers back a step. He fumbles for the radio on his belt, his hand shaking. "Backup!" the guard yells. "Intruders, in the—"

Before he gets any further, Leah's fingers twitch. The radio jerks out of his hand and drops to the floor.

Heath storms toward him. The guard reaches for his belt again, but his hand comes back empty. "Where's my taser?"

Phillip appears on the other side of the room with it.

Heath is two steps from the guard, pulling back a fist. Rob jumps on his back, locking an arm around his throat and jerking him backward.

Ash jabs an elbow to my face and wrangles free. I lunge forward, expecting her to go for the guard, but she darts the other way. I sprawl out on the floor, and look back to see her shove Phillip and grab the taser—then she spins around and pulls the trigger.

The probes launch and bury themselves into the guard's chest. His whole body spasms wildly as the arcing sound fills the room. Then he drops to the floor like an empty sack, still convulsing.

"You didn't have to do that, Ash!" I yell.

"He's still breathing, isn't he? More than he deserves." Ash jabs a finger at the safe. "Get that open again before the other guards get here!"

Heath throws Rob off of him and shakes his head. "No time. They're already on their way, and one of them's calling the cops right now."

"I'm not leaving here with nothing!" Ash yells.

Heath holds up the bundle of bills he pulled from the safe earlier. "Not nothing."

Ash chews her lip, then grabs the bills from him. "Fine. Let's go."

Heath takes Leah's arm and pulls her toward the door. Leah gives me one final glare before disappearing through it.

Rob tugs on my arm. "We need to get out of here too, man."

I nod and pull myself up to follow him when someone taps my shoulder. I look to see it's Tess. She points to the guard on the floor, then her hand goes back to her phone.

Something wrong with him, she says.

"Yeah, he got tased," Rob says.

But Tess is right, it's more than that. His breaths are quick and shallow, and he's got sweat covering his face. I touch his forehead, and his skin is cold.

"Shit," I mutter. "I think the taser did something to him."

I grab Ash's arm as she runs for the door. "We can't leave him like this. We have to help him."

"Why the hell would I do that?" Ash snaps.

"He could die."

"So what?!" she screams, her voice cold.

"You don't mean that," I plead. "Ash, you can use your Ability to feel what's wrong with him. Please. Just for once, don't you want to make a difference?"

Ash yanks her arm away, clenches a fist, and punches me right in the face. I land hard on the floor, rubbing my jaw out of pain and utter shock.

"You made your choice," Ash spits at me. "You're one of *them* now."

I sit there watching her storm out in a daze until I feel someone shaking me and realize it's Phillip.

"Matt!" he yells. "Come on, we've got to do something now!"

"Right. Sorry." I push myself up.

"You good?" Phillip asks.

"Yeah. We need to help this guy."

Rob darts a glance toward the door. "Uh, maybe we get out of here before the other guards show up, and we let *them* help him."

I shake my head. "No. We can do things they can't."

"I appreciate your idealism, Matt, but what can we do to help with this?"

I turn to Tess. "Do you know what's happening to him?"

She shakes her head. "*Not yet. I need his name to find his medical history.*"

"Sure, why not?" Rob says with an eye roll. He kneels down and starts going through the guard's pockets. "Sorry for getting personal on you, man, but we're trying to help."

The guard doesn't say anything. He's still struggling to breathe.

"*You need to do CPR,*" Tess says to me.

I swallow. "But I don't know how to—"

My phone buzzes, and I stare blankly at the CPR instructions on the screen. Guess I'm gonna have to learn fast.

Rob pulls out the guard's wallet. "Carl Jacobs," he announces.

Tess's fingers pound anxiously at her phone.

I'm still speed-reading the CPR instructions when a voice shouts from the trophy room. "Carl! You okay? What the hell happened in here?"

Our eyes all dart toward the door, where the second guard is approaching.

"I've got this," Phillip says.

"No," I bark at him. "You're not going to—"

But he's already disappearing through the doorway.

I set my hands on Carl's chest. "We're going to get you through this, Carl," I tell him, even though I'm not sure I believe it. He nods faintly.

I put my weight into the first compression, just like the instructions said. *One.*

"Hey!" the guard outside yells. "Who're you? Stop right there!"

Two.

"... wait, where'd you go?"

Three.

"There you are! I said... Damn it, now he's gone again!"

Four.

The guard's footsteps fade as I keep compressing. I finish the first set and look at Carl's face. He's still dripping cold sweat.

"I don't think this is working, Tess," I say anxiously. "Please tell me you found something."

"*He has a pacemaker,*" she says. "*CardioRhythm Technologies model 300AR.*"

"The taser must've messed it up," Rob says. "Can you hack into that?"

"*No. For security reasons, pacemakers can't be controlled over the internet.*"

I gulp, and start another round of compressions into Carl's chest. "Then what're we gonna—"

"*But I can reset the pacemaker with magnetic signals,*" Tess says.

Rob nods with a subtle smirk. "And I'm guessing you can get your phone to make those?"

"*Almost there.*" Her fingers intensify. I finish my compressions and pull my hands away.

Tess steps forward and kneels down over Carl. As she holds the phone out toward his chest, she makes eye contact with him and holds it for longer than I've seen her make eye contact with anyone, until Carl's chest spasms, and he coughs. I hold my breath.

"Did it work?" Rob asks.

Tess straightens up and her hands go back to her phone. "*Unit operating normally. Heart rate stabilizing.*"

I let out a long breath and look Carl in the eye. "Are you okay?"

He wheezes, and his eyes come back into focus. "I... think so."

Someone else is shouting outside, the voice getting closer. Rob grabs my arm to pull me up.

"We need to get out of here, man." Rob looks at Carl. "Maybe, uh, don't give our descriptions to the cops, huh? That'd be really nice."

I hurry behind Rob and Tess out the door and back through the trophy room. I look at the aftermath of my fight with Leah.

We did it. We stopped them... but at what cost?

44

Matt

The living room is dark and quiet as I step inside the house. I trudge toward the stairs to throw myself into bed and sleep for about a week when I hear the shuffle of feet.

"Matt?" comes my dad's voice. "Is that you?"

Damn.

"Who else would it be, Dad?" I snip at him.

"It's late. Where have you been?"

"Saving the world," I say sarcastically. "And alienating the only people who understand me. You know, just normal freak-superhero stuff."

Dad switches on the light. He stands there in his sweatpants and a ratty old T-shirt. His cheeks seem to sag more than usual, and his graying stubble stands out against his skin.

"You're not a freak, Matt," he says softly.

"If you say so."

He rubs his hands awkwardly. He steps toward me, his eyes fixated on the carpet. "Saving the world, huh?" he says, forcing a levity to his voice.

"No. Well... maybe a small little part of it. I hope." I shake my head. "You wouldn't understand."

"You're right, I don't. Or, I haven't. But I want to, Matt."

"I don't have the energy for this right now, Dad. I've already lost a lot tonight." I start up the stairs.

"You can move things with your mind," Dad says behind me.

I stop and slowly turn around. Dad looks me in the eye for just a second, then goes back to the carpet.

"You can move things with your mind," he repeats. "And Sue... your mom... she could, too. There, I've said it."

I look at him for a long time. Part of me wants to snap something back at him. That's been my go-to reaction with him for so long, and he's given me plenty of ammunition to use against him. But he just looks so... tired. If I'm honest, I'm tired too.

Instead of all the hurtful things I could throw at him, instead I just say, "I know it's not an easy thing for you to accept."

"I'm sure it's not an easy thing for you to live with, either," Dad says. "I'm sorry about that. I'm sorry I... haven't been there for you."

I smile to mask the sadness underneath. "It's okay."

"It's not. You should have someone you can talk to about this."

"I did. For a few days, at least."

"You did?" Dad asks. "But you don't anymore?"

I shake my head. "I lost any chance at that. It was the price of saving the world."

Dad scratches at his stubble, as if deciding whether to ask what I'm talking about. In the end, he just says, "I'm sorry."

"It was just nice for once, to talk about it with someone who actually knew what it's like. I wish I could've talked about it with... Mom."

Dad's eyes flick toward me, surprised. "You didn't?"

"I didn't know she had the Ability until after she was gone."

A pale regret washes over his face. "I thought you knew."

"She didn't want me to know, I guess. She was trying to protect me. She probably did, in her own way. But it would've been nice to talk to her about it."

Dad looks down. "I always thought you two were talking behind my back about things I wouldn't understand. Like your little private club that I could never be a part of."

"I would've talked to you about it, if you'd let me."

"I know," he says, his voice heavy.

"Did you ever talk to Mom about it?" I ask him.

There's a pain, a loss in his eyes. "I didn't know how. I still... don't know how. Maybe that means I'm weak or insensitive. I'm sorry. You deserve to have someone to talk to about this."

As I look at him thinking about what I've lost, I feel sorry for myself for a moment. I do deserve that, right? I deserve to have my mom still here to talk to. I deserve to have Ash and Leah not hate me. But then I think about what I *do* have—the friends that risked everything to help me tonight. The friends that accept me, freak of nature and all.

"It's okay," I say. "Because I do have people I can talk to, actually. And I was taking them for granted. That's on me."

"That's... that's great, Matt."

"Yeah. I have some great friends. They really came through for me tonight. I couldn't have done that without them."

"Saving the world?" Dad asks, smirking.

"Something like that. But we did some good."

Dad shifts on his feet, trying to come up with what to say.

"You know I love you," Dad finally says. "Right, Matt? And... I loved your mother."

I step toward him, slowly reaching my arms around him. He pats me on the back before we step apart again. Not a real hug, but it's a start.

"I love you too, Dad."

45

Matt

I watch the students milling around outside the school, joking around, griping about stuff that doesn't matter. They're all oblivious to what went down last night. I guess that's okay. I'm not looking for them to thank me, and this isn't the first time I've played hero. But as I keep looking over everyone, I realize that what I'm looking for is a glimpse of not-quite-brown, not-quite-red hair. Or a bunch of floating pebbles. Hell, I'd even settle for Heath's ugly bald head.

They were long gone by the time we resuscitated that guard and got out of there. I knew they would be, and I knew they wouldn't be here today. I'm sure Ash got them on the interstate and never looked back. I don't even know what I'd say to them if they were here, but... I can't help wondering if last night could've gone any other way. If there was some version of last night where I didn't alienate them. Where we could have all walked away together.

As I stand there watching everyone, it takes me a minute to notice the person standing next to me.

Phillip pulls his hoodie back and roughs at the dark spikes of his hair. "You're looking for Ash, aren't you?"

I think about denying it, then nod reluctantly. "I just hope they're okay, wherever they are. Wherever they're going."

"After everything that happened last night, you're still worried about them?"

Rob slides up before I can come up with a reply. He shoulder-bumps me hard enough to knock me off balance. "Don't tell me. Matt's worried about whether Ash and her fellow delinquents are okay?"

"I had to stop them," I say. "That doesn't mean I wanted to see them get hurt."

"Awfully generous of you," Rob says, "since they tried to kill us last night."

"They didn't try to *kill* us."

Rob cocks his head and raises an eyebrow.

"Okay," I admit. "Heath was coming for you pretty heavy."

"Leah was coming for you pretty heavy, too," Rob says. "Never thought she'd have that in her."

I chew my lip. "That's the thing, I feel like it's my fault. I'm the one who pushed her over the edge, let all that anger out."

Phillip shakes his head. "Anger like that doesn't just happen. It must've been lurking under the surface for a long time."

"You think so?" I ask him.

His pale green eyes study me closely. "Going through life being... different... can be tough. You don't have anything building under the surface, do you?"

I smile. "I'm okay. Thanks to you guys."

"Better believe it," Rob says. "Of course, we can't take all the credit. Hey, Tess! Come join the party."

Tess walks over and gives a wave. *"What are you guys talking about?"*

"Well," Rob says, "you'd *think* we'd be talking about how we saved the day last night. But somehow Matt has found a way to feel bad about it."

"All I'm trying to say," I protest, "is that I hope they can redeem themselves someday. Just because someone got on the wrong track doesn't mean they can't get back on the right one."

"Even Crossman?" Phillip asks.

"Even him. Being a villain doesn't have to be forever."

"Can you at least admit we did good last night?" Rob asks. "Hell, Tess saved a guy's life!"

"I couldn't have done it without all of you," Tess says.

"You're being modest," Rob says. "I still say you could've managed the whole thing by yourself, at home in your pajamas."

"Phillip could have done it without anyone knowing he was ever there," Tess says.

I can't help but laugh. "You're right, guys. We did good last night. Thanks."

"We did do good." Tess turns her phone around. The screen shows a confirmation of another armored car pickup a few hours ago, then the final deposit to the Crossman Foundation for Emergency Response.

"See, Matt?" Rob says. "Now you'll get your fire station, so they can come running the next time you burn popcorn."

He slaps me on the back and smiles. I smile back, because I know what he's really trying to say. Sometimes you don't have to say it out loud. Other times...

"Hey, Emily," I call out, as I see her and Scott heading up the sidewalk. I'm not looking forward to this, but there's no getting around it.

Emily avoids my eyes for a second, like she's trying to decide if she should just pretend not to see me. Then she lets out a frustrated breath and walks over. "Matt, I—"

She doesn't get any farther, because Scott pushes past her and storms straight up to my face. "You've got a lot of nerve after what you said to her," he barks at me.

"I'm trying to apologize," I tell him.

"Well, maybe she doesn't *want* you to—"

"Cool it, Scott," Emily says. "I can take care of myself."

Scott looks down and takes a step back. "I was just trying to—"

"I know," she says, "but I'm not some damsel in distress."

He sulks back a few steps, but keeps his glare firmly fixed on me.

Rob scratches at his hair. "Uh, I should probably get to class..."

"Don't worry," Emily says, "we're not going to get into a screaming match."

I raise an eyebrow. "We're not? Because I probably deserve that."

"You do deserve it. But we've known each other long enough to get past crap like that." Emily shrugs, ruffling the red waves of her hair. "And maybe I was pushing you too hard anyway."

"You were just trying to look out for me," I admit.

"Yes I was, and I only brought that up because I'm trying to be nice right now," she quips. "You were a prick. But everyone is a prick sometimes. We'll be okay."

I look up at her. Her green eyes seem particularly piercing today. "Really? We're okay?"

"I said we'll *be* okay." Emily tries to scowl at me but can't hide a hint of a smirk. She walks off, and Scott follows. He manages to scowl at me just fine.

Rob slaps my back. "She let you off easy."

"Yeah. I deserved a lot worse."

"Even superheroes mess up sometimes, huh?" Phillip asks.

I chuckle. "I guess so. Thanks, guys."

"*We'll always be here to save the day,*" Tess says.

"I know you will." I glance at my watch. "I, uh, need to talk to someone else before class starts. I'll catch up with you guys later."

"You'd better," Rob says.

I step toward the building, listening to them continue to chat with each other behind me. I push through the doors and into the hall, where lockers are slamming and everyone's talking about football games and cat videos and who's having a party on Friday night. I walk past all of it, to the science room.

Mr. Plask shuffles around inside, carrying some bottles toward the closet. He spins when he hears me, looking startled like he usually does, his eyes popping even wider than normal behind his glasses.

"Oh... Matt," he says, taking a breath. "I didn't see you there. What brings you by?"

"Do you think having an Ability can corrupt someone?" I ask him.

Plask sets his armful of bottles down with a clank. "That's a rather deep question for this early in the morning. What brought this up?"

"I thought I could use it for good, to make a difference. Nothing big, but I can do something no one else can do... well, I *thought* no one else could do it. Anyway, I felt like I was helping people. But then I started wondering if it was worth it, if those people I was helping would even accept me for who I am. And… maybe I should just look out for myself."

"You don't believe that, Matt." It makes me feel a little better that Plask says that so quickly.

"No, but I thought about it for a lot longer than I should have."

"Does this have anything to do with the new kids you've been hanging out with?" he asks. "The ones who have Abilities too?"

I look up at him, shocked.

"I'm not a complete idiot," he quips.

"What they said made a lot of sense," I say. "The rest of the world doesn't understand us. They wanted to fight back."

Plask nods. "At the heart of it, everyone is scared that someone will hurt them or take something from them. You can either fight everyone you meet, or you can take a risk and help them."

"They've been hurt by a lot of people. I've been hurt by a few, too."

"That happens sometimes. Like I said, it's a risk. But you can feel better about yourself after what you did last night."

I raise an eyebrow at him. "I didn't tell you what we—"

Plask smiles. "Like I said, I'm not an idiot."

"I'm… sorry I didn't tell you about that earlier." I shuffle on my feet. Then I glance at the bottles on the desk, and it suddenly dawns on me. "Wait a minute, what's in those bottles? Are those like the bombs you used to stop Crossman at the factory?"

He scratches at the tufts of his hair. "I wouldn't call them bombs…"

"You know what I mean."

"Well, I may have prepared some, uh, surprises that could have helped out last night. I told you, chemistry is my superpower."

"So why didn't you show up at the house to use those?"

He shrugs. "I decided that if you wanted me to be involved, you would have asked me."

I grimace. "I didn't want to drag you into it. To get you hurt."

"I figured, and I decided to respect that," Plask says. "But sometimes being a hero means asking for help. Remember that next time."

"I will. Thanks."

"But it still turned out okay?" he asks.

I nod. "Yeah. I just didn't ever think I'd be fighting people like... me."

"Sounds like they've gotten themselves off the track. Lost sight of what's important."

I hesitate. "Do you think they could ever find their way back to what's right?"

Plask gives me a piercing look, and smiles. "You did, didn't you?"

46

Matt

My steps carry me over the crumbling sidewalk that should've been replaced years ago, past the laundromat where half the machines don't work and the barber shop that always smells like cheap hairspray. I imagine the new fire station going in between those, or maybe they'll tear down that fitness center that nobody uses. But either way, it'll be *here,* ready to jump into action, because of what we did last night. Maybe now, the fire truck will get there in time to pull someone else's mom out of the house before it burns. Maybe someone can have a better life because of me. Because of us.

I keep going, taking in the blue sky and the crisp air. A couple blocks later, I pass by the diner. I look at the dirty pickup trucks parked out front, and a hatchback with mismatched fenders, and...

A car with out-of-state plates and a crumpled front end from where it ran into a trash can.

As I walk toward the door, I know it's a bad idea. But somehow it feels like this is something I have to do, maybe for me as much as for him.

The door chimes as I step through it onto the scuffed tile floor. A couple of retired guys sit in the back, chatting over coffee. Steve, Ash's dad, sits on one of the bar stools at the counter, staring with dead eyes at a half-eaten sandwich that looks like it's been sitting in front of him for a while. He glances over slowly at the door chime. Then his eyes lock onto me and they ignite with fury.

I stumble back a step and put up my hands. "I don't know where she is," I say quickly. "She's gone."

Steve slumps back down in his seat and his eyes go dead again. I hesitate, then shuffle over and drop myself onto the seat next to him. The plastic cushion wheezes as it smushes underneath me.

The waitress saunters over and glares at me through her thick glasses. "You gonna order somethin' this time?"

"I'm, uh, sorry about the other night," I say sheepishly. "That was out of line."

She stands there, noisily smacking at her gum. She taps a pencil irritably against her pad.

"Oh, right. Order something," I sputter. "A chocolate milkshake. Please."

She gives me an unimpressed look, scribbles on the pad, and strolls off. I turn back to Steve; I don't think he's blinked since I sat down.

"I'm surprised you're still in town," I say.

He keeps staring straight ahead. "She was here."

"Well, yeah. She was."

"Thought I'd have another chance at her." Steve glances over at me suspiciously. "I almost had her this time. Twice. *You* broke it up both times."

"Well, you punched me in the face. We can call it even."

He grunts. It doesn't sound like an apology.

"Do you really want to hurt her that badly?" I ask him.

"She hurt me." Steve looks at me, and I can see the pain in his eyes, going on and on inside. "She hurt you too, didn't she?"

I think about denying it for a second, but I feel the jab in my heart. "Yeah."

"It's what she does. The worst part is, she draws you in first. Makes you think she cares. Then you figure out she's just manipulating you. Using your pain against you."

I'm about to agree with him when I stop myself. "Ash only lashes out because she's scared. She's been hurt too. People don't understand people like her."

"You mean people like *you*, right?" Steve looks at me sharply.

I meet his stare. "It can be tough."

Steve glares for another second, then gives up and takes a bite of his sandwich.

"Look," I say, "I'm not here to defend her. She's made some bad choices. She got on the wrong path. Maybe she'll find her way back... maybe not. But you can't spend your whole life chasing her, plotting revenge."

"Don't tell me you've forgiven her already," he says.

I have to think about that one. "No, I haven't. But I'm not going to carry it with me."

"Good for you," he mutters.

"Look, I know she hurt you—"

"You don't know the half of it."

"All right, maybe I don't," I admit. "But I know the reason Ash has hurt people is because of what happened to her, and now you're trying to hurt her because of what happened to you. Someone has to end the cycle, or it's going to go on like this forever."

"Maybe I want it to." Steve looks over at me. "You really don't know where she is?"

I shake my head. "No."

He keeps his eyes on me until he convinces himself I'm not lying. "Too bad. But someday, I'll make her pay, if I have to strangle her with my dying breath."

The waitress shuffles over and plunks my milkshake on the counter. I leave it untouched and push myself off the stool, dropping a couple bills on the counter to pay for it, along with enough of a tip to make up for going off on her the other night.

"I hope not," I tell him. "Not just for her sake, but for yours too."

"Are you really that idealistic?" Steve asks me, his voice cold.

"Yeah. And I hope I can bring a few people with me along the way."

He still looks dead inside as I walk out the door. I leave him behind me and step outside, taking a moment to appreciate the sun on my skin.

47

Matt

I stand with my hands in my pockets, looking through the big plate-glass window at the suits and ties and bottles of cologne. Rob saunters around inside the store, pretending to be interested in a silk shirt. He flashes a smile at the sales clerk and asks him something I can't hear. The clerk reluctantly drags himself over to him and responds to his question with a lot of effort. After a few more questions that I know Rob doesn't even care about, he flashes another smile, slips the shirt back on the rack, and wanders out of the store. The clerk lets out a long sigh, like he's questioning his life choices, and goes back to folding sweaters.

"You enjoy my performance in there?" Rob asks me as he steps out.

I chuckle. "It looked like you were enjoying yourself."

"What's wrong with that?"

I shake my head and turn to Tess. "You take care of the cameras?"

"*They'll never know we were here,*" she says.

"Some of my best work, and no one's going to get to see it," Rob says.

"We needed to be discreet," I say. "And speaking of discreet..."

Phillip reappears next to me and pulls back his hoodie.

"You get the wallet back in there okay?" I ask him.

He gives me a thumbs up.

"Seems a shame," Rob says. "We have Phillip's ninja stealth mode, and he uses it to put something back in?"

"That was the whole point, Rob," I tell him.

"What? I'm just saying, Phillip could've walked right out with that silk shirt. That would've looked good on me."

I shake my head. "This was about fixing something I did wrong. I should never have stolen that wallet in the first place."

"*We all make mistakes,*" Tess says.

"I let my Ability go to my head for a minute," I admit. "I can't use it to take things like that."

"Must be tough," Rob says. "Having a superpower and not being able to use it for yourself once in a while." He turns to Tess. "You've never thought about hacking into the bank and making a few withdrawals?"

"*It had crossed my mind,*" she says with a smirk, "*but Matt's idealism rubbed off on me.*"

"He rubbed off on all of us," Phillip says.

"Come on, you're gonna make me blush." I give Phillip a nudge. "Thanks again for slipping it in for me."

"I didn't need Rob's performance to distract the clerk, you know," he says.

"I know you didn't," I agree. "But when something needs to be made right, we're all here to play our part."

"You say that like playing hero is your job now," Rob says. "You planning to save the world again anytime soon?"

I do my best to hide a smile. "You never know."

Epilogue

Leah

She rubs the thick towel over her hands, over and over, in an almost hypnotic rhythm. Her hands are already dry by now, but the towel is so warm and soft and comforting, not thin and scratchy like at most of the places they've stayed at. Leah keeps rubbing her hands through the fibers, letting the softness soothe the tangle in her gut that's always there. A muffled bang thuds through the wall—just the TV in the next room turned up too loud, but it still makes her flinch, makes the tangle twist and prick her again like a knotted ball of barbed wire. Leah takes a strained breath and presses her hands deeper into the towel. The softness helps, a little.

Heath looks over from where he's stretched out on one of the beds. For once, it's big enough that his feet don't hang over the end. "You're smiling," he says.

Leah drops the towel, suddenly self-conscious.

"You don't have to stop," Heath says. "I don't see you smile often enough."

Leah steps timidly away from the sink, letting her bare feet sink into the thick carpet. "It's just nice, after everything, to stay in a nice place for once."

"I'll admit, this hotel doesn't suck. I guess the question is how long we can afford to stay here. Speaking of—"

The door flies open and bangs into the wall. Leah immediately hunches over, an instinctive reaction she can't repress. The tangle twists inside her and cuts a little more, shards of repressed memories jabbing through the surface, the image of her mother's crazed eyes...

Leah stifles a shudder as Ash storms in and slams the door shut.

"So I guess it went well at the car dealership?" Heath says casually.

"The little prick didn't have anything I could use," Ash fumes. "It pisses me off to see someone that happy. It's not natural."

"So you weren't able to get inside his head," Heath says. "There are other ways to negotiate, you know."

"I *tried* that," Ash snaps back. "For as happy as he is, he didn't wiggle much. To get a decent car will take most of that measly wad of cash we got away with."

"It's still a lot more money than we've had in a long time."

"It's not enough, and it's way less than we deserve! Damn it, that job was our ticket, and Matt ruined it! He was supposed to help us, and instead he turned into a traitor."

"I told you we never should've trusted him in the first place."

"You're saying this is *my* fault?"

The tangle inside Leah twists again, but there's something more in the jumble of feelings this time, something she's not used to. She squishes her toes into the carpet, using the softness to push the tangle back down for one more moment.

Leah steps to the window while Ash and Heath keep yelling at each other. She looks down at the parking lot, trying to calm herself by tracing the painted lines with her eyes. The lines are straight and crisp, unlike the faded, weed-infested mess at the last place, and there's an island in the middle with decorative gravel and some bushes. It really is nice here. She rubs her feet against the carpet again and tries to take comfort in the softness. But then she swallows a scream and the tangle explodes into rusty nails inside her when she sees the car pulling into the lot.

The all-too-familiar one, except now the front bumper and hood are smashed up from the last time he chased Ash.

Leah feels the cold fear drench over her and paralyze her as she watches Steve's face through the windshield down below, wondering how he found them again. The tangle cuts her, forcing images through of him with his hands around Ash's throat. But the fear is only getting started. Then it becomes her mother's face, screaming at her, throwing her into the closet until the demon in her is gone. It becomes the face of that guard at the detention center, when... when he...

And after all that, it becomes Matt's face.

Matt was like her. He was supposed to *help* her. But he hurt her too. He chose the other people over her. The tangle keeps twisting inside her, but it's not just fear now. There's something else pricking her, something new.

Leah can't make herself move or even speak, but her eyes dart to Ash and Heath. They haven't seen Steve yet. They're still arguing over the money. She looks back at the car, where Steve is getting out now, looking back and forth intensely. She draws in a shaking breath.

Matt told her she should forgive people like him. That she should *love* them. How could Matt turn on her like that? Didn't he know how many times they've hurt her? She feels her whole body shake, her legs twitching to run away, if she could just tear her way out of this cocoon of fear...

No. The voice booms from inside her, as the tangle in her gut heats up and the barbs singe her from the inside. That's what that new feeling is—anger. She's tired of flinching at every loud noise, tired of running away, tired of always waiting for the next person to hurt her again. Ash had said they're better than everyone else. Leah had never believed that, always thought she didn't deserve anything... but that was just her mother's voice screaming at her that she was unholy.

Her mother doesn't deserve love, and neither does Steve. People like that will never stop trying to hurt her. But she doesn't have to run away anymore.

She can hurt them back.

Leah twitches her fingers, and the gravel from the parking lot island down below floats up, hovering like a cloud of hailstones.

Steve marches angrily toward the building, not seeing the floating stones behind him. As Leah watches him, she finally lets her fear harden to hate. Matt's voice pushes through her head one last time, saying it doesn't have to be this way. That she doesn't have to hurt him; that he doesn't have to hurt her anymore. But as the rage boils all the way to her fingertips, finally crowding out the fear, finally straightening her shoulders, she suddenly realizes... it feels *good*.

Leah flicks her fingers, and the rocks launch themselves like a shotgun blast.

And look for book 3 of the Hidden
Abilities series...

But I'm (Not) A Sidekick

Acknowledgements

First off, thank you to everyone who supported me by reading the first book in this series, *But I'm Not A Hero!* (If you haven't read that yet, you should!) Thank you to my incredible critique readers Fran, Nicole, Anika, Vince, Erik, Sarah, and Jenna. Thank you to Jeremiah and Caleb for listening to me blabber about plot ideas on multiple occasions, and to Jennifer for acting as my "technical consultant" for all my medical questions. Most of all, I couldn't have gone through this journey without my wife and my parents, who have always supported my dreams and cheered me on.

Soli Deo Gloria.

Eric Demarest spent most of his childhood living in his imagination. His adult life isn't much different, except now he writes his imaginings down and makes other people read them. He loves how stories can make us understand ourselves and others more fully. His work has been featured in Spider children's magazine. When he's not writing (or reading), he loves watching science fiction movies, and imagining what life is like in the parallel universe where he became a film music composer instead. He lives in the suburbs of Kansas City with his wife and their cat.

Scan this to find out more about Eric and
the other stories in the Hidden Abilities series!
Or follow Eric on social media @authordemarest

www.ingramcontent.com/pod-product-compliance
Lightning Source LLC
Chambersburg PA
CBHW050138120726
47903CB00002B/407